VIGILANTE SEASON

VIGILANTE SEASON

A LUC VANIER NOVEL

PETER KIRBY

Cover design : Debbie Geltner

Cover photo : Roumi Photos http://www.roumagnac.net

Book design and typesetting : WildElement.ca

Author photo : Jocelyn Michel

Library and Archives Canada Cataloguing in Publication

Kirby, Peter, 1953-, author
     Vigilante season / Peter Kirby.

(A Luc Vanier novel)
Issued in print and electronic formats.
ISBN 978-1-927535-23-3 (pbk.).--ISBN 978-1-927535-24-0 (epub).--
ISBN 978-1-927535-25-7 (mobi).--ISBN 978-1-927535-26-4 (pdf)

    I. Title.
PS8621.I725V54 2013   C813'.6   C2013-902016-0
                                            C2013-902017-9

Printed and bound in Canada by Marquis Book Printing.

Legal Deposit, Library and Archives Canada
et Bibliothèque et Archives nationales du Québec

Linda Leith Publishing acknowledges the support of the Canada Council for the Arts.

Linda Leith Publishing Inc.
P.O. Box 322, Station Victoria
Westmount, Quebec H3Z 2V8 Canada
www.lindaleith.com

To Jess

One

Inspector Luc Vanier was standing in a rainstorm at the intersection of Sherbrooke and Pie-IX, surveying the remnants of a car accident. A dark blue body bag was at his feet. The bag's zipper had been pulled down by the ambulance crew, and the broken face of its occupant stared up into the night. Another man, his face obscured by a breathing mask, was being lifted into the back of the ambulance on a stretcher, while the rain washed away the blood that had pooled on the ground from his head wound. The blue, red, and amber lights of emergency vehicles circled like spotlights, and the people who had gathered outside the perimeter of yellow tape were beginning to drift off, sensing the show was winding down. Vanier looked around him, feeling like the ringmaster in a bleak circus.

Detective Sergeant Sylvie Saint-Jacques said, "Don't worry, they're collecting names and contacts. The pedestrians first, then the cars. Someone must have seen something." She walked off towards a police cruiser parked at the edge of the intersection.

The duty coroner, Jean-Louis Nadeau, had been speaking through the window to the ambulance driver. He stepped back, watched the vehicle pull away, and walked over to Vanier, smiling.

"Inspector Vanier, how good to see you again."

"Good to see you too, Doctor. What's the story?"

Nadeau nodded towards the body bag on the ground. "He was in the bag when I got here. Male, white, in his mid-forties.

He's been dead for a few hours, but that's all I can tell for the moment. It's best to leave him in the bag for the trip. That way we won't miss anything."

Vanier squatted down to get a closer look at the man's face. It was bruised and crusted with dried blood. The man's nose was broken, and a piece of his cheekbone stuck out through skin.

"Jesus," said Vanier.

"I doubt it." Vanier looked up to Nadeau and rolled his eyes. The Doctor shrugged and continued. "But we'll see. He was beaten, but there's no obvious cause of death yet. We need to get a good look at him."

The morgue van arrived, and a uniform pulled back the yellow tape to let it pass. It stopped next to the body bag, and two men in grey coveralls got out. Dr. Nadeau supervised as they loaded the bag onto the stretcher and into the back of the van. He turned to Vanier,

"Not often you get into an accident on your way to dump a body. We'll do the autopsy tomorrow morning and get something to you quickly."

"Can we go through his pockets tonight? Get an ID?"

"Sure. I'll see what's in there. I'll call you. Any ideas?"

"Nothing. Just questions. Don't often see people moving bodies around. The psychos do it, but he doesn't look like your average sex-crime victim. Maybe it's a gang hit. We'll have a better idea when we can identify the corpse."

"I'll call you."

Saint-Jacques came back over, hunched against the rain. A uniformed cop was following her. She gestured to him. "Constable Adams was first on the scene."

Vanier reached out his hand, and the constable shook it. "So what do we know?"

"I was parked down the street and I heard the crash. No mistaking the impact of two vehicles. I was here in a minute or so. There was a collision between the Buick over there and a pick-up truck." He pointed to a white Buick with its front end smashed in. "The truck was still in the intersection when I got here, but the driver must have seen my lights. He took off north on Pie-IX. I was ready to pursue, but I saw the old man on the floor bleeding, and I had a choice. I decided to stay with him and call in the truck."

"What kind of truck."

"Red Toyota Tundra. I'm certain. My brother-in-law has one. This one was maybe four years old. No dents that I could see. Two guys inside."

"Did you get a look at them?"

"No. They were back in the truck, pulling away, by the time I got close."

"So what happened?"

"Collision, like I said. The Buick hit the truck, and the truck spun out and hit the traffic light. The bag seems to have fallen off the flat bed. The guy in the Buick got out to inspect the damage and was wacked pretty bad by one of the guys in the truck. He was unconscious when I got here. I called in the ambulance, and then I called in the truck. I thought for sure somebody would get them, but no. They were lucky."

"Losing a body isn't lucky."

"I suppose. But maybe I should have chased them."

"You did the right thing. You didn't get a plate?"

"No."

"Okay. Thanks. Send me your report when it's ready."

Vanier handed the officer his card, and turned to watch the morgue truck take off. A tow truck was hooking up the Buick to take it to the Police Lab. The accident scene officers were winding down; one was packing away the video camera into the trunk of a cruiser, another was cranking a fifty-metre measure back onto its roll. Inside the cruiser, another officer was writing on a clipboard, sheltering from the rain in the passenger seat. Vanier let himself into the driver's side and nodded a greeting.

"Inspector Vanier, Serious Crime."

"Looks like you've got one here, Inspector." His name badge said Jacques Allard.

"What do you think?"

"The missing truck ran the red. We know that from the Mazda."

"Mazda?"

"Yeah. He was behind the Buick. Traffic on Sherbrooke was cruising along green, so no reason to slow down. The guy in the Mazda says they were all doing fifty. More like sixty-five if you ask me. Anyway, the Buick enters the intersection on a green, and the truck comes barrelling through on a red and gets hit. It keeps going, but the rear fishtailed and hit the light post on the north-east corner." He nodded his head in the direction of the downed traffic light post.

"The impact must have popped the lock on the flatbed, and the bag dropped down. The Mazda said two guys jumped out of the truck and went straight for the bag. They were lifting it up when the Buick came over."

"The Buick?"

"Yeah." He looked at his clipboard. "Mr. Clement, the driver of the Buick. Sixty-three years old. Seems he was pissed mad, screaming and waving his arms. The two guys were struggling with the body bag, and Clement put his hand on the shoulder of one of them."

"There was an argument?"

"No argument. One of the two guys drops his end of the bag, wheels around, and punches Clement in the face. The old man drops to the floor and bangs his head. That's when the truck guys see the lights from the cruiser and take off."

"Leaving the body behind."

"No choice. The cruiser got here as they were leaving. They didn't have time."

"When will you finish the report?"

"It's not complicated. Tomorrow afternoon if I'm lucky."

Vanier handed him his card. "Can you send me a copy as soon as it's done?"

"Sure. Not a problem."

Vanier got out of the cruiser and shivered. The rain had seeped through his coat, and he was feeling the cold. A city truck had arrived, and workers were putting metal *ARRÊT* signs at every corner. Two others were sizing up the traffic light pole that was leaning over into the traffic lane. The intersection of Sherbrooke and Pie-IX was going to be a star attraction for the morning commute.

The Maisonneuve Tavern on Ontario Street was full and loud, the sound system was competing with the hockey commentary from the television, and shouted conversations filled whatever space was left. It was the day when direct deposits of welfare payments hit empty bank accounts, and everyone has money to spend for a day or two. Hugo Desportes was reading *God Bless You, Mr. Rosewater* and getting buzzed. A month ago he had found a copy of *Slaughterhouse Five* in a charity shop and was amazed to find a writer who understood how life works. He decided to read all the Vonnegut books, one after the other.

It was a few seconds before he noticed the stocky man beside him. A small guy, but built like a stone wall.

The man said, "I can sit down?"

Desportes was feeling charitable. "Sure. Sit down." He closed the book and picked up his glass.

The man sat down and reached out his hand. "Hi. My name is Alfredo Cortina. People say that maybe you can help me."

Desportes said nothing.

"I want to get a job with the city. For many years, I have tried. But they ignore me. It's because I'm not from here, I think."

"Everyone needs help to get a job with the city."

"So I'm asking for help. I can pay."

"You want a beer?"

Cortina nodded and Desportes waved for two quart bottles. The waiter was there in an instant. Desportes paid.

"So if you need a job with the city, why don't you go see your Councillor, Madame Farand. That's part of her job, to get local people into city jobs."

"I did this. It does not work. She said I am over qualified."

Desportes spent most of his time pushing people away. He couldn't take every on every cause that came his way. But he let Cortina talk. Listening didn't cost anything. Cortina was an engineer from Guatemala. It had taken four years for his refugee claim to be accepted, and then he brought his wife and two kids to Montreal. His French wasn't good enough to qualify as an engineer in Quebec, so he worked at any job he could get. And any job meant crap jobs, with more hours than he could manage and less money than he needed to live. He had given up hope for himself. Being an engineer in Guatemala meant nothing here, but his kids were still young and they had a chance. A job with the city would mean he didn't have to work two jobs. He could spend time at home. He could help his kids with their schoolwork.

Cortina's story was the same as that of thousands of other immigrants in Montreal. Helping him would be arbitrary, but everything is arbitrary – and he was the only one talking to Desportes. Plus, Desportes knew he could do it. He was sitting on information that gave him leverage with City Hall, and most information has a shelf life, use it or it goes stale. Right now, he didn't have anything better to use it on.

Desportes asked Cortina if he had a photograph of his wife and kids. The engineer reached into his wallet and pulled out small colour photos of all three, his face changing from hard to soft at the same time. Then he bent down to open a brown, hard-plastic briefcase, the kind that had gone out of fashion thirty years ago. He took a fistful of worn photographs from a zippered pocket.

Desportes looked through them. "Nice kids."

"Very good kids. They're going to make it here."

He reached into the briefcase again and pulled out an envelope. He passed it across the table. "This is my cv. How much will it cost?"

Desportes took the envelope. "No cash. An exchange. I help you, and maybe one day you help me. If you ever hear of something you think might interest me, you tell me. If I need something, I'll call you, and you'll deliver. Simple."

"I understand. But what kind of help would you need?"

"Let's get you a job first. Then we'll see."

It was 2 a.m. when Vanier got back to his apartment. He was wet and cold. Alex's boots and sneakers were outside the door, so Alex was home. His son had moved in when he came back from Afghanistan, said it was temporary, but he wasn't finding it easy to get back into civilian life.

Inside the apartment, Vanier looked up the hallway to Alex's bedroom door. It was closed, and there was no light through the gap at the bottom. He went up the hall and eased the door open quietly. The room had that thick, fetid smell that only a night of drinking can produce. Alex was in a deep sleep.

He went back to the living room, poured himself a Jameson and checked his phone. Dr. Nadeau had sent him a text: *No wallet, Medicare Card in back pocket says Émile Legault, 28 April, 1968.* He flipped the text to Saint-Jacques and asked her to get someone to put Legault's name through the databases in the morning. He had a feeling Legault would have a record. If he did, things would be easier.

He stood in the living room in boxers and T-shirt and looked around, trying to reconstruct what Alex had been doing all day. The pile of brochures and forms from Veterans Affairs and the Department of National Defence was untouched. Next to it was a plate with congealed egg yolk and crumbs from toast, easy food, but at least he'd eaten. The armchair had been pulled close in front of the television set. Beside it, a videogame hand-set lay on the floor, its long cord leading to a jumble of consoles and cassettes.

Vanier poured another drink and sat on the couch. He downed it quickly, lifted his legs onto the couch, and stretched out.

He was awake at 4 a.m., the dead part of the night when the terrors that have been held in check all day start groping around in the dark. There was the slow ebb of street noises from outside and the familiar grunts of struggling from Alex's room. Sometimes Alex would settle again into a restless sleep. Sometimes he wouldn't. Vanier didn't yet understand the patterns, so he sat up and waited.

Then the first shout came, more a scream than a shout, and Vanier was on his feet, stopping in the bathroom to grab a washcloth and soak it in warm water. He pushed on the door. Alex was still asleep, but thrashing around like he was running, making grunting noises without words. Vanier sat on the bed and cradled his son's head on his knees, wiping his forehead with the washcloth. Alex struggled some more and then relaxed. Vanier knew he was awake when the tears came, silently, with a racking of the body. He had no idea what to do, except what he had done when Alex had nightmares as a kid, just be there, speak soothing words, reassure him, and hold him close. Vanier couldn't imagine what beasts were tormenting the boy, all he could do was mumble, "It's okay, Alex. It's going to be fine. I'm here. Everything's going to be fine," over and over until the beasts left, and the boy fell asleep. It took an hour, and then Vanier lay down on top of the bed and dozed off himself.

An hour later he was standing under a scalding shower trying to shake off the fatigue.

Two

The database search for Émile Legault had turned up an address about ten blocks from where his body had tumbled from the back of the truck. The apartment was a semi-basement in a triplex. The two front windows were half underground and covered on the inside with what looked like blankets.

Saint-Jacques fist-pounded the door, listening for any sign of a response, then nodded back at Vanier and waited. A woman shouted from behind the door, "Émile's not here. Go somewhere else."

"It's the police, Madame. Can we come in?"

The door opened with a chain on it, and a woman with a shrunken-eyed face and junkie's pallor stared out at them, the face of someone who had spent too much time in dingy apartments and crack houses. She said,

"Like I said, Émile's not here. You need to come back later."

"We're here to talk to you about Émile. Open the door so we can come in."

The door closed, and they could hear the chain being detached. Then it opened wide, and she stood there looking confused.

"What's it about?"

"Can we come in?"

"I suppose," she said, turning to walk back into the apartment.

They followed her into the usual cheap, one bedroom set-up, a front room with a small kitchen area; the bedroom and toilet would be in back. The front room was all sofas, one against each wall and a fourth in front of the kitchen area. The room was lit by a single, weak floor lamp, and it stank of stale beer, cigarettes, and something rotting in an overflowing garbage can. Saint-Jacques went through to the back to make sure there was no one else in the apartment. The girl sank down onto one of the couches, and it barely registered her weight. She put her head back, as though she was going to fall asleep.

"What's your name?" Vanier asked.

"Maude."

"Maude what?"

"Maude Roberge."

"Truth?"

"Truth."

"How do you know Émile?"

"I live here. He lets me live here. It's his place."

"For how long?"

"He always says, for as long as I like."

"No. I mean how long have you been together?"

"Oh. Six, seven years. I met him just after I finished high school." Even in the gloom she looked years older than five or six years out of high school.

"I've some bad news, Maude. Émile was found dead last night. He was murdered."

There was no reaction while she absorbed the news. Saint-Jacques came back into the front room, "Back door's broken, like a forced entry."

Maude stirred, she said in a low voice. "I figured they'd kill him. After they took him yesterday. I knew he was in trouble."

"Who took him?"

"I don't know who it was."

She rambled through a story. Vanier and Saint-Jacques had to drag it out of her with questions and prodding.

She thought they broke in around ten o'clock in the morning. Émile had been partying all night, and there were people in the place until dawn. She was asleep in the bed when some guys crashed through the back door. Émile must have been in the front. There were three of them, she thought. One of them put a gun to her head and told her to put her face into the pillow and stay quiet. The others went and got Émile. She could hear him swearing and arguing with them. The guy holding the gun to her head told her if she didn't see anything she had nothing to worry about. So she just lay there and stayed quiet and waited for them to leave. She said she got really scared when she heard Émile shrieking, like he was really hurt, but not like he was dying, just really hurt. She heard them going through the place for about half an hour. The guy with the gun never moved. She thinks that she fell asleep again and when she woke up, Émile was gone and all his stock was gone with him. No money, no drugs, they had taken everything, even her welfare money.

"You didn't call the police?"

She raised her head for the first time and looked at him like he was crazy.

"I was waiting. Either he'd come back or he wouldn't. Either way, I still had a place to sleep."

"And you have no idea who they were?"

"I told you. No. I think there were maybe three of them. All dressed dark. White guys, I think. But that's it. Wasn't anyone I knew."

"Any ideas?"

"They didn't seem like the usual guys. Not any of the gangs, and not Angels. They were quiet, you know? Not screaming and shouting. They talked low, did their business, and left. You know, like you see in the movies. Like professionals. Not the usual assholes. The only one screaming was Émile."

"We're going to have to go through this place. It's a crime scene, Maude."

She raised her head again. "But I live here. I've got nowhere else to go."

Vanier looked at Saint-Jacques, who shrugged her shoulder. "I guess I can stay with her until the crime scene people get here, make sure she doesn't touch anything."

"No need. She's been here since he disappeared. Another hour won't make a difference."

Saint-Jacques punched numbers on the phone and began organizing the work.

Vanier kept up the questions, afraid she was falling asleep. "Where did he keep the drugs, Maude?"

"Drugs?" She said, like a bad actor trying for indignation, but only showing how little energy she had left.

"Stop fucking around, Maude. Where?"

"He had four or five spots, but they took everything, even the money."

"He showed them?"

"He didn't have much choice. I remember him screaming like a kid with its finger caught in a car door. I couldn't do anything. I had to keep my face in the pillow."

"And?"

"Over there. On the counter."

Saint-Jacques moved into the kitchen space.

"Near the salt. In a Kleenex. I found it after they left."

Saint-Jacques saw the red-stained Kleenex and tore it apart. It was a finger cut at the knuckle. She held it up for Vanier to see before dropping it into an evidence bag.

"You'd need garden sheers to cut off his finger off like that," Maude said.

Saint-Jacques put the evidence bag into her pocket.

Vanier made a mental note to talk to Dr. Nadeau about the hand with the fingertip missing.

"You do that to someone, and they're going to show you everything," Maude said. "I kept it for if he came back. You know, maybe the doctors could re-attach it."

"And Émile showed them everything?"

She looked at him like a child caught in a lie. "Well no. He usually kept some cash, about $1,500, in a pair of jeans at the bottom of the laundry basket. He didn't show them that. But they got everything else."

"$1,500. You counted it?"

Maude's her hand went instinctively to her pocket. She saw that Vanier had seen it.

"It's all I have."

"So they took all of the money and the drugs, is that the story?"

"Yes. And his guns."

"I thought you had your face in the pillow all the time."

"I checked, after they left."

"Maude, will you tell his family?" Vanier was thinking that Maude didn't seem like the family sort. It was more likely she would just close the door and walk away. Or, maybe, not even close the door.

"Don't need to. They'll read about it in the paper. They don't like me."

"Are his parents alive?"

"Yeah. More's the pity."

"What's the address?"

Maude had to think. Eventually she gave them an address about fifteen blocks away.

"So where are you going to be, Maude? If we need to talk to you."

"Got nowhere else to go. I guess I'll wait till someone throws me out."

Vanier got up and handed her his card. "If anything else comes to mind, call me. And Maude, it's important. If you move, let me know where you're going. I don't want to have to come looking for you."

She put the card in her jeans. "Yeah. I'll let you know." She put her head back on the couch, closed her eyes, and started scratching her arm.

"We'll let ourselves out."

"Sure. Whatever."

The Mayor of Montreal lives behind walls, both the real and the artificial kind. He gets driven everywhere, and nobody bumps into him at the mall. He's delivered to his office every morning in a city car, and he returns at night the same way. His phone numbers are unlisted, and his arrivals at functions are always choreographed to avoid impromptu meetings with citizens. He's not an easy man to speak to.

He likes to think of himself as a man of the people and prides himself on his normality, eating breakfast every morning with his wife and two children, as normal as any family where the father eats breakfast in a suit while reading three newspapers. It's left to his wife to maintain contact with the rest of the world.

Her cell phone rang, and a voice announced itself.

"Madame Chambord, it's Lucien Houde here, I wonder if I could have a word with Raymond. It's kind of urgent."

She was puzzled. "Why don't you call him on his cell? You have his number, I suppose?"

"Of course. We've being trying for the last fifteen minutes, but there seems to be a problem. Perhaps he has it switched off."

Her husband was watching, noticing the questioning look on her face. She passed the phone across the table.

"It's for you, Raymond. It's Lucien Houde. He says it's urgent."

He didn't know any Lucien Houde, and he had a choice: he could take the phone and speak to some lunatic who happened to have his wife's cell phone number, or he could leave the problem with his wife. No choice. He reached across the table and took the phone.

"Hello … ah … Mr. Houde. What is this about?"

"Good morning Mr. Mayor, and thanks for taking my call. It's so difficult to get you during office hours."

"This better be good, you're disturbing my family time."

"I won't keep you, Mr. Mayor, rest assured. But first, a couple of preliminaries."

The Mayor listened.

"First, your initial reaction will be to hang up on me. Don't. It's a common reaction, I know, but it would be unfortunate. Just hear me out. Second, a name: The Sons of Lebanon Charitable Trust. You must remember them, they've been very generous to you."

"Just a second. Hold on."

The Mayor pushed the hold button. His wife had been trying to understand what the conversation was about. She had as much invested in his career as he did, and made it a point to know as much about her husband's life as possible.

"I have to take this in the office," he said, and got up from the kitchen table. There are secrets in every marriage.

He went into a small office off the kitchen, closed the door, and sat down, breathing out slowly, composing himself. Then he pushed the resume button on the cell.

"Now, Mr. Houde, what is this about?"

"Nothing to worry about, Mr. Mayor. I just want to ask you a very small and simple favour."

Again, the Mayor said nothing, letting the silence hang.

"Please write down this name. Mr. Alfredo Cortina. A simple and hardworking Guatemalan who has been in Canada with his wonderful wife and three children for ten years. Every year for the last ten years he has applied to the city. Nothing much, just a humble blue-collar job, anything will do. But guess what? In each of those years his application has been turned down. Have you written down his name, Mr. Mayor."

"I'm taking notes."

"Well, Mr. Mayor. This year is his lucky year. This is the year he finally gets a job with the city. Isn't that wonderful?"

The Mayor didn't answer.

"This afternoon, your office will receive an envelope with Mr. Cortina's application form, employment history, and references. It will be addressed to you and marked 'Personal and Confidential,' so you should alert your staff. I would hate for it to get lost in the bureaucracy. I would like Mr. Cortina to receive an offer of employment – full-time, full benefits, and no probationary period – within one week. That's not a lot to ask, Mr. Mayor. Is it?"

Perhaps it was the insignificance of the request, but the Mayor started to push back. "This is an outrage. Are you blackmailing me? That's a criminal offence, you know."

The voice responded calmly. "Mr. Mayor. Don't forget the good Sons of Lebanon. If I wanted to blackmail you I would be asking for a lot more. I am simply offering the city an excellent candidate and helping him overcome the usual cronyism of the city's hiring practices."

The Mayor recalled a cash donation of $100,000 from the Sons of Lebanon in the last election. A donation that required some finesse to accept and distribute, given that it was all cash and a receipt was not required. He also knew that he had already handsomely repaid various members of the Sons of Lebanon in city contracts.

"Listen, if you have anything to bring to my attention respecting on behalf of The Sons of Lebanon, I suggest you do it through them. I'm sure that if you speak to their Mr. Nabil, I believe, he will provide you with sufficient information to demonstrate that our administration has worked very closely with the Lebanese community and continues to do so. All requests should be addressed to him, and when he brings it to my attention, I will do my utmost to assist your … ah … client."

"Mr. Mayor, my request has nothing to do with the Sons of Lebanon. I simply mentioned their name because I thought it might motivate you to take Mr. Cortina's application into consideration."

The Mayor was confused. This was information that shouldn't be known by anyone except those involved, and it was worrying to think that others knew. But it all came down to politics — do favours and receive them.

"Look, Mr. – " he looked at his notes. "Mr. Houde, send me the application and I'll see what I can do. You know that times have changed. I don't control hiring by the city. I can't get involved in those day-to-day decisions."

"I understand. But Mr. Cortina needs work. He's a good man, he's qualified, and he will improve the city's minority hiring record. These are all good things. I'm sure that the city can find a place for him."

"I'll pass along his file, with a recommendation."

"With a strong recommendation. Make it a really strong one."

"Listen. I don't want you to call me on my wife's number, do you understand? If you need to speak to me, and I hope that our business is finished, call my cell phone number." He recited numbers to the caller.

"Mr. Mayor, I hope we won't have to talk again."

"So do I. I will see what I can do."

In the car ride to the office, the Mayor went over the call. He felt he had handled it well. It was politics, just somebody exercising a bit of leverage. There was nothing to worry about. He would have to speak to Réjane Cloutier, the head of the blue-collar union,

24

about the hiring, but he was sure that they could reach an understanding. It wasn't a big favour, so Cloutier couldn't expect too much for agreeing. The Mayor wondered what he would want.

Vanier stood next to the cash machine in a greasy spoon on Ontario Street watching four eggs cook on the grill behind the counter. Saint-Jacques sat in a booth by the window, talking on her phone.

A kind review would have called the place unpretentious. The colour scheme was red, white, and black – the shock version of each colour. Below waist level, the tiled floor, the booths, the round plastic tops of the counter stools, and the bottom half of the walls screamed fire-engine red. Above the red, the white walls were covered in a series of black and white posters that listed more meal choices than a buffet at the United Nations. But it wasn't the kind of place where you ordered anything other than breakfast, burgers, hot dogs or fries, anything else might have been growing mould in the back of the fridge for months.

The owner loaded eggs, bacon, potatoes, beans, and toast onto thin plastic plates and finished them off with a limp postage stamp of lettuce and an anaemic slice of tomato. He put them on a red tray, took Vanier's money, and mumbled, "Bon Appétit." Vanier carried the trays over to the booth.

Saint-Jacques looked doubtfully at the offering as Vanier slipped into the booth opposite her.

"Food for the masses," he said, tearing at sachets of salt and pepper.

"That's why the masses are having so many coronaries."

Vanier picked up a plastic knife and fork and started ripping the eggs apart.

"I have a triathlon coming up in three weeks. Bacon and eggs aren't exactly recommended. It makes you flabby."

"Flabby?" Vanier feigned hurt. "Look at me. I'm not flabby."

"Have you been tested for tapeworm? Maybe that's what's keeping you slim?"

Saint-Jacques started to cut an egg carefully around the yolk, then she forked the whites and ate. Vanier watched.

"How far do you run?"

"It's an easy one. Swim 1.5 kilometres, bike 40, and then run 10."

"You're kidding, right?"

She smiled. "I'm thinking of doing the Ironman in a couple of years. That's a 4 kilometre swim, 180 kilometres on a bike, and a 20 kilometre run to finish things off."

Vanier put his plastic utensils down and looked up. "So maybe you shouldn't eat junk." He looked at her plate and realized she wasn't. Her breakfast was largely untouched, except for one egg. She had eaten the white around the yolk, and he watched her slip the plastic fork under the yolk and raise it to her mouth. The yolk disappeared into her mouth and she closed down on it.

"Now that's how to eat a fried egg," she said, grinning.

Vanier went back to eating.

"I hope you don't mind me saying this, boss, but you look like shit."

"Thanks," he said, looking up. "I wasn't sure. Just thought it was the lighting."

"Alex?" she asked. Vanier said nothing, spread jam on his toast. "Tough night?"

"We'll get through it. I could do with a good night's sleep, though." Which meant, end of conversation. Pick another subject. Saint-Jacques got the message.

"Laurent says they're waiting for the garage to report on the Buick, but without the other vehicle there's not much to go on."

"How's the driver?"

"In a coma. His brain was swollen with fluid, so the doctors put him out while they drain it. Could be a couple of days before we can we can talk to him."

"And Legault?"

"That was easy. Flood got the prints early this morning and ran them through. Legault's got a record going back years. His juvenile is sealed, but when he hit eighteen he was already in his stride. It's all small, crappy stuff, break and enter, assault, possession, one for trafficking put him away for three years, actually served eight months. A typical loser cv."

"Gangs?"

"Flood says no. There's nothing to suggest he was part of any gang. He didn't seem to be a joiner."

Vanier took a paper napkin and wiped grease and egg yolk from his mouth. Then he picked up the styrofoam coffee cup, sipped, and winced. It was warm, and that was the most distinctive thing about it. "So they lifted Legault at 10 a.m., took him somewhere, and he shows up at midnight in a body bag, looking like he spent the day in a cement mixer with a couple of bricks. What do you think?"

"Why kidnap him. Why not just kill him where he was?" said Saint-Jacques.

"To get information? To avoid publicity?"

"Kidnapping would get a lot more publicity than just another drug murder."

"Yeah, but only if anyone found out. Maude wasn't in a hurry to call it in."

"What kind of information could he have had?" asked Vanier.

"Who knows? He wasn't exactly a kingpin."

Vanier was using the last slice of toast to mop up egg yolk and ketchup. "Were we using him? You think he could have been an informant?"

"I've seen worse. We could check."

"You can try. But nobody is going to come forward to volunteer that their informant was killed. That always looks bad."

Saint-Jacques was writing notes. "What about the body bag?"

"It's better than a rolled-up carpet for disposing of a body."

"Lighter, too. It's even got handles."

"The body bag's interesting. Who the hell uses body bags? I've never seen that before."

"Worth tracking down?"

"I don't suppose you can buy them at Canadian Tire. Sure, have someone look into it."

Saint-Jacques pushed her plate away and pulled out her cell phone. She'd left everything else except that one egg. Vanier took her plate, put it on top of his own, and finished off her breakfast while she made the call.

She watched him eat, then hung up the phone,

"Flood's going to do both: the body bag and the informant possibility. You hungry?"

"Got to feed the machine."

"Clog up the machine is more like it."

"We've been through that. Tapeworm, remember?" Vanier stood up. "Okay. Let's go visit Mom and Dad and break the bad news."

"I never get used to breaking the bad news."

"Try not to," said Vanier, carrying the plates to the trash.

The address Maude had given them was a social housing block on Vimont, a four-story brick building with a wheelchair ramp, electric doors, and an elevator. It was probably the best place any of the tenants had ever lived. It wasn't often that bureaucrats shelled out the money to build social housing, but when they did, they made sure to spend enough. It was a great way to repay favours to contractors. You can't have graft without fat in the contracts.

The Legault apartment was on the first floor, and Madame let them in. She pegged them for police immediately and didn't see the need for conversation. Instead, she turned and walked back into the apartment, leaving the door open and expecting them to follow. They navigated around an electric scooter – the kind you find outside Walmart – that took up most of the width of the hallway.

The air was poisonous with cigarette smoke, and Madame was lighting another when they walked into the living room. Except for a single chair at the table, every flat surface was covered with the kind of assorted junk and gadgets you'd find in a down-scale charity shop. It looked like they had given up balancing the incoming stock against sales; the room was bulging with a hoarder's trove of mismatched cutlery, chipped glasses and cups, food mixers, toasters, a microwave oven, even a George Foreman grill. The kind of junk the pawn shops teach kids not to steal. Madame stood by the chair and flicked cigarette ash into a dinner plate already brimming with spent butts and ashes.

She said, "It's about Émile."

"Yes, Madame. Is your husband here?"

"He's in the back. This way."

She led them past more piles of crap into a small bedroom where Émile Legault's father lay in bed sucking oxygen through a face mask under loose pages of the *Journal de Montréal*. He pulled off the mask and said, "It's Émile?"

"I'm afraid so," said Vanier. "Your son Émile was found dead last night. He was murdered."

The old man reached for a cigarette. Vanier was expecting tears but there were only the resigned looks of people beyond surprise.

"We'll have to arrange a funeral," Madame said to her husband. He ignored her.

"I always told him drugs are shit. Sure, he made some money, but drugs are shit. There are other ways to make money."

"You don't seem surprised," said Vanier.

"Do I look stupid? You don't retire selling drugs, or using them,

29

and Émile did both, he had a bad habit."

Vanier said nothing. Saint-Jacques was looking at Legault's mother, who had raised her arm up and was scratching the fat at the back, like it helped her think.

Legault coughed and said, "He was his own best customer. If it wasn't for Maude, he would've gone bust long ago."

"Maude?" Vanier had trouble imagining that the wasted junkie had been a lot of help.

"She was the brains." He coughed again, this time from deep within his lungs. Then he leaned over and retched a tennis ball of phlegm into a pint glass on the bedside table. "Maude's a junkie too. But she knew enough to sell enough to keep it going. Émile thought he was in charge, but she was the business woman."

"You guys got along?"

"Hell no. I hate the bitch. Every time I saw her she was asking for money. Like their problems were mine."

"Like you've got money," Madame said.

He flashed her a look that said shut your mouth, and she ignored it.

"Did he say anything recently to suggest why someone would want to kill him?" Saint-Jacques asked.

"Émile said a lot of things," said the father. "Most of it was bullshit. He was a junkie first and a dealer second. His problem was selling enough to keep going. His customers stole from him. His girlfriend stole from him. There had to come a time when he couldn't pay."

"Any names? Who he owed money to? Did anyone threaten him?" asked Vanier.

"You sure you're a cop? His suppliers would fuck him over for the thrill of it. His customers were junkies. Fuck, they'd steal your eyeballs and come back for the lashes. You want names, go ask Maude. That bitch wrote everything down. I've seen her. Her mind is shot, so she had to write everything down. She'll know how much he owed and to which fucker he owed it. Not complicated." He turned to his wife. "Should have been a cop myself."

Then he laughed.

Madame turned to Saint-Jacques. "The funeral place will know where to collect him?"

Saint-Jacques handed the card to the woman. "If they don't, have them call me."

"He was a good kid when he was young," she said.

"I'm sure," said Saint-Jacques.

The old man's laugh had turned to a hacking cough, and neither of them wanted to stay around for the birth of the next ball of phlegm. As they were making for the door, the old man managed, "Hey, officers, see anything you like, make me an offer."

Poste de Quartier 23 is Hochelaga's police station. It sits back from the street on a grassy incline, with a large plate-glass door at the top of a white stone staircase.

Vanier was inside, sitting in front of Commander Lechasseur. They were on page six of a PowerPoint presentation on crime reduction in Hochelaga. Vanier and Saint-Jacques had been looking for information on drug dealers who had disappeared in the last few years, and the desk officer had suggested they talk to the Commander. The desk officer was probably still laughing about it now. Saint-Jacques had made an excuse and left as soon as she saw Lechasseur pull out the PowerPoint.

Vanier stared at a graph. Lechasseur said, "The X-axis measures time, in years. The Y-axis is the number of establishments known to sell drugs."

There was a chart, with columns for each year. In case Vanier missed the point, Lechasseur leaned over and traced his finger along the declining red line above the columns.

"We went from twenty-eight establishments four years ago to six last year." He tapped his finger on the column that represented last year. "Émile Legault would be in here. And next year he won't."

He turned the page to reveal a map of Hochelaga with printed stars. "The stars represent the illegal establishments. This one is four years ago. The next four show progress over time." Lechasseur leaned over again and turned pages for Vanier. He was obviously enjoying himself, honing his presentation skills. "From twenty-eight to eighteen, to ten, to six. We think they'll all be gone next year."

"Impressive, sir. Where did they go?"

"Go?"

"Yes. What happened to them?"

"Some, we arrested and closed down. The rest have just left my jurisdiction and haven't come back. I assume they've either reformed or that they're someone else's problem. Someone else's problem, more likely."

The Commander didn't seem to care whose problem they became. His job was limited to his jurisdiction. The message from the PowerPoint was clear, Commander Lechasseur had led a transformation in Hochelaga. The brass loved statistics, and everyone loves success. Careers are built on a lot less.

"Commander, if you don't mind me asking, how did it happen? It is remarkable." Vanier wasn't above flattery when it would get him somewhere. And the Commander was beaming at the attention.

"A very good question, Detective Inspector." He sat back in his chair. "There's no point mopping up the water if you don't fix the leak."

"You have a point, sir," he said, not sure if he understood what the point was.

"We have implemented a dual focus. We put pressure on the existing establishments to close, and we're quick to respond to any new businesses opening up. Word soon gets out."

"Pressure?"

"Immense pressure. If I can say so. We might park a cruiser for twelve hours outside an establishment. That's two men and a cruiser. That's very risky from a manpower perspective, but I was willing to take the risk. Two or three times a month. I also convinced the fire service to make regular inspections. They would show up to check the batteries in the smoke detectors once a month. The city inspectors would be in and out looking for mice and rats. Believe me, it sounds like nothing, but it's all very bad for business. Eventually, the bad guys get the message and leave.

"What's really interesting, Inspector, is that the more attention we paid to a place, the more likely the neighbours were to put pressure on these people. Now I don't agree with some of the things that have been done, but I understand it. We are giving honest and law-abiding citizens hope that things could change, and they respond. It's as though attitudes changed when we showed them the police were committed. The neighbours start taking a stand for themselves. I'm still trying to come up with a way to measure that, you know, to prove my hypothesis: increased police attention translating into increased community involvement. Combatting crime is everyone's job, Inspector."

"What sort of things?"

"Pardon?"

"You said you didn't agree with some of the things people did. What sort of things?"

"I've heard stories of different kinds of pressure tactics," Lechasseur replied. "You know, graffiti on doors, bricks through windows, that sort of thing. Nothing too serious. Last year there was an unfortunate incident with an incendiary device that caused a lot of damage, but it was an isolated event. Obviously, we don't get a lot of complaints about these incidents, the victims are not the complaining sort. But when ordinary people lash out, it's usually not very sophisticated. Hochelaga's a complicated place, Inspector. It takes a while to get to understand it. Tell you what." He leaned forward, as though he just had a good idea. "Why don't we ask Constable Wallach to give you the tour?"

"Constable Wallach?"

"He's the station's Community Relations Officer. He knows what's going on around here better than any of us. I'll see if he's around."

Lechasseur picked up his phone to track down Wallach. When he finished, he turned back to Vanier.

"He's on his way. He'll drive you and your partner around for a tour. Constable Wallach's been a great help with collecting the data for this." Lechasseur tapped his finger on the presentation. "He knows everyone. It's his job, I know. But he hears within a day or two as soon as a new establishment opens, and we get to work. Dissuasion, that's the key. The bad guys have to know that things aren't what they were. What we have here, Inspector, is Community Policing at its best. Nothing new opening and the old businesses closing down. It takes time." He leaned forward to make his point. "But it's a hundred times more effective than the damn justice system."

Vanier listened while Lechasseur continued to practice his presentation skills, extolling the virtues of effective community policing in a speech he'd obviously been rehearsing.

When Vanier was wondering how much more he could take, Wallach knocked on the door and walked in. "You were looking for me, sir?"

"I was. I've just been giving Inspector Vanier some background on the progress we've been making over the last few years. He's investigating the death of Émile Legault."

"Murder," said Vanier, rising to shake hands with Wallach.

"Yes. Of course. Murder. Émile Legault's murder," said Lechasseur.

"Who's Legault?" asked Wallach.

"You know him. Had a place on Joliette," said Lechasseur.

"Oh, that Legault. He's dead?"

"Left the planet," said the Commander.

"Does anyone care?" Wallach looked at Vanier.

"Me," said Vanier. "Any idea who would want to kill him?"

"Any one of his customers. His suppliers. Maybe his girlfriend. His neighbours. Is that enough to be going on with? He was a piece of shit, Inspector. He won't be missed."

Lechasseur said, "I thought it would be a good idea for you to give the Inspector and his partner a tour of the neighbourhood. A bit of local flavour might help them." He reached out to recover his PowerPoint printout, and Vanier put his hand on it.

"Can I keep it?"

"Absolutely. The more circulation it gets the better. Real Improvement Through Focused Community Policing. That's the working title."

"It gets the point across."

"You ready to go now?" asked Wallach.

Vanier stood up. "We'll pick up Saint-Jacques on the way."

They took an unmarked car, and Constable Richard Wallach seemed happy to play the tourist guide, hatless but in uniform, with the obligatory bullet-resistant vest with Police written across the back. Saint-Jacques was in the passenger seat, and Vanier was spread out in the back.

"I grew up here, on Davidson, below Sainte-Catherine. There were maybe eight or ten Jewish families on the street, all from Germany. There were no Jewish schools, so we were put in with the English, along with anyone else who wasn't French. We went to Memorial on Préfontaine, and the French went to St. Émile. The big divide."

Vanier was staring out the window.

"So how did you feel about coming back?" Saint-Jacques asked.

"I wasn't sure at first. So many people had left. The only people still here are those who couldn't make it out. It was hard at the beginning. The place has changed. But I'm happy now. It was a tough place when I was growing up, working-class, poor, and pretty much ignored by everyone outside. But it was a neighbourhood with stable families. The crime didn't seem to affect daily life. Sure, you could buy a gun in most taverns, but only if you bought two draft at the same time. It was almost civilized."

He turned back to Saint-Jacques. "Then it got worse. Much worse, the whole place fell apart. Drugs were everywhere, prostitution, muggings, break and entries. Nobody from here was getting rich, and everyone was suffering. Things are on the mend now. They're looking up. But before we talk about the present, let's visit the past."

Wallach pulled into the parking lot of Marché Maisonneuve, and they got out. He led them past the indoor market to the plaza. The old market building that now serves as the City Hall dominates the square, an imposing Beaux-Arts building from the early 1900s topped with a fifty-foot high cupola tower. You can't look at the City Hall without noticing the chalk-white, leaning tower of the Olympic Stadium looking over it like a jealous neighbour. The Stadium is a gaudy, modernist display of the artist's creativity with poured concrete, but Marché Maisonneuve was built to serve, like a community matriarch with tough muscles and callused hands imposing order and comfort in equal measure. The Stadium keeps legions of professionals busy finding ways to make it useful while the Marché Maisonneuve is just used, as it has been for over a century.

In the middle of the plaza a bronze statue of a farmer's wife, La Fermière, standing atop a huge fountain surrounded by bronze children and animals. Someone had poured detergent into the fountain, and the water was covered by a thick layer of dirty white suds.

They were standing at the top of the steps of City Hall looking down at the fountain and beyond, to the wide Avenue Morgan where the public baths were housed in a temple-like building fronted by massive Tuscan columns.

Vanier had driven by the plaza countless times and had never stopped. He turned around, taking it in for the first time, like a tourist in Rome.

Wallach was holding his arms out. "This was all built when Hochelaga still had ambitions. Back then, it was called Pittsburgh North because of the industry and the port. The place was thriving, a serious competitor to Montreal. It had shipbuilding, heavy industry, factories making shoes, textiles, cigarettes, everything. The city fathers wanted it to be a Garden City, to have workers and bosses, everyone living together in harmony.

"What happened?"

"They ran out of money in the depression at the end of World War I."

"The end of a dream," said Vanier.

"The end of many dreams. Things went downhill from there."

Standing between La Fermière and City Hall, Vanier could imagine the ambition and pride that went into building the place. Nothing projects a city's pride like decorative public spaces and monumental buildings meant to last for hundreds of years. The city fathers had tried for immortality and had lost.

"The decline took decades. First the bosses left to live in the smarter parts of Montreal, and then, over the years, the factories closed, work went overseas or just dried up, the shipbuilding yards closed, the Angus yards that used to build locomotives closed down. The engineers left, there was no work for the skilled guys, families fell into poverty. Eventually, there wasn't a good job to be had. The place spiralled into decay.

"Hochelaga never got its fair shake of anything, except bad

breaks. And it got more than it needed of those. With the City of Montreal in charge, nobody gave a shit, and the place was left to rot. But things are getting better, Inspector. You wanted to know if any other dealers have gone missing. Truth is, they've been bailing out, like rats off a sinking ship. But the ship's not sinking. The opposite. It's just the rats can't take the improvements."

They got back in the car, and Wallach started cruising up and down residential streets, stopping every now and then to point out an apartment or a small house that looked just like the others, except it used to be a crack house or a brothel.

"In the last couple of years we're getting new people coming in. The old landlords are selling out, and then the pressure is on us to clean up. It's bizarre, people buy a house cheap because it's next to a dump, and then they start calling City Hall, screaming that someone should close down the dump. The poor bastards who owned the place before had probably been doing the same thing for years, and nobody listened to them. I guess it's who you know."

"So the complaints worked?" Vanier asked.

"We haven't been doing any more raids, but the bad guys are leaving. Either down to the zone or just disappearing."

"The zone?"

"Yeah, the zone. The great experiment."

Wallach took Davidson down to Sainte-Catherine and drove slowly west. "It starts here. It's not official, but south of Sainte-Catherine to the river, from Moreau west to the train tracks, it's a no-go zone for us. A zone of tolerance. We don't arrest anybody for anything. We don't even go in there unless we're called."

Vanier counted six prostitutes working the street in three blocks, and it was only 11 a.m. "Can we do a drive-through?"

"Like I said, Inspector, we don't go in there unless we're called."

Vanier made a mental note to visit. He'd ask Saint-Jacques if she wanted to go.

Three

It was Sunday. Vanier had hoped to spend the day with Alex, but that hadn't worked out. Alex didn't get up until one o'clock, and he left at two. He had things to do, he said, and wouldn't be back till late. So Vanier called Anjili.

Dr. Anjili Segal was one of Montreal's six coroners, and she and Vanier had been dating for over two years, each of them giving up bits and pieces of their lives to the other, growing inevitably closer. They were wandering cautiously to the moment when they might consider living together, but neither of them was hurried.

Anjili got lost in her work as much as Vanier did. That was part of how well they got along together. They each understood hastily arranged dates and last-minute cancellations, and each lived with the erratic schedules and last minute crises that doom most relationships. They had found a way to make the relationship work, despite the obstacles. When he thought about it, he liked to think that she understood Rilke's definition of love: *Two solitudes that protect and touch and greet each other*.

But Alex's return had changed things; Vanier was no longer just distracted with work. He had a sick son who occupied his time and his mind. Anjili hadn't said anything, but she didn't need to. He could feel the strain in the innumerable other ways that people communicate. With anyone else, he would have pulled back and let the relationship slow down and die, but he didn't want to lose her.

So he found himself apologizing more often than ever and making promises that he didn't know if he could keep. He kept telling her it was just a matter of time before things would be back to normal. And she kept wanting to believe him.

He punched the speed dial number on his phone, and she picked up on the third ring.

"Hey, stranger," she said.

"Ah, don't say that."

"I haven't heard from you in so long." There was a smile in her voice. She was glad he called.

"Three days, Anjili. That's all."

"That's all? It seems like so long. I forget what you look like."

"Funny. Are you up for dinner tonight?"

"Dinner? With a handsome stranger? Did you get the night off?" Vanier let out a sigh. "Yes, I've got the night off."

"School night or weekend?"

"What?"

"You staying over?"

"I can't, Anjili. Just dinner."

"So a school night. I suppose a girl's got to take what she can get. What time?"

"I'll pick you up at seven. Okay?"

"Wonderful. I'll waiting downstairs, my love. Maybe you should wear a rose so I'll recognize you."

"Sure. I'll wear a rose."

The waiter in the Maisonneuve Tavern placed another quart bottle of Export in front of Desportes. Desportes handed him a twenty.

"And, Jacques, give me a bacon cheeseburger to go, with some fries… and beans. Lots of protein."

The waiter looked at Desportes. "You leaving? You're still hungry?" It was 10:30, and the kitchen was about to close.

"Maybe I'll get hungry later on. Who knows?"

Desportes went back to reading. It was Sunday night, and the tavern was quiet. The Canadians were on another losing streak. They wouldn't make the Playoffs again, and people had given up caring. It was raining outside, and only the die-hard lonely drinkers were out.

By the time Desportes got up to go, he had enough beer in him to ensure that he would sleep for five hours. The styrofoam container of food in a white plastic bag dangled from his hand. He walked along Ontario Street until he reached Bennett, then he turned, walked half a block north, and disappeared into an alley. He felt more comfortable in the alleys that crisscrossed Hochelaga than on its main streets.

The previous night, he had seen her pretending to sleep behind a dumpster as she watched his footsteps pass by. He pretended he hadn't seen her. Now, when he approached the same spot, he saw that she was there again, motionless, curled up in some kind of blanket under a torn cardboard box. He bent down and dropped the bag of food near her head. She didn't move, but he could see she was holding her breath. She was young, but he couldn't tell how young. He looked at her for a few seconds and then walked slowly away.

Twenty minutes later he was trolling through emails received over the last few days by Leon Kaufman, a partner in one of Montreal's largest accounting firms. Desportes had unrestricted access to Kaufman's emails because a woman he had helped out returned the favour. She supervised the overnight cleaning staff in Kaufman's office building and let Desportes in one night. She had turned her back while he installed a small program onto Kaufman's computer. She turned her back a bunch of other times that night, too, while Desportes did the same on a half dozen other computers. Now, going through the emails was a bit like fishing and, given it was close to the end of the first quarter, Desportes was fishing for information on upcoming quarterly reports from listed companies.

Quarterly earnings move the market. If a company beats expectations, the stock will rise. Disappoint, and it will fall. The market is predictable if you have more information than the average Joe, and Desportes worked hard to have more information than the average Joe.

It didn't take him long to find an email chain discussing the surprisingly bad results from Emphram Corp., a technology company that went public three years before, buoyed by glowing reports from analysts and a multi-million-dollar contract from National Defence. It was now trading at fifteen dollars a share. But it had oversold the technology and underbid the Defence contract, and, as Kaufman delicately put it in his email to Emphram's CFO, "the shit is about to hit the fan." The quarterly report would show the company was losing millions a month on the contract, and the technology had more bugs than a rooming house mattress. Kaufman predicted the price would drop five to ten dollars as soon as the results were released.

Desportes had no trouble buying a put option with a thirteen dollar strike price that expired two weeks after Emphram's report hit the street. If the price fell below that any time before the option expired, he would make serious money, or rather an obscure Cayman company would make a bundle and, given the Byzantine corporate structure he had put in place, nobody would be able to trace it to him.

Vanier lay in bed beside Anjili. Not touching. The clock radio said 1 a.m., but it was only 12:45. She kept it fifteen minutes fast, thinking it helped her in the morning.

He knew he had to leave, but there isn't a good way to get up and go home after lovemaking. No matter how many times she said she understood, he knew it hurt her.

She was pretending to be asleep. He shifted his weight carefully, trying not to disturb the bed, and dressed quietly in the dark. Then he moved around to her side and bent down to kiss her. Her face was buried in the pillow, and a blanket covered her shoulders. All there was to kiss was the back of her head.

"Don't."

"I'm sorry, Anjili."

"I don't know how much more of this shit I can take." Her voice was muffled by the pillow.

"You don't have to talk like that."

She turned and looked up at him. "You want me to be more polite? This shit. It's horrible. I can't take it."

"Anjili, I can't help it. You told me you understood."

"You think I don't understand?"

"That's not what I mean."

"Of course I understand. That's the problem. I can't blame you, so I can only blame myself. Luc, I'm too old for this. I hate you for leaving, and I hate myself for feeling that. Maybe I should just stop caring."

He knew he should stay, talk it through, but they'd had the conversation too often in the last few weeks. He'd tell her it was temporary, that Alex would work his way through things, and then they could think about moving in together. And she would pretend to agree.

"We're like teenagers, stealing moments," she said. "But without the fun."

He sat down on the bed, tired, unable to have the conversation. She rolled over to look up at him, and caught him looking at the clock.

"Let yourself out," she said and rolled back into the pillow.

All he could say was, "Sorry."

"Luc. Go. I'm tired. We'll talk about this another time."

Vanier stood up, and the cat jumped onto the bed, curled against her, and began purring. She reached an arm around it.

"Okay. I'm off."

"Lock the door on your way out."

Four

Vanier was reading the autopsy report on Legault. Even in Dr. Nadeau's medical jargon, it wasn't easy. Dr. Nadeau concluded that Legault had been restrained – there were rope marks on his wrists and ankles – and beaten over a period of several hours. The precise cause of death was unknown; each of the five blows to the head had fractured his skull, and it was impossible to tell which was the fatal one. It didn't really matter. There were plenty of other injuries, including an inch missing from the index finger of his right hand, but none would have been fatal on their own.

Most of Legault's injuries were to his upper body, but there was serious bruising around his groin. He had three broken ribs. His front teeth and a large molar in the back were gone. His nose was broken in three places, and his cheekbone jutted out through torn skin. Legault's last hours had been brutal.

Vanier wondered what Legault had done to deserve the beating. In gang wars, people get shot, knifed, or even blown up by homemade bombs, not tortured to death over an afternoon. He couldn't believe that Legault had information that could only be beaten out of him, Legault wouldn't have been that brave. So why go to the trouble? It didn't look like an accident – like they wanted to teach him a lesson, but went too far. Vanier knew people who could work you over so badly in a few minutes that you would remember it forever.

It seemed Legault was doomed from the start. The key was finding out why. And right now, Vanier didn't have any ideas.

For the second time, Vanier and Saint-Jacques went down the five steps to Legault's semi-basement apartment. The door was wide open, and you couldn't miss the smell of fresh paint. Inside, the floors were spread with painters' sheets. The guy rolling paint on the walls didn't stop when the two cops walked in.

"It's closed. No drugs here. Fuck off."

"Police. What's going on?" said Vanier.

The man stopped painting and turned to Vanier. "I'm painting. What does it look like?"

"Funny. Where is everything? The tenant's stuff?"

"Moved out. The woman went into a shelter, and we were told to clean the place up for new tenants."

"We?"

"Yeah. My partners. They left an hour ago. They're driving all the shit to the Eco Centre."

"Who decided?"

He put the roller down reluctantly and pulled a paper from his top pocket. "Here's the Work Order."

Vanier unfolded the paper and read the instructions:

- Clear out contents
- Repair minor damage
- Quote on major repairs
- Repaint all walls

The Work Order was from the *Société des Patriotes de Montréal*.

"Who are these guys?" Vanier read the name, "*Société des Patriotes de Montréal*?"

"The *Patriotes*. It's a community organization. They run a lot of programs around here. Listen, you have a problem with this, you go see them. Me, I've got a job to do."

He picked up the roller, dipped it in the paint, and went back to work.

"And if you think we robbed the place, there was nothing to rob. The woman took her clothes in a garbage bag and that was about it. The rest was crap, filthy couches, mattresses that looked like they'd been pissed on more often than a lamppost. I don't know how people live like that. It's a disgrace. And his customers have been coming in here all morning. Scum, they are. Filthy scum."

While he was talking, Saint-Jacques had done a quick tour. "It's empty."

"Yeah. It is now. You should have seen it earlier. Empty beer bottles and syringes everywhere, and enough dirty ashtrays for a smokers' convention. If you ask me, it's a good thing. Going from a crack house to social housing."

"You know where the woman went?"

"Haven't a clue. A lady from the *Patriotes* was with her. She said something about a shelter."

Vanier turned to leave, and Saint-Jacques followed him out.

"Where to, boss?"

"Let's go visit the *Patriotes*. Whoever they are." The Work Order had an address on Ontario Street.

The *Patriotes* operated out of a former store. You couldn't miss it. There was a large sign over the entrance with *Société des Patriotes de Montréal* painted in blue letters, three feet high, framed at each end by small renditions of the Quebec flag.

From the outside, it resembled a political campaign office. The store's plate glass windows gave passersby an unobstructed view of everything inside, cheap desks and chairs, filing cabinets, posters on the wall, a coffee machine, and little else. The three women sitting at the desks all looked up when Vanier and Saint-Jacques set the bell on the door jangling.

"Police officers," Vanier said. "We're here to see whoever is in charge."

"That would be Colonel Montpetit," said a woman with a bright purple streak through her black hair. "I'll call him." The other two women continued to stare.

There was a threadbare couch against a wall, but Vanier and Saint-Jacques remained standing. Sitting down sends the wrong message – that you're expecting to wait. A wooden staircase at the back of the room led up to a doorway. It opened after a few minutes, and two men in vaguely matching military jackets and pants and green button-down shirts came down the stairs.

"Shit, I hate uniforms," Vanier whispered to Saint-Jacques.

The first man was shaved bald. You could see the shadow where hair still sprouted, and where he was really bald. He would have looked years older if he didn't shave his head. The second man was older and had enough hair for both of them, dyed black as a crow. At the bottom of the stairs, the bald guy did a bodyguard impression, looking around and then stepping aside for the boss.

The hairy one made straight for the two officers, flashing a big grin and holding his hand out.

"I'm Colonel Montpetit," he said. "You asked to see me."

"You're in charge?"

"I am the leader of the *Société des Patriotes de Montréal*. So, yes, I'm in charge."

Vanier shook his hand. "I'm Detective Inspector Vanier, Serious Crimes. This is Detective Sergeant Saint-Jacques."

The Colonel took in Saint-Jacques. She was used to men ogling her. She lived in what was still a man's world, and had learned to deal with it. For a second her eyes locked on Montpetit's, and he got the non-verbal communication: *Never in a million years, asshole.*

He took a step back. "Perhaps we should go up to my office. Corporal Brasso will lead us."

They followed Brasso up the stairs, with the Colonel bringing up the rear. He led them down a corridor into an open office space that faced onto the street. It was a contrast to the Spartan furnishings below; carpeted and well furnished, with a boardroom table at one end and a heavy wooden desk at the other. The long room was divided by a rectangle of two leather couches and two armchairs. The Colonel herded them to the long table, and Brasso sat down in one of the armchairs.

"So what can I do for you, Inspector?"

"We're investigating the murder of Émile Legault."

The Colonel furrowed his brow, as though he was trying to remember.

"Legault? The name doesn't mean anything." He turned to the other man. "Corporal Brasso, do you know this man Legault?"

"Never heard of him, sir."

The Colonel turned back to Vanier. "Perhaps with some context. Does he work for us? I know almost everyone."

"Not that I know of," said Vanier. "He was running a crack house on Joliette. Your group was his landlord."

"Can't be, Inspector. We don't have that many tenants, and I would recognize the name. And if he was selling drugs out of one of one of our apartments, I would have known about it and stopped it. We're very strict. No illegal activity and certainly no drugs. We're trying to improve this place, not continue its destruction."

"We went to his apartment this morning. You had people cleaning it up for the next tenant."

Montpetit thought for a second. "Oh, I think I understand."

"What?"

"Your confusion, associating us with this Legault fellow. Absentee landlords are one of the big problems in this neighbourhood. Imagine, Inspector, people think they can own an apartment building and rent apartments to anyone they want without any responsibility. Well they can't. If you own property in Hochelaga, you have a responsibility."

He emphasized the point by pointing a finger down at the table. "We've been working hard to convince these absentee landlords that if they want to take money out of the community, they must take their community responsibilities seriously." He stood up. "What's the address?"

Vanier gave him the address on Joliette Street, and the Colonel walked over to a filing cabinet. He pulled out a thin folder, reading as he walked back to the table.

"That settles it. The owner is a Mr. Panagopoulos. He seems to have finally realized the harm he was doing. He's agreed to allow the *Patriotes* to take over the apartment to show him how it can be managed properly."

"When did this happen?"

"A few days ago. Of course, I didn't speak to him myself. A leader needs to be disciplined. I have a method: Do, Delegate, Defer, or Drop, and this would have been delegation. We convinced him that allowing his property to be used as a crack house was a bad idea. So now we're managing the place. We'll be able to house a deserving family in there. Much better than a drug dealer, wouldn't you agree?"

"So what happened to Legault?"

"You've just told me he was murdered."

"With the apartment, I mean. Was he given notice?"

"Once again, not my department. I imagine it was the same as the others. Someone would have had a word with him and told him that he was no longer welcome, and he would have left."

"And if he didn't want to go?"

The Colonel smiled. "They always decide to leave. My people can be persuasive."

"Someone kidnapped him two days ago, and he showed up

dead ten hours later." Vanier heard Brasso shifting in his seat. He was paying attention.

"You're not suggesting that we were involved, are you, Inspector? That would be a very serious allegation."

"You just said your people were very persuasive. Who went to see him?"

He looked through the papers in the folder. "Not clear from the file, Inspector. But I could find out for you."

"Please do."

Vanier sat back, waiting.

"Not just now." The Colonel was getting irritated. "I need to make enquiries."

"This is a murder investigation, sir. I would appreciate it if you could do whatever you need to do and get me the names. Right now."

"I'm not sure anyone even visited him."

"Why don't you find out, one way or the other. We can wait."

The Colonel sat back, closed the file and said, "Corporal Brasso. Can you make some calls and see if anyone went to see this Legault man to give him notice?"

Brasso got up. "Yes, sir." He headed for the door.

"And Mr. Brasso," said Vanier. Brasso stopped and turned. "Why don't you do the same for Mr. Panagopoulos? The Colonel probably doesn't have the names of whoever went to see him either."

Brasso looked at the Colonel. The Colonel shrugged, said, "Do it."

Then, as Brasso was at the door, Montpetit added, "But maybe Mr. Panagopoulos approached us. That's a possibility."

"Yes, sir."

The Colonel turned to the two officers. "It could have been Mr. Panagopoulos that approached us. He signed a document allowing the *Patriotes* to manage the apartment. Maybe he wanted to make amends for renting it to scum."

"Scum?"

"Scum, Inspector. We don't need any Legaults in the neighbourhood. Life is hard enough here."

"And the *Patriotes* care about that?"

"Unfortunately we may be the only ones who do."

"So what do the *Patriotes* do?"

The Colonel was relieved to be back on familiar ground. "Everything the government doesn't do. And believe me, Inspector, that's plenty. We're a charitable organization."

He got up and went back to his desk again, rummaging through a drawer. He returned with two flyers and handed one to each officer. Vanier looked at the pictures, hungry mothers, scared looking seniors, and kids playing sports.

"This describes our work: housing, pre-school programs, after-school programs, employment centres, a food bank, two kindergartens, a summer camp. You name it, we do it. If there's one thing we have a lot of in Hochelaga, it's need. We even have a program on the care and maintenance of Hochelaga taxis."

"Hochelaga taxis?"

"Otherwise known as electric scooters. You'd be amazed how many people have mobility problems around here. We fill needs, Inspector. The government does less and less every year, and we keep picking up the slack. Do you want to make a donation? It's tax deductible."

"We'll think about it," said Vanier, answering for both of them before Saint-Jacques was tempted to put her hand in her pocket.

"We started five years ago. Back then, we were simply preparing ourselves to defend Quebec. The Federals didn't give a shit, and the Provincial government is just a tool of the Feds. So we decided to be ready to protect Quebecers in any emergency. Back then, we

thought the threat was in the future, but it didn't take long to realize that Quebecers were under attack right now, every day, and
none more so that the people in our own back yard, here in Hochelaga. So we decided to do something about it.

"Now, we employ eighty people, local people who care about
this place. And we're giving people hope. There's talent in Hochelaga, Inspector, and we help people help themselves. Workers who
can't find jobs but can put in an afternoon to install a boiler in one
of our apartments. Young people with good degrees from UQAM
can't break into the job market downtown, but there's all kinds of
stuff that they can do right here. We have nurses, social workers,
teachers, lawyers. There's so much unused talent here, our biggest
challenge is putting everyone to work. But we're doing it."

Vanier was getting tired of the pep talk, he almost believed it.
But he had been staring at the pictures on the wall behind the Colonel, pictures of guys with guns. He got up to take a closer look.
They were all pictures of men in uniform wearing berets, and the
Colonel was in most of them. One showed a bunch of them marching in formation along a residential street, another had guys in combat fatigues posing with guns. Most of the photos with weapons
were taken in the country, but there was one posed in a back alley.

"And you play at making war?"

The Colonel stood up. "Nobody's playing, Inspector. We're
going to be ready, believe me. This community needs services, and
if the government won't provide them, we will. And the people
need protection. We will protect them."

Vanier tapped one of the pictures with his finger. "Nice cos-
tumes, Mr. Montpetit.

The Colonel moved closer to Vanier, and Saint-Jacques stood up.

"You should be careful. We're not playing games, Mr. Vanier. And
unless there are further questions, I think this interview is finished."

"Playing is all you'd better be doing. But we're not finished.

Mr. Brasso, remember?" "Corporal Brasso will call you with the information you need."

"Tell him not to forget. In the meantime, why don't you give me Mr. Panagopoulos's address. Maybe he remembers which of your persuasive people went to see him."

The Colonel sat down and copied an address from the file folder onto a piece of paper he handed to Vanier. Vanier turned to Saint-Jacques.

"Let's go. We've got work to do."

When the door closed behind them, the Colonel pulled out his cell phone. "Corporal Brasso. The next time Inspector Vanier pays us a visit, I'd like you to arrange something special for him. Nothing too serious, but a little surprise to help him realize that Hochelaga can be a difficult place. He needs to appreciate the work we're doing."

Before he got into his car, Vanier looked up at the second floor window and saw the Colonel watching. He wasn't smiling.

Vanier and Saint-Jacques were in Park Extension, the first home for the wave of Greek immigrants that arrived in Montreal in the 1950s. Vestiges of the community still remain in cafés that sell thick, black coffee to old men who watch football from Greece on tired television sets, and in postage-stamp parks that draw people out from dark apartments in the spring to sit and talk in the only comfortable language.

Those who prospered have long since moved on to bigger homes in the suburbs, and the children of those who couldn't escape have gone, leaving their parents behind. Succeeding waves of new immigrants from Pakistan and Bangladesh have set up their own outposts. As with most immigrant communities, eventually, all that's left is a hollow shell for the permanently displaced who can't go home because home has changed beyond recognition, and who never managed to become Canadian and move on.

Constantine Panagopoulos lived on Bloomfield Avenue, a street that sounds more up-market than it is. It was still lined with white plastic car shelters, the ugly but efficient way to keep driveways clear of snow during the winter. The driveways on Bloomfield slope down from the street to semi-basement garages, and without a shelter you'd have to shovel snow uphill all winter like a Canadian Sisyphus.

Panagopoulos led them into a living room that had the unused look of a museum display. Vanier guessed that the living was done in the kitchen. Three matching armchairs flanked a straight-backed sofa on pedestal legs. Saint-Jacques made a show of looking at the framed pictures on the wall: the Parthenon, whitewashed villas, islands in an azure sea. There was a collection of framed pictures of children at various ages on top of a glass-fronted cabinet that held the family china. Three of the kids were beaming smiles in graduation gowns.

Panagopoulos gestured for them to sit on the sofa and let himself down slowly onto one of the armchairs. "I never had police here. What I can do for you?"

Before they could answer, an older woman in a blue flour-stained apron came in with a tray of coffee and biscuits.

"My wife, Yelani," Panagopoulos said.

She smiled at Vanier and began pouring out the coffee. Vanier and Saint-Jacques took theirs, and Vanier reached for a biscuit and bit into it.

"Very good" he said, holding it up.

"*Efharistó*. I make."

"My wife. She no talk good English."

Vanier turned back to Panagopoulos. "We're here because you're the owner of the building where Émile Legault lived."

Panagopoulos's face clouded, and his wife sat down on the edge of one of the chairs. "Legault. Don't talk to me about this bastard. Only trouble since he move in. He no pay rent for months, and now I lose the apartment. So, you going to help me?"

"We're here to understand what happened. Legault was murdered, and we are investigating that."

Panagopoulos sat back, his arms out with his palms facing the officers. "Is not me. You think I could kill someone?" His wife looked worried, trying to follow the conversation.

"No. That's not it," said Vanier. "But you were the landlord. And we heard that you gave the apartment to the *Patriotes* to manage."

"Give? I no give the apartment to no one. They steal it. For ten months I try to kick Legault out. I make application to *Régie du logement*. You need *Régie* to give the okay to kick someone out of apartment. So I fill out the forms. It takes six months, then we have a hearing. But Legault, he get a lawyer to say he's sick and need more delay. So, another three months. Now I have a date for May."

He got up and went over to a sideboard cabinet against one wall, opening it with one hand, and using the other to stop the pile of papers and file folders inside from sliding to the floor. It looked like everything had just been thrown inside. He grabbed a manila folder from the pile and pushed everything else back behind the door. He handed Vanier a letter from the *Régie du logement* advising of a hearing in *Panagopoulos v. Legault*.

"So I get this. I think maybe now I get okay to kick him out. But I have to wait. And he no pay rent. I no rich. I drive taxi. But I buy this house," he raised his arms to indicate what he was talking about. "And then the building on Joliette. For thirty years I work, collect rent, pay mortgage. I keep the building good. I think someday I have something to leave my kids, you know? But these bastards, they come and make me sign document. Say it's only temporary."

He pulled another paper from the folder and handed it to Vanier.

Vanier scanned it. It was a one-page contract, Panagopoulos hands over the management and administration of the apartment to the *Société des Patriotes de Montréal*. In return, the *Patriotes* keep the rent. The contract said the arrangement would continue until both parties agreed to end it. That's the kicker, Vanier thought, temporary is until the *Patriotes* decide to end it. He handed it to Saint-Jacques.

"When did you sign?"

"It says there. March 23," Panagopoulos stood up to show Saint-Jacques the date.

"Morning? Afternoon?" asked Vanier.

"Morning. Early. Maybe eight o'clock. Two guys come and say they want to talk to me. And they come in. Big guys, you know? They fill this room. They start to talk about I'm a bad guy, letting my building be used for drugs. Maybe the police get involved, they say. One of them picks up pictures of the kids. Says I look after my kids but let other kids get ruined by drugs."

Vanier reached for another biscuit.

"I tell them it's nothing for me. I tell them about the *Régie* and all that, how I try to kick Legault out, but they don't care. Like it's my fault. And Yelani, she's crying."

Yelani nodded.

"So they give me document and say why wait for the *Régie*? Say the *Patriotes* help me, that it's only temporary. The keep saying this, temporary, like maybe fifty times. And I sign."

"Can I take this?" Saint-Jacques asked. "I'll make a copy and send it back to you."

"You want copy? I make. I have scanner."

He stood up and took the contract from Saint-Jacques and handed it to his wife, saying something in Greek. She disappeared out the door.

Vanier thought about the fact that if these guys had come in and stolen one of the pictures off the wall, it would be a crime.

But paper up theft with a contract and it's legal, not a police matter. And this one was small potatoes. He had seen family businesses stolen with lawyers' letters and bullshit legal procedures. With enough money and the right lawyer, you don't need to throw a brick through a window, you just hired a bailiff and deliver a writ.

"You know the names of the two men?" asked Vanier

"No. One time they say their names but that's all. They don't sign paper. Say it needs to be approved first. They say they send me signed copy after."

"You have signed copy?" Vanier noticed he was dropping articles.

"No. They supposed to send to me. No have yet."

Vanier handed Panagopoulos the brochure the Colonel had given him. "Are the men in any of these pictures?"

Panagopoulos studied the photo. "Yeah. That's one of them," he said, pointing.

Yelani came back in and handed a copy of the contract to each of the officers. Panagopoulos said something in Greek and pointed at the photograph in the brochure. "*Ναί*," she said.

"No?" asked Vanier.

"That's Greek for yes," said Saint-Jacques.

"Yeah. This is one of the guys," said Panagopoulos. He was pointing to a guy holding a soccer ball beside a team of eleven year olds.

"You're sure?" asked Vanier.

"*Ναί*."

Vanier looked at Saint-Jacques as if to say, I get it.

They got up to leave, mouthing thanks to Panagopoulos and promising to keep him up to date if they heard anything. Yelani reached into the deep pocket of her apron and took out two Ziploc bags of cookies. She gave one each to the officers.

"Enjoy," she said, almost giggling. Before he realized it, Vanier was leaning down to give her a kiss on both cheeks.

"Thank you," he said. Saint-Jacques awkwardly did the same

thing and followed Vanier out the door.

As they were walking to the car Saint-Jacques asked, "Since when do you give the cheek kiss to witnesses?"

"You haven't seen enough of my good side."

"There's a good side?" she said, opening the car door.

Five

This time, when Vanier and Saint-Jacques walked into the *Patriotes'* storefront on Ontario Street, they didn't wait to be escorted up to the Colonel's office. Vanier led the way up the staircase and down the hall. He knocked and entered at the same time. The Colonel looked up from his desk, surprised for a second, and then he forced an artificial smile.

"Officers, officers. What a surprise. Come in, come in," as though he were inviting them.

Montpetit was alone, and the three of them sat around the boardroom table. Before Vanier could say anything, the door opened, and Brasso walked in.

"I heard you had visitors, Colonel," he said, ignoring the officers.

"Corporal Brasso. You remember Inspector Vanier and his assistant. They're just about to tell us what they want. You haven't missed anything."

Brasso sat down. This time he sat at the table, completing the foursome.

"Mr. Montpetit," said Vanier, deliberately forgetting the rank, "We met Mr. Panagopoulos."

"Mr. Panagopoulos?"

"Legault's landlord," said Brasso.

"He tells me that two of your guys showed up at his home at eight o'clock in the morning of March 23rd and forced him to sign a contract giving up his apartment."

"I'm sure he didn't use those exact words, Mr. Vanier."

"He said he didn't have a choice. He had to sign."

"Neither of us were there, were we? And I'm sure the documents will show that he signed everything of his own free will. We have a standard form. Very legal."

"Who were the two men?"

"Corporal Brasso. Weren't you looking after that?" He looked at Brasso, who said nothing.

"Mr. Montpetit. We're in the middle of a murder investigation. Shall I put you down as cooperative, or non-cooperative?"

Montpetit had lost his smile, wondering where Vanier was going. He assumed it was a question of timing, when his men had shown up at the Panagopoulos's house.

"Cooperative, of course. Anything you need, we'll get for you."

"So can I get the names and addresses of the two men?"

Montpetit rose slowly and walked over to his desk. He made a show of checking things on his computer, and scribbled on a piece of paper. He walked back to the boardroom table and handed the paper to Vanier.

"These are the names and phone numbers of the two gentlemen who spoke to Mr. Panagopoulos. Wonderful men, both of them. Veterans. Now, will that be all?" Vanier looked at the names, Jules Leclerc and Antoine Savard. He put the paper in his pocket.

"Émile Legault was kidnapped. Three men took him from his apartment. Took his drugs and money too." Vanier didn't tell them about the fingertip left behind. It was always useful to hold back something. "Know anything about that, Mr. Montpetit?"

"Kidnapped?" He seemed to think about it for a moment. "I know nothing about that. But it probably goes with the profession. You told me he was selling drugs. Maybe he forgot to pay his supplier. I'm sure it's a very dangerous profession."

"I thought about that. But why was he kidnapped? That's what bothers me. If someone wanted to kill him, why didn't they just shoot him where he was? They had the guns to do it. But they took him away. That's what I don't understand. Then they beat the shit out of him, killed him, and then lost the body on the way to dumping it."

"He was the guy? I read about that," said Montpetit.

"Émile Legault."

"An awful business. It's like I've always said, this community is being destroyed by drugs. Wait, let me get you something. It won't take long."

Montpetit went over to his desk again, picked up the phone and said, "Melissa? Three coffees in here when you have a chance. Thanks." Then he turned to the computer and started typing.

Saint-Jacques stood up and stretched, walking over to the window to gaze down on Ontario Street. She watched a kid riding a bike slowly up the middle of the street like he owned the place, forcing the traffic behind him to slow down. The kid turned onto the pavement below the window, where Vanier's car was parked, and leaned his bike against a tree. He was young, barely looked fifteen, with an oversized white quilted jacket and a white New York Yankees baseball cap worn sideways. She was only half paying attention when the kid walked back into the street and stopped in front of Vanier's car. Then he pulled a knife out of his back pocket, flipped it open and plunged it into the rubber of the front tire.

"Shit," said Saint-Jacques, turning for the door. "Some kid is slashing your tires, boss."

Vanier followed her, running down the stairs, and both got outside in time to see the kid riding off on his bicycle while the car gently settled on the deflating tires.

Saint-Jacques did a circle of the car. "All four. He got all four tires."

"Fuck," said Vanier, contemplating running after the bastard. Instead, he watched the kid raise his cap in a kind of salute and disappear up a side street.

"That's why they have pool cars, sir."

Vanier gave her a long look and sighed. "The pool cars are crap. You know that. Everyone drives them, and no one looks after them."

Vanier turned and looked up to the window. The Colonel was looking down at them with a mug of coffee in his hand. He held it up, as though reminding them he had ordered coffees for them. That's when Vanier noticed the camera over the door. They turned and walked back into the *Patriotes'* offices, while Saint-Jacques was on the phone calling in the tire slashing and trying to arrange replacement transport.

Three women at the desks were staring at him.

"Which one of you is Melissa?" he asked.

"That's me."

"Could you give me a copy of the images from the last half hour from the camera outside?"

"Well, I'll have to ask the Colonel. But if he says okay, I could email the images to you."

Vanier gave her his card. "I'll tell the Colonel to okay it. Send it as soon as possible. I want to see everything from when I parked my car twenty minutes ago to now."

"Sure." She smiled at him and turned to her computer. Vanier wondered why she had chosen purple to streak her hair.

The two officers went back upstairs. The Colonel was behind at his desk looking at the screen. He looked up when they entered.

"Now you see what we're up against. Criminal behaviour is rampant in Hochelaga."

"Colonel, could you call down to Melissa and confirm that she can send me the images of my car's tires being slashed?"

The Colonel hesitated for a second, then realized he didn't have much choice. "Certainly, we'll get those to you."

"Just call her now and tell her it's okay. Then Saint-Jacques can go down and make sure it's done."

The Colonel reluctantly picked up the phone and told Melissa she could send the images. Saint-Jacques went downstairs, and the Colonel returned to the computer, punched keys, and the printer began to spit out documents.

"Before we were interrupted, Inspector, I said that I had something to show you." He grabbed papers off the printer, sorted them into three piles, and handed them to Vanier.

"The first document is a report of crime in Hochelaga last year. It was prepared by your people."

Vanier took the PowerPoint. It was the same one he had sat through with Commander Lechasseur. "It shows Hochelaga four years ago as a crime-ridden sinkhole without any kind of future. And today, there's hope."

"The second is a study by a UQAM criminologist. He shows that if you eliminate the drugs and prostitution, and the other crimes that flow from them, Hochelaga is as safe as Westmount. With the dealers and addicts, this place is going nowhere. That's all I'm saying. It's drugs that are causing all the problems in this community, and nobody cares about a scumbag dealer that got himself killed."

Vanier took the papers. "I care."

"Perhaps you have a bigger heart than the rest of us, Inspector. But frankly, I have a lot more important things to worry about."

"Are you saying murder for the common good is okay?"

The Colonel refused to debate.

"All I'm telling you is don't waste your time. One less drug dealer is not worth it."

"And I'm telling you, Mr. Montpetit, I like to hunt down murderers and put them away. Don't care who they killed, or why. I just like to lock them away."

"Are we finished?"

Vanier was already on his way out.

Alex pushed open the door to the dentist. The waiting room was as crowded as a bus terminal on a long weekend. All the seats were taken, and people were talking to each other like old friends catching up on gossip. They ignored him as he crossed through the room to the narrow corridor where the receptionist sat behind a high counter. Two sliced loaves of banana bread in cradles of aluminum foil sat in front of her. The receptionist looked up.

"Mr. Vanier?"

"Yeah."

She smiled. "Sandra will be with you in a few minutes. Why don't you take a seat?" gesturing towards the waiting room.

Alex looked at the banana bread, but a mouth full of crumbs probably wasn't the best way to start a visit to the dentist. He turned back to the waiting room and wandered back and forth in what little floor space was available, trying to ignore the noise of conversation. He tried not to think about someone picking at his teeth with sharp tools. He didn't have long to wait.

"Mr. Vanier?"

He turned. A short woman, more a girl, was smiling at him from inside an oversized white coat.

"I'm Sandra," she said. She led him into an examination room opposite the receptionist counter. He took off his coat and lay down on long chair. The chair reclined, and his head was lower than his feet. Sandra sat out of sight, behind his head, and he grunted responding noises and half-pronounced words to her chatter of how had he been, and wasn't it great to see winter shifting into spring. Then she got down to business.

"We're going to start with the Florida Probe. It's a new system for periodontal examinations. It does everything automatically. It registers the results automatically and calls out the results as you go along.

"Hm."

"I need to do six probes on each tooth, the corner, the middle and the corner, outside and inside."

"Hm."

"And if the numbers are high, she'll say *Warning* or *Danger*. *Warning*, if you're at 5 or 6, and *Danger* at 7 and up. Oh, and she's got a strange British accent. Don't know why."

"Can you change the accent?"

"Apparently. But I haven't figured out how to do it yet. And you can have male or female voices too. You can even change the language."

"To something I don't understand?"

"Ha. Not sure if it would do any good, *Warning* and *Danger* are recognizable in most languages."

"*Wadareya.*"

"What?"

"Nothing. It means *Watch Out* in Pashto."

Sandra got busy with the switches and dials of the machine, and Alex tried to relax, watching the clouds roll over the building across the street.

"It's crowded out there," Sandra said, bringing him back.

"Yeah. No seats."

"It's a study group. Dentists. They have an expert coming in this morning to talk to them about gold."

"Gold? That's just an excuse for someone to kick your teeth out when you're dead."

"What?"

"Gold fillings. They're valuable. People will take them out of

66

your mouth."

She laughed. "Not gold fillings. Gold for investment. It's a dentist investment group that Dr. Boivin belongs to."

"They must be making too much money."

She didn't reply, and he drifted off to images of swollen faces with looted mouths. Enough faces that it was hard to keep them separate. She held his head with one hand and the business end of the Florida Probe with the other.

"So we'll start at the top, in the back, and go all the way around the front. Then we'll do the lower ones. Then we'll do the same thing on the inside. Okay?"

"Okay."

He twitched as he felt the needle probe between the back molar and the gum. The pain wasn't bad, he could take it. Six times on each tooth, outside and in.

A woman's voice said in a British accent: 3. 5 *Warning*. 2.

It was okay. He was expecting it. And the pain was bearable.

Three more probes: 4. 6 *Warning*. 7 *Danger*.

He tried to concentrate on the different noises, to separate them. The close noises of the vacuum tube sucking saliva out of his mouth, the water rinse, the squeaking of her chair wheels as she arched her back to manoeuvre inside his mouth.

4. 7 *Danger*. 5 *Warning*.

He could feel the blood pumping through his head as he listened to the scraping of metal on teeth that softened as she pushed the probe beneath the gum line.

He listened to the distant noises of conversation from the corridor. The gold-digging dentists must have gathered in the hallway around the banana bread. Then he thought back to the close and distant noises on patrol. The machine noises of overburdened motors, the tapping of metal on metal, and the soft, human sound of flesh stopping shrapnel. There were no boots in the small room, but he heard the fall of boots on hard ground. He heard the distant murmur of people watching a passing patrol, waiting for something to happen. The soldiers knowing they were waiting for the interesting part of the script, the one that ends in an explosion or gunfire, and then bleeding and death.

The noise outside the glass door was louder. Dozens of dentists seemed to have crammed into the narrow corridor outside the glass doors, grabbing at of the banana bread and slurping coffees like the bun eaters and tea drinkers in cafés watching passing patrols. They were the audience, watching him.

3. 2. 4.

3. 3. 4.

His teeth were in better shape at the front. He was sweating, but in control, aware of everything, even of the noise of cars passing in the street below. As she rounded the front teeth on the outside and moved towards the back of his mouth, he tried to pick out individual voices from the murmuring behind the glass door.

3. 7 *Danger*. 7 *Danger*.

5 *Warning*. 7 *Danger*. 8 *Danger*.

Then the watchers went quiet, and quiet was never good; the silence of breaths held, of birds deserting the street, of kids being pulled back to safety, of an audience that knows the climax is approaching. He listened hard, to the numbers, to the warning and to the danger, feeling the sweat on his back pooling above the waist of his pants. Behind his closed eyes, the dentist's light became the blazing desert sun. He strained, listening.

Then he felt fingers rubbing gently on each side of his jaw.

"Relax. We're almost done."

Her fingers were softly massaging the flesh over his jawbone. No woman had touched him with tenderness in years, and it felt good. But it didn't slow the adrenalin pumping through his system.

Her fingers left his jaw and she picked up the probe again. He drifted back to foot patrol, back to moments when awareness was superhuman, when everything was crystal sharp, when he could see, smell, and hear with godlike intensity.

He focused on the probe, following it down between tooth and gum. He listened to his heart, felt his muscles tight and ready and closed his eyes again to the blinding sun. Then she was scraping tartar off his teeth with a sharp pick, the metal scratching on enamel for the listeners in the hallway. Then he smelled the blood.

"There's always a little blood." As though she knew what he was thinking. "It's normal."

She pumped short jets of water around his mouth and vacuumed the bloody mixture. Rivulets of sweat ran down his back. His calves stuck to the chair through his jeans. His heart was beating too fast.

And then she scraped an exposed nerve, sending pain shooting to his brain. His eyes opened wide in terror and he was on his feet, pushing past Sandra, upsetting her tray of instruments.

"Mr. Vanier – "

She followed him out of the small room, but he was already opening the main door.

He didn't wait for the elevator, taking the stairs down in leaps, all the time screaming, wanting to fight back and terrified of doing it.

You could always tell when Chief Bedard was stressed. He sweated. And he was sweating profusely now. Vanier was sitting in front of the Chief's desk, waiting for one of the old handkerchiefs to come out. The Chief had graduated to tissues for blowing his nose, or table napkins at a push, but he couldn't break the habit of handkerchiefs for sweat.

"I know it's a murder investigation, Luc, but you have to use some discretion when talking to citizens."

"I treat everyone the same way, sir. It's my job to ask questions. And there are consequences if people lie to me. It's my job to push them."

"You know what I'm talking about. Some citizens can make a lot more noise than others. You have to think about that."

"And treat them differently?"

"Don't put words in my mouth. You know what I mean. Treat people with respect. That's all I'm saying. Everyone's entitled to respect."

"Did he call you?"

"Colonel Alfonse Montpetit? No, he didn't call me. He doesn't have to call me. He calls politicians, and they call me. Luc, you have to understand who you're dealing with."

"A lunatic who likes to play soldiers and thinks he runs the neighbourhood?"

"A lunatic maybe, but a lunatic who is responsible for any number of charitable programs and can rely on all kinds of political support. The guy's dug in deep in Hochelaga. And if you cause problems for him and can't make it stick, you've got big problems. Is he a suspect?"

"I don't know. No he's not a suspect. But there's lots he knows that can help us, and he's not helping."

"And why isn't this just a regular drug death?"

"Someone cared enough to package Legault up for disposal. He wasn't just killed, he was tortured to death over a couple of hours. Angry junkies don't do that. Maybe it was his supplier, but why go to the trouble? They took his stash, his money, his weapons, but they also took him. Why didn't they just kill him there? It's not an ordinary drug killing. I don't know what the hell it is."

"You don't have to swear, Luc. So what do you think? Who would go to so much trouble to get rid of a lowlife, bottom-of-the-ladder pusher?"

"Someone who just wanted him to disappear without a trace."

"Like the *Patriotes*? You've got to be kidding, right?

"Maybe. Well, maybe not. I don't know."

"You seriously think the *Patriotes* might have had a hand in it?"

"I said I don't know, sir. But they seem to be out there cleaning up the neighbourhood."

Bedard took out the handkerchief and wiped his neck, trying to dry the sweat accumulating around his collar where the fat had formed an impenetrable barrier.

"Because if the *Patriotes* are involved, we have a problem. These guys are a serious community organization."

"So I heard. But hours after they take control of Legault's apartment, Legault is lifted, and then the apartment's being cleaned up for a new tenant."

"Okay. It's not a typical drug-related death. You think you may be able to figure out who did it?"

"I think we have a shot. But you know the statistics on solving drug deaths."

"And you're following leads?"

"Yes, sir."

"Okay. So keep at it for a day or two and we'll talk then. So I have enough to work with for now."

"To work with?"

"Luc, we all have to answer to someone. When it's my turn, I have some answers." Bedard turned his attention to papers on his desk.

"That's it?"

Bedard looked up. "That's it."

Desportes was walking in an alley through mottled patches of dark shadows and weak light from bulbs above back doors. Rusting dumpsters leaked stinking liquids that collected with the rainwater in the middle. He was doing his best to avoid the stagnant puddles. The rain had been enough to hasten the rot of the food that spilled from the dumpsters, but not enough to wash it away. Halfway up the alley he stopped next to the sleeping figure and bent down to place another take-out container next to the bundle.

The bundle stirred. "Mister." A girl's voice. "Kyle's sick. He needs help."

He couldn't make out her face in the dark.

"Who's Kyle?"

The girl pulled the blanket down to reveal a blond spiked-hair head.

"My brother. He's sick."

Desportes got down on his knees and reached his hand out to feel the boy's forehead. The boy opened his eyes but didn't move. Desportes felt a fever heat.

"How long has he been like this?"

"He was feeling sick yesterday, but it got worse this morning. I don't know what to do."

"He needs to get off the street." Desportes looked around, as though searching for someone to help. "I suppose you better come with me. Help me get him up."

She jumped to her feet, rolling the thin blanket that had covered them both and stuffing it into a hold-all. With the blanket gone, the boy shivered, and they both reached for him, helping him to his feet while he looked vacantly about him. The girl was supporting him and trying to grab the bag at the same time.

"You take the bag and the food. I'll carry him." Desportes grabbed the boy's arm and placed it around his shoulder. Then he slipped his left arm behind the boy's knees and stood up. The boy lay in his arms without struggling, much lighter than Desportes had guessed. The girl waited for directions with the bag and take-out container in her hands.

"Follow me," said Desportes.

They started walking, and it started raining again, heavy drops at first, and then sheets of water. At each intersection, Desportes waited in the alley until the street was clear of traffic and then hurried across with his load. The girl followed silently. After five blocks of garbage-strewn alleys, Desportes turned to the girl and almost whispered, "We're here."

They were walking in the middle of another alley, all brick walls except for a solitary, unlit door on one side. Desportes turned a key in the lock and pushed. Then he stepped over the threshold and looked back at the girl.

"Come in."

The girl followed Desportes down a long hallway into the kind of kitchen she had only seen in magazines, with gleaming black counters and stainless steel gadgets. She followed him through the kitchen into a living area where he let the boy down lightly on a couch. He opened a low cupboard and pulled out a thick blanket that he spread over the boy. He turned to the girl,

"I'm going to call a doctor, and then we'll get him into a cool bath."

"No," she said. It was more of a plea than an order.

"Don't worry, just medicine. No social work."

He pulled out a cell phone and punched in numbers. The girl listened to one side of the conversation.

"Doctor," he said.

. . . .

"Yes. It's me."

. . .

"No, not that kind of problem. No bleeding. I have a kid that needs help. He has a bad fever."

. . .

"Great." He clicked the phone off and put it in his pocket. Turned to the girl. "He'll be here in twenty minutes."

The girl nodded and knelt down beside the couch, reaching out to brush her brother's hair back off his forehead. Desportes disappeared up the stairs. He returned a few minutes later with a thermometer and placed it in the boy's mouth. She was still kneeling beside the couch, resting on her heels while she watched.

"We need to get him undressed and into a cool bath. It's running upstairs."

The thermometer beeped and he read aloud, "38.7."

"Is that bad?" she asked.

"It's not good. But we'll let the doctor decide. You said his name was Kyle?"

"Yes."

"And yours?"

"Star."

"Well, Star, we need to get his clothes off."

Star leaned over and started unbuttoning Kyle's shirt.

"What's yours?"

"I'm Hugo."

She was unbuttoning Kyle's pants but hardly needed to. He was so thin she could have just pulled them off. Lying on the couch in his shorts he looked anorexic, as though he hadn't eaten in a month. Desportes replaced the blanket, picked him up, and carried him up the stairs to the bathroom. He used his foot to close the lid on the toilet and sat the boy down while he checked the water and turned off the taps. Then he pulled Kyle's shorts down and gently placed him in the bath. The girl was watching him, and taking in the bathroom. She'd never seen one so big. Desportes handed her a washcloth and a bar of soap.

"Here. You might as well clean him up while we're at it," he said, and left her to it.

When he got back, Kyle was standing unsteadily on the thick carpet while Star dried him. When she finished, she wrapped the towel around his waist, draped another one over his shoulders.

"Let's get him into bed." Desportes said, walking over to Kyle and taking him up in his arms. "You best get the doors, Star."

She held the bathroom door and then scooted in front of them. Desportes showed her which room, and she opened the door to a bedroom.

"I suppose both of you can sleep here?" He nodded at the double bed.

"Thanks," she said.

They put Kyle in the bed and pulled blankets over him. He was shivering again. A buzzer sounded, and the television on the wall lit up, showing the image of a man standing in the alley, looking up into the camera. Desportes pushed a button on a console next to the television.

"It's open, Doctor. We're on the second floor."

A few minutes later, a bearded man in an Adidas tracksuit stood in the doorway, clutching a gym bag. He nodded at Desportes and pointed at the boy.

"This is the patient?"

It was one o'clock in the morning, and Vanier was sitting on the couch, knowing he should go to bed, but putting it off. He had been trying to reach Alex for hours without success. All his calls went directly to voice mail. He had stopped drinking an hour ago and was fighting the urge to have a nightcap. It wouldn't make a difference, because he wouldn't be able to sleep anyway, he could think of too many ways that Alex could get into serious trouble. So he sat and waited, and hoped.

At one-thirty, the silence was broken by the sound of the elevator opening and closing, then heavy, uneven footsteps down the hallway and the thud of a body bumping against the wall. The footsteps stopped, and he heard the scratching of a key trying to find its place, a noise only drunks make, when opening a door becomes skilled labour. Eventually, the door swung open and Alex stood in the entrance, looking relieved to have arrived at a destination.

"Hey."

"Hi, Alex. You had supper yet?"

"Gotta go."

Alex turned and lumbered down the hallway to the bathroom. Vanier listened to the retching, hoping it was in the bowl and not the sink, or the floor. Then he heard Alex's bedroom door opening, and then closing with a thud.

At least there wouldn't be nightmares tonight, thought Vanier, as he reached for a nightcap.

Six

It didn't take long to identify the tire slasher. First thing in the morning, Saint-Jacques had sent prints from the *Patriotes* video to Constable Wallach in Station 23. She figured if he was doing his job as the community relations officer, he would know the local troublemakers. He called her about fifteen minutes after she sent the email.

"Sergeant Saint-Jacques."

"Please, call me Sylvie."

"Sylvie, the kid is none other than Serge Barbeau, local idiot and troublemaker."

Saint-Jacques was writing the name down.

"He's one of those kids that you know is going to jail one day. It's his destiny. A total loser. And when I said he was an idiot, I meant that. He's dumb as an ashtray."

"So, do you think he could have just randomly chosen Inspector Vanier's car?"

"That, I'm not sure about."

"Think it's worth talking to him?"

"Can't hurt. But don't expect him to care."

He gave her Barbeau's address. "Say hello for me."

"Thanks, Richard."

"Any time."

In ten minutes, she had collected Vanier and was sitting in the passenger seat beside him on their way to Barbeau's home.

"$600. That's what it's going to cost to replace the tires," said Vanier.

Saint-Jacques knew that he wasn't looking for a response, just an audience.

"And if I claim on the insurance, they'll just jack up the premiums till they get their money back, and then some. I can't wait to see Barbeau."

Saint-Jacques couldn't stop herself, "I've told you before. You should use a pool car. Most people do."

"A pool car? That's like using a Rent-a-Wreck. Look at this," he said, pointing to the dashboard. "Only 100,000 kilometres, and it's ready to die underneath us."

"I don't see why we're not just calling it in, get someone to deliver a summons to him."

"The shit slashed my tires. It's personal."

"That's it?"

"And I want to know why he did it. I mean, who goes around slashing tires?"

"Wallach said he wasn't that smart."

"The golden rule in slashing tires is that you should know who owns the car. You don't want to slash the tires of someone who's going to beat the shit out of you. It's not usually random."

"You're kidding, right?"

"I'm not kidding. Think about it. Unless you know you're not getting caught, you want to be sure whose car it is."

"Like I said, Wallach said he wasn't that smart."

"Maybe someone put him up to it. The Colonel didn't seem too surprised."

Barbeau's apartment was in a worn-out building on Bossuet Street, about as close to the port as you can get without living in a container on the dock. Vanier dropped Saint-Jacques at the alley-way that ran behind the row of buildings.

"It's the second house in. Twenty bucks says he'll walk out the back."

There was an outside staircase to the second floor and then two doors, one for the second floor apartment, the other for the third. He pushed the buzzer marked "Barbeau," and heard a door open, and then footsteps coming down the staircase from the third floor. A woman pulled the door open and looked at him. She was wear-ing a tight skirt and an even tighter yellow T-shirt with a glitter flower, like she was going out to a party, or maybe just coming home from one.

"Inspector Vanier, Montreal Police. Is Serge Barbeau here?"

She hesitated a second too long. "He's out. Give me a card and he'll call you."

"Why don't you just let me in to see him, Madame Barbeau. It'll be easier."

She shrugged, and turned to walk back up the stairs. Vanier fol-lowed. Then she called up the stairs, "Serge. You up there? It's the police, for you."

Vanier pushed passed her up the staircase and got into the apart-ment just in time to see Barbeau heading out the back door. Vanier ran after him. Barbeau didn't notice Saint-Jacques until he was fac-ing her at the bottom of the staircase.

"Shit," he said.

"Yeah. Shit."

He turned to let her put the cuffs on. Then he looked up to the third floor where his mother was leaning over.

"Don't worry, Serge. I'll call legal aid. Maybe they'll send someone up."

Then she yelled at Vanier who was standing in the alley. "Where are you taking him?"

"Station 23. Have the legal aid lawyer ask for me. Here's my card." He pulled out a card and made a show of sticking it in a crack of the staircase railing.

"No, Mom!" Barbeau called up. "Don't call legal aid. Call the Colonel. He'll know what to do."

Neighbours had appeared on back staircases, watching while they led Barbeau off down the alley. Barbeau was strutting, enjoying the attention.

Paul Brasso put his phone away and looked up at the Colonel from the armchair. "That was Barbeau's mother. Your buddy Vanier and his partner have just arrested the kid and taken him to Station 23. They even handcuffed him."

"Handcuffs? He's just a kid. They should have come to us. When are they going to learn that they have to start treating us with respect?"

"The real problem is that we don't want him talking to the police. We put him up to it."

"He doesn't have to say anything to the police. He can just keep quiet."

"Yeah, but they can keep questioning him. That's the drill. Keep reminding him he has the right to remain silent, and keep asking him questions for hours."

"Send the lawyer, what's his name? Dufrene, that's it. Send him up there. Right now. Tell him to get the kid to keep his mouth shut and just wait it out."

Brasso pulled his phone out and began scrolling for Dufrene's phone number.

"And we're going to show these bastards what it means to ignore us. This is an opportunity. When you've finished with Dufrene, we need to get people mobilized. Let's give them something serious to think about. You call Dufrene, I'll call the Mayor to protest. Then we organize trouble for these bastards. Big fucking trouble."

"What do you have in mind?"

"A demonstration. This is just the kind of opportunity we've been looking for. We'll show them that the *Patriotes* are a force in Hochelaga. We won't be ignored."

The Colonel fished out his phone and used his address book to connect.

"Hello, Mr. Mayor. We have a problem."

There were no windows in the interview room, just a two-way mirror from the observation room at the side. A camera high up in the corner captured everything that happened. Vanier and Saint-Jacques sat at one side of the table, Serge Barbeau at the other, his dirty white parka dumped at his feet. He had two gold chains around his neck and was still wearing the white baseball cap askew. Vanier had pocketed the knife he had found in Barbeau's back pocket.

"I said it wasn't me."

"Of course it was you, Serge. Look at the photos."

He was picking his nose. A cocky fifteen-year-old, going on twenty, with no fear of the police. He reached out and grabbed one of the coloured prints.

"Pretty shitty quality, I'd say."

"It's you. You didn't even have the sense to change your clothes."

"If it was me, do you think I'd be stupid enough not to change clothes?

"Seems you were," said Saint-Jacques.

He looked at her without saying anything.

"So why my car?" said Vanier.

He looked at Vanier again. "I told you. It wasn't me."

"Get fucking serious, Serge. You're in trouble here."

"Yeah, big trouble. And I've got an alibi too."

"How could you know you have an alibi if we didn't tell you

when it happened?" said Saint-Jacques.

"If I didn't do it, I must have an alibi, right? If I wasn't there, I was somewhere else, right? What time was it then?"

"Yesterday, 10 a.m."

"I was with my Mom all morning. Good boy, I am."

Vanier picked up one of the photos. There was no question it was Barbeau, but he knew Barbeau was just going to keep denying it. The kid knew the system, whatever they wanted to charge him with, the lawyers would bargain it down to next to nothing. Pay a fine and move on. He knew enough not to make it easy for the police. The lawyers would only be interested in closing the file, and nobody would be going to trial for a tire slashing. Vanier knew this was his one chance to get anything from Barbeau.

"Just tell me why. Why my car? Anyone ask you to do it?"

Barbeau stiffened. "I want to see my lawyer. I've got nothing more to say."

"And why did you tell your mother to call the Colonel?"

"In case I get hungry, like."

"What?"

"Colonel Sanders. KFC."

Before Vanier could respond, the door opened, and Constable Wallach put his head around the door.

"The Commander wants to see you two upstairs. Pronto."

As they were leaving, Barbeau held up a print. "Can I have a copy?"

Vanier turned back, "I thought you said it wasn't you."

"It's not. But I like the photo."

Vanier stood up. "You stay here. I'll be back."

They left the interview room, locking the door behind them.

Place Valois is one of Hochelaga's village squares, half a block of public space designed as a meeting place, with wooden benches and concrete tubs with plants. At four o'clock on a darkening afternoon made gloomy by constant showers, it was filling up. Pot-bangers were wandering in conga lines through the crowd bashing spoons on metal. Pot-banging was the preferred mode of expression because it translated the general malaise so well; slogans are too specific, pot-banging just says: *I'm pissed off.* And lots of people in Hochelaga are pissed off, most of them with good reason.

It's easy to start a fire when you know where to touch the match, and in Hochelaga, the *Patriotes* knew that as well as anyone. Every group had their activists, and a phone call to one or two quickly became a call to everyone, and the calls had been made to get people to Place Valois. They hadn't used social media because the police monitored everyone, and a Facebook invitation to a protest was an invitation for the police to get there first. The square was filling quickly with anarchists, anti-poverty activists, women's rights supporters, union people, and the just plain disaffected who couldn't resist a chance to let people know, and that covered most of the people in Hochelaga. Most of them were vaguely aware of another arrest, another example of how the police brutalized citizens of Hochelaga. They weren't particularly interested in the details.

News spreads fast in a crowd, but it's rarely accurate. But, before long, everyone knew that one of their own had been lifted off the street in front of his mother by plain-clothes police officers for no good reason. And they knew he was being held in Station 23.

By five o'clock, protestors had spilled onto Ontario Street and were blocking traffic. They were getting itchy to move and, as though by some unspoken suggestion, a crowd began forming on Valois Street. There were no obvious leaders as people started to wander north on Valois with a vague sense that they were heading for Station 23.

The crowd grew as it meandered slowly through the streets, picking up anyone who wanted to share the excitement. By the time they got to Hochelaga and turned right towards Station 23, there were about two hundred people. There wasn't a cop to be seen.

When word got out about people gathering in Place Valois, Commander Lechasseur had ordered everyone back to the station to prepare for crowd control. Inside the station, they were scrambling. They had alerted headquarters, and the riot squad was gearing up to get to Hochelaga, but it would take time before they arrived. The helicopter was already in the air, tracking the mass of people as they advanced towards the station.

The original plan had been to get half a dozen cars down to Place Valois to calm things down, but now the crowd was coming to them. The Commander hadn't expected that. He watched from a second floor window as twenty officers in flak jackets took up position outside the station. Squad cars blocked the street at each end, and all the doors to the station were locked, except one in back. A riot was never good, but a march on his station was a disaster. He knew if he didn't handle things properly he'd be finished, and no PowerPoint of declining crime statistics would change that.

"Shit," he said, turning to Wallach. "What the hell is this about?"

"They're mad because we picked up some kid."

"Kid? What kid?"

"Inspector Vanier and his partner arrested a kid about an hour and a half ago. They're interviewing him downstairs."

"About the murder?"

"Not even. Apparently the kid slashed the tires on Vanier's car."

"Jesus Christ. Since when are we arresting people for vandalism?"

"Seems the Inspector doesn't take kindly to someone vandalizing his car."

"Get both of them up here. Right now. I want that kid released."

"I'm not sure you can do that, sir. It's Vanier's arrest. Maybe it's better the decision comes from him."

"Perhaps you're right. Get him up here so I can tell him what goddamn decision to make."

Wallach turned and left, and the Commander kept himself busy shouting orders, glancing out the window every few seconds. A flash of movement caught his eye. A large camera truck from TVQ pulled up opposite the front door. Then a CTV truck pulled into the entrance of the parking lot, taking up a prime spot for a wide view of the street.

Three blocks away, two men were sitting in a stolen car, its motor idling. The passenger was listening on his cell phone to a play-by-play commentary from someone in the advancing crowd.

He turned to the driver. "They'll be here in five or ten minutes."

The driver said, "It'll be dark in about half an hour. Fuck, I love riots."

Just before the crowd crossed Jeanne d'Arc, fifteen youths walked out of an alleyway and blended into the front half of the crowd. They all had their faces covered, some almost casually, with scarves, others were wearing ski masks. People felt the tension mount, but what do you do to someone in black and a ski mask who wants to join the mob?

You do nothing.

Serge Barbeau was sitting in the front seat of an SUV like he belonged there. He didn't know the driver's name, but he had seen him around. He had wanted to stick around for the riot, but the guy refused, said Barbeau's job was done. So now they were driving away from the station in the opposite direction from his home. Barbeau didn't care. He was part of things now.

The driver turned to him. "You did well, Serge, you're a hero. A fucking symbol."

Barbeau wasn't sure what he meant, but he grinned. He felt like he had been allowed into the big boys' club.

"I didn't say fuck to the police. Man, they were pissed. You should have seen their faces."

"All those people back there. They were there for you."

Barbeau laughed the kind of laugh that begs for company, and the driver joined in. "You're one of us now. You've got a future. Like I said, Serge, you're a hero."

"Thanks."

"But it's not finished, not by a long shot."

The car slowed on Sicard Street and pulled into a narrow alley. It was dark, brick walls with no windows on both sides, and the only lamp was broken.

"You can count on me."

"We know that. But there's one more thing. It's not personal, it's part of the plan. It's going to be rough. You ready?"

"Anything."

"It wasn't good that the police let you go so easily. We should have forced them to do it."

"Yeah, but still, they only did it because of the crowd."

"We lost the advantage. We had a bunch of people on their way to demand your release and they let you go before we could get there."

"Yeah, but they knew you were coming. That's enough, no?"

"We looked stupid. So the boss had an idea. They let you go alright, but they beat the shit out of you beforehand."

Barbeau turned to face the driver just in time to see the fist aimed at his face. The first punch broke his nose and blood began pouring down onto his jacket. The second burst his lip and loosened a tooth. Before he had time to get a grip on the door handle, two more blows landed on the side of his face.

The driver reached for Barbeau's chin and turned his face. The boy seemed groggy.

"Listen kid. I'm going to call an ambulance soon. Listen to me." Barbeau opened his eyes and stared at the driver. "The police did this to you during the interrogation. Got it?"

Barbeau didn't answer, and the driver squeezed his cheeks until pain brought him back into focus.

"Remember the story. Get it right and you're one of us. You understand?"

Barbeau nodded.

"I'm sorry kid, I really am." He pulled back and drove his fist into Barbeau's ribs. On the second blow, he felt a bone give. Barbeau groaned.

"That's all." He whispered into the kid's ear. "Now, what's the story?"

Barbeau didn't say anything, his head lolling around like a newborn. The driver grabbed his face again and turned it, bringing his own within inches of the kid's, and screamed, "What's the fucking story, kid?"

"The police did this."

"More. Make it believable."

"Huh?" was all Barbeau could manage.

"Details. Tell me the story."

"I don't remember much, but the police started beating me in the interview room. Then they let me go. Told me not to tell anyone, or they'd kill me. Please, I need an ambulance."

"Not the police. Only one guy. Who did it?"

"The guy who picked me up?"

"That's right. The guy who picked you up. He was pissed at you because you slashed his tires. So he beat the shit out of you and then pushed you out the back door. You ran as far as you could go but then you collapsed. That's the story. Got it?"

Barbeau nodded.

"Say it."

"The guy who picked me up." Barbeau was whistling through the gap from the missing tooth. "He started to punch me. I couldn't fight back. It was awful. Then he brought me to the back door and pushed me out. So I ran. I don't remember much more."

"That's it kid. Remember. You'll be a hero for this."

Barbeau nodded, again.

The driver reached into his pocket and pulled out a cell phone. He punched numbers one-handed and spoke.

"Call an ambulance to the alley between Sicard and Leclair, south of Adam. Got it? Tell them you don't want to give your name, but you just saw someone collapsed on the floor. Tell them it's an emergency. And call from one of the disposables. Don't use your own phone."

He reached past the kid, and opened the passenger door.

"Now, get out and lie down. Don't move until the ambulance gets here. Remember the story."

Barbeau struggled out of the car and slumped to the wet ground, moaning. He curled into a foetal position and bled into puddles. The driver got out, leaving his door open, and went around to where the kid was lying. He pushed the passenger door closed.

"Don't forget the story. We'll have lawyers all over this before you're seen in the emergency room. Nothing to worry about."

Barbeau moaned that he understood, and the driver pulled a short black cosh from his pocket. He raised his arm and brought the cosh down hard on Barbeau's head.

Barbeau grunted into unconsciousness.

The driver was three blocks away when the speeding ambulance passed him, rushing to respond to the emergency call.

Commander Lechasseur had ordered two patrol car parked at each end of the block to keep the protesters away from the front of the station, where the temptation to throw rocks would have been too great. Ten uniformed police in flak jackets formed a barricade in front of the squad cars and stared down the approaching crowd. The mob stopped moving forward, except for a few kids who would run out in front to taunt the police and then run back into the crowd.

The driver of the stolen car that was now parked half a block away clicked his phone closed and pushed it into his pocket.

"They're coming," he said to the passenger as he leaned forward to pop the trunk. They both got out and went around to the trunk as five kids in ski-masks came running up.

The driver said, "Come on, quick. They're in the trunk."

The kids lifted their masks, there was no need to hide their faces. The passenger pulled a beer case out of the back filled with twelve primed Molotov cocktails. He handed it to the first kid and then handed out the other three cases. Forty-eight Molotovs in all.

The kids were eager to get back to the action. The driver said, "Don't throw them to hit the cops. Drop them in front of them. Nobody's to get killed. But get rid of them all. Don't hold back. And get the fucking cars burning. Remember, when the Colonel says to stop and go home. You fucking drop everything and get lost. Got it?"

The kids had beaming smiles, already leaving while he was talking. One yelled back over his shoulder, "Sure thing. But tell the Colonel to give us time to get the cars burning."

The kids ran back up the street pulling the ski-masks back into place, and joined the crowd out of sight of the police. Then they pushed their way towards the front of the crowd, picking up friends on the way. There were three kids to every case of Molotovs; two to guard the case and move it through the mob, and one to throw. They took it in turns to throw.

The mob and the police hushed and watched as the first lit Molotov traced a slow arc and spun down towards the police line. It fell five feet short, and the crowd cheered as it burst into flames.

The flames went out quickly, and another kid ran out from the crowd and lobbed a second, its tail trailing sparks in the night sky. It was more accurate. It dropped two feet in front of a cop and exploded in flames, splashing his pants with burning gasoline. He jumped back against the cruiser and started swatting at his legs. He put the flames out easily and looked back at the crowd. Then he looked at the other cops as though checking they were still there.

The third was on a clear trajectory for the chest of a bulky cop in the middle of the line and he dived out of the way. It missed him and smashed against a squad car. The crowd cheered again as flaming gasoline dripped down the door.

Before the next one came, there was a shouted order, and the police retreated behind the two squad cars, leaving the empty vehicles sitting like an invitation. The crowd surged forward, and a kid with a scarf wound around his face pulled out a hammer and started hitting the windows. It took three or four blows to each before they gave, but he was methodical. He ran back into the crowd to cheers, and the Molotovs began to fly again. They were breaking inside and around the cars, and in seconds both cars were on fire.

The cops pulled back further, and more flaming bottles were dropping into their ranks. The mob stayed on the one side of the burning cars, using them as a barricade. From that side the kids with the Molotovs had a clear shot into the Station's parking lot, and within minutes two more squad cars were burning. Behind the crowd, a fire engine was stopped on Hochelaga Street behind another burning car. The two guys who had handed out the Molotov cocktails had parked the car they had stolen horizontally across the street and used the left over gasoline to torch it.

The mob was at a pitch of excitement, but everyone knew it was just a matter of time before the riot squad showed up. Then, seemingly out of nowhere, Colonel Montpetit was standing at the side of the street, his face bathed in the flames from the fires. He was in full dress uniform, dark pants, crisp white shirt with epaulets, and a *Patriotes* beret pulled down tight on his head. He held a megaphone up to his mouth and shouted, "Wait."

He had to repeat it a few times, but the crowd went quiet.

"Good news. I have good news. The police have listened to the people of Hochelaga. Thirty minutes ago, they released Mr. Barbeau. We have won!"

The crowd roared and started chanting: *ACAB, ACAB*, the acronym plastered on walls all over Montreal, *All Cops are Bastards*.

Montpetit struggled to be heard. "Now is the time to show them that we are responsible people. More responsible than the authorities."

The mob roared its approval, and watched as another Molotov took a long arc over the parking lot fence and exploded on an already burning squad car.

Montpetit shouted into the megaphone "No. That's enough. We've won. Now is the time to show them who we are."

The crowd quietened down as the SQ helicopter hovered overhead and lit up the street with its searchlight. The Colonel basked in the light.

"My friends, the riot squad is on its way. Please. Disperse peacefully. And as quickly as possible. We have won."

The crowd cheered again, and men and women who had been part of the mob took out berets with the *Patriotes* insignia and put them on. Then they started breaking up the crowd, paying a lot of attention to the kids, working hard to calm them down.

People began to leave like fans streaming out of a Habs game in the third period when the Habs are down 3 to 1 — a few at first, then a crush for the exits, leaving only the die-hard fans behind. The *Patriotes* roughly cleared the remaining protestors from the street while the police watched.

Seven

Barbeau's press conference was being held in the *Patriotes'* storefront office on Ontario Street. The three desks had been pushed together to form a line in front of twenty folding chairs for the press. The previous nights' riot was the morning's lead story on all the news programs, and the room was overflowing. Serge Barbeau had become the day's star attraction.

Barbeau was centre stage, behind the desk, grinning madly under the bandages that held his nose in place. His favourite New York Yankees baseball cap was perched sideways on his head, and his matching white quilted jacket was slung over his shoulder, covering his arm in a sling. His lawyer, Dufrene, was on one side, and his mother and the Colonel on the other. Dufrene was doing his best to look like a crusading lawyer protecting the downtrodden. He knew that television could do wonders for his career.

The Colonel started to talk, and the room hushed.

"Good afternoon, ladies and gentlemen, and thanks for coming. Last evening the peace and tranquility of Hochelaga was shattered by a spontaneous outpouring of protest from its beleaguered citizens. Once again, as happens too often around here, one of their own was snatched off the street by a police force more interested in showing their authority than in using that authority for the good of the community.

"Mr. Serge Barbeau was arrested in his home where he was quietly watching television. He was handcuffed, pushed into an unmarked car and whisked off. All this because he was a suspect in a minor vandalism incident.

"The brutal arrest and disappearance of Mr. Barbeau was one incident too many, and the people of Hochelaga decided they had had enough. They were successful in obtaining Mr. Barbeau's release. If they had not been, who knows what would have happened to Mr. Barbeau?

"But Mr. Barbeau was not allowed to walk out the front door. No, he was hustled out the back entrance under darkness, as though the authorities were ashamed. Now we know why. On his release, Mr. Barbeau ran. He was badly injured and scared. He was found shortly after, unconscious in an alleyway. He was treated for four hours at hospital, and the conclusion is obvious. While he was in police custody, he was severely beaten, resulting in a broken arm, nose and rib."

He turned to Barbeau, who was still grinning at the crowd, and then continued. "The Police Service of Montreal will be held to account. Not just for this incident, but for their continual disregard for the rights of citizens in this neighbourhood.

"The *Patriotes* are ready and willing to continue to work with the police to ensure that Hochelaga is a peaceful and crime-free neighbourhood, but cooperation with us must be the rule, not the exception. We will not stand by and let our people be brutalized. I am, therefore, calling on the Mayor to instruct the Police Service to work through us to ensure that law and order is maintained with the consent of the people. Anything else is oppression, and the people will no longer accept oppression. Times have changed.

"Now Mr. Barbeau will read from a prepared statement, and we will then field some questions."

The room went silent. Barbeau continued to scan the crowd with a big grin on his face until Dufrene touched him on the shoulder and whispered, "Read the statement, Serge."

Barbeau picked up the single sheet of paper and squinted in concentration. His grin disappeared. He spoke haltingly, with long pauses between each word. When he wasn't saying anything, he realized there were thirty people waiting for his next word. He had never been good at reading.

Dufrene was getting nervous and stopped making eye contact with the journalists. Nobody had thought to check Barbeau's reading skills.

"I was arrested last night by two people that I later ... discovered ... were police officers ... "

He knew he was having trouble and began focusing on the silence between his words, on the long pauses when people were waiting for him and he had nothing.

"While I was in ... custony ... no, in custody. While I was in custody, I was subject ... subjected to a several ... a severe beating at the hands of the police. I ... suffered a broken nose – " he pointed to it – "and a broken arm – " he pointed to the arm in a sling – "and numerous ..."

He leaned over to Dufrene pointing out the word. Dufrene whispered in his ear. "Abrasions."

"What's that?"

"Cuts."

"Oh yeah." Barbeau turned back to the journalists. "Fuck this," he said, dropping the page onto the desk. He looked up at the room full of reporters. "Like it says, I was arrested and then I had the shit kicked out of me by the police. I didn't do nothing. The pigs, man, they just like to beat up on anyone. And you can't do nothing. You fight back, you get worse!"

Dufrene put his hand on Barbeau's shoulder and squeezed, sending a searing pain through Barbeau's arm. Barbeau winced and shut up.

Dufrene addressed the audience. "We'll take a few questions, but Mr. Barbeau is obviously very tired and still suffering from his ordeal."

A journalist from *La Presse* was first. "Mr. Barbeau. You were found in an alleyway a good distance from the station. How come you didn't ask for help as soon as you were released?"

Barbeau looked to Dufrene as though asking for help. "I dunno. I was scared. Running. I just ran."

"Mr. Barbeau, did they tell you why you were arrested?"

"No ... Yeah. They said vandalism. That's bullshit."

"Have you been charged?"

"Yeah. They said they'd send it in the mail. Vandalism. That's it. It's bullshit, you know?"

"Mr. Barbeau, getting back to your running away from the station."

"Yeah?"

"So, you're bleeding from the nose. You've got a broken arm and a broken rib and you're running along the street. Where were you running to?"

"I was running home. To my mother." He grinned again, happy to have found the right answer.

"But why go past dozens of people and then into a dark alley. What were you thinking?"

Barbeau jumped to his feet. "You calling me a liar? You calling me a liar, fuck?"

Dufrene tried to calm Barbeau, but the kid wasn't having it. "You heard him. He's calling me a liar."

The Colonel turned to Brasso. "Get him upstairs. Now." Then he addressed the audience.

"Ladies and gentlemen. As you can see, Mr. Barbeau's still in shock. This has been a traumatic experience for him. The press conference is ended. Thank you all for coming."

He had done it before. But it didn't get easier with time. Vanier resisted the urge to give the two men sitting across from him a smile. Two Detective Sergeants from Internal, Brisette and Pilon. He was in anger-control mode, doing his best to look calm, but not particularly friendly. It's just business, he told himself, just get through it and move on.

Brisette fiddled with the recording device and looked up. "This is Detective Sergeant Brisette. It's 2 p.m., April 6, and I am beginning an interview with Detective Inspector Vanier. I'm accompanied by Detective Sergeant Pilon. Inspector Vanier has been advised of his rights to be accompanied by a lawyer and he has declined to exercise that right."

"Inspector Vanier, could you confirm that?"

"I am Inspector Vanier."

"No. That you have been advised of your rights to a lawyer and have declined to exercise that right."

"I have been advised of my right to have a lawyer and I have declined."

"Thank you."

Bisette opened a file in front of him and began. "Inspector Vanier, we're investigating an allegation made by Serge Barbeau that you beat him severely while he was in custody during the afternoon of April 5th. Have you read his statement?"

"Yes. I have read his statement."

"And what's your response to it?"

"It's not true. I questioned Mr. Barbeau for about half an hour and then I was called away. I returned about twenty minutes later and told him he was free to go. He left through the back door of Station 23. He was unharmed while he was in custody."

"Let's start at the beginning, from when you picked him up."

Vanier went through the entire afternoon. He spoke in a monotone, placing words on the transcript carefully, like the footsteps of a hockey coach crossing the ice to an injured player. It was a stilted and unnatural way of talking, but Vanier knew it would look crisp and confident in the written transcript, no faltering or wandering, just a straight story from start to finish. The story ended was when he left Saint-Jacques with the Station Commander and went down to get Barbeau out of the interview room and send him home. He didn't tell them about Barbeau mocking him as they went down the stairs. How Barbeau had been laughing at him.

"Why the back door? Why not the front?" asked Brisette.

"The front entrances were locked. There was a crowd of angry people outside. I thought it was safer for the kid."

"But the crowd was there to get Barbeau released, wouldn't that have defused things? If they saw Mr. Barbeau walking out the front door."

"I don't know what the crowd was looking for. And I wasn't about to predict how the crowd would react. He might've got hurt."

"So you led him down the stairs to the back door and shoved him out?"

"I didn't shove him out. I led him down the staircase, opened the door, and he left. It was 5:30 p.m."

"How do you know it was 5:30?"

"I called Saint-Jacques to let her know he was out the back door. The call was logged on my cell phone."

"Did anyone see you escort Mr. Barbeau out of the building?"

"I don't think so. Everyone was either out front or looking out the windows. There was a riot going on."

"Did anyone see him as he left the building?"

"Me."

"Anyone else?"

"Not that I know of."

"Who made the decision to release him?"

"He was my witness. So it was my decision. I told you, Saint-Jacques and I were questioning him in the interview room, and I got a call to go see the Station Commander. We left Barbeau where he was and went upstairs to the Commander's office. There were three of his men with him. The Commander told me that a crowd was marching on the station to demand Barbeau's release. He asked if it was important to hold him. He said if it wasn't, to let the kid go. That's all. I said I'd let him go and went back to the room. When I left the interview with the Station Commander, the rest of them were looking out the window to see what was happening in the street. The community relations officer, Wallach, said to let him know when the kid had left the building and he would make some calls to the crowd outside. He thought it would defuse things."

They took him through the story three times, and Vanier was careful to make each telling as close to identical as the last. Then they moved to his past.

"Inspector Vanier, this is the fifth complaint of brutality made against you. That's quite a lot." Brisette looked at Vanier, waiting for a response.

"Is that a question?" said Vanier.

"An observation, I suppose. What do you think?"

"About your observation?"

"About the fact you've had five complaints against you for getting too physical with members of the public."

"They were all investigated, and I was cleared. They're closed."

"Perhaps. But at some point, people might think there's a pattern."

Again the wait. He knew he had to keep focused on the transcript. In real-time, the silence filled the room with tension, but on the transcript there would be nothing until the next word was spoken. So he waited. If there wasn't a question, he didn't have to answer.

Brisette rephrased his observation. "Do you think there is a pattern to your actions generating complaints from members of the public?"

"Absolutely not. Each case was different, and in every case, there was a full investigation. None of the complaints were found to be justified. I was cleared of any wrongdoing."

Brisette closed the file before him, shuffled through his notes, and looked at Pilon, who responded by shaking his head back and forth.

"You told us that you knew it was 5:30 p.m. because you made a call to DS Saint-Jacques. Do you have a record of that?"

"I told you, yes."

"Could you give us that phone so that we can verify the calls that were made?"

Vanier needed his phone. Alex could call anytime, or someone could call about Alex. He pointed at the tape machine, and Brisette leaned over and switched it off.

"You can have the records. I'll give you permission to look at whatever you want to look at. But I need my phone. Personal reasons."

Brisette and Pilon exchanged glances, and Pilon gave a faint shrug.

"Okay. Give us the password to your account, and we'll go online and get the information."

Vanier didn't have an online account. He promised to set one up and send them the details. Brisette leaned over again and switched on the machine.

"Inspector Vanier has promised to give us full access to his phone records. One last thing, Inspector. Can I see your hands?"

Vanier held his hands out and Brisette took them, turning them over, back and forth.

"It's 4:30 p.m., almost twenty-four hours after the alleged incident. I am examining Detective Inspector Vanier's hands, and they show no obvious indication of bruising."

He released the hands, and Vanier pointed to the tape machine again. Brisette reached over and switched it off.

Vanier said, "Obvious indications? What the hell does that mean?"

Brisette shrugged and switched the recorder back on. Said, "Correction. Detective Inspector Vanier's hands show no indication of bruising. I am now terminating the interview with Detective Inspector Vanier." He looked up at Vanier, "That will be all for the moment Detective Inspector."

Vanier forced himself, "Thank you. Glad to be of help."

Another drop for the transcript.

Colonel Alfonse Montpetit knew the importance of morale to any fighting unit. Soldiers had to believe in what they were doing, and they could do anything for the right cause. So he spent a lot of time making sure that they understood the importance of their role. History was strewn with examples of small groups of trained soldiers standing up for what was right, and often history proved them right. The *Patriotes* were a small group whose time would come. They had to be ready.

According to Montpetit, the West was rotting from the inside, and he was lucky enough to have been chosen to participate in saving it. The *Patriotes* were starting from zero in their own little patch of Quebec, but they were going to succeed.

Ten of the faithful were relaxing with beer and pizza in the Colonel's office, lounging over the sofas and armchairs. The storefront below was closed for the day.

Montpetit stood in front of a blank television screen.

"Gentlemen. The job's well under way. It's not easy, but you have all shown that you have the will and the strength to do the tough stuff. Across the continent, people like us are organizing for the inevitable day when we can take back society. The institutions are crumbling because the corrupt political class has looted the treasuries until there is nothing left, and now they can't deliver anything to the people except more taxes. The people know that the current political class has reached the end.

"And in Hochelaga, we're in the vanguard. We're an example to our brothers in arms everywhere. We are making government irrelevant, and the leeches are only too happy to see us take up the slack. The people look to us for help before they call the government, and we give them peace and security. We are making Hochelaga better than it ever was under the thieving bastards in Quebec City and Ottawa.

"We have taken the first steps and we're making great strides. Much is left to do. Hard work and sacrifice. But the battle is engaged. I salute you, gentlemen."

He raised a can of beer in the air, and the men cheered.

"Yesterday, we showed the people of Montreal and, more importantly, the politicians and police, that they don't control the streets. We do. From now on, they have to talk to us, to consult us. Or there will be hell to pay. If they want to get elected from Hochelaga, to operate in Hochelaga, they have to go through us. We are the people."

There was a murmur of support.

"Their Inspector Vanier disrespected us, and he's paying the price. And he's going to be an example to his bosses, and to everyone else in the force. We're in charge of Hochelaga and they have to recognize that."

The men were listening intently. They knew it wasn't an illusion, the *Patriotes* were beginning to matter. They were supplying more and more of the services in Hochelaga, and government from City Hall, or even further away, was becoming irrelevant.

Montpetit picked up a universal remote and pointed it at the screen. "Sergeant LaFleur, the lights, please."

A tall guy in the back got up and flicked a switch on the wall. The room darkened, lit only by the lights from the street. Montpetit clicked the remote. On the screen, images of battlefield brutality.

First, there were similar scenes, a desert country, or maybe several desert countries, and sand-coloured armoured vehicles moving forward through villages, alongside walls, or out in the open until, time after time, the vehicle lifted, sometimes from the front, sometimes from the back, sometimes straight up or sideways. The clips were short, just enough time for the viewer to register what he was looking at: an armoured vehicle with soldiers inside, then the vehicle lifted into the air or jumped sideways with the puff of an explosion, first the image and then the sound, repeated time and again: *Watch your buddies get killed, watch your buddies get killed, again, and again, and again.*

Then the images changed to ramp-side ceremonies of coffins being loaded onto planes for the trip home. In one, the camera slowed to focus on one of the saluting officers and then faded into his face in a different setting, before the flag of a US militia organization. The man, still in his US Marines uniform, looked into the camera.

"My name is Paul Kerry, Lieutenant Paul Kerry of the US Marines, and I lead the Veterans Militia. Like all of you, I've said goodbye to too many unnecessary heroes, too many sons and daughters sacrificed for profit and politics. But, together, we are going to stop the slaughter.

"We were sent overseas to fight someone else's war, and it's time that we brought the war back home. If the politicians think that we're good enough to be blown to bits in some hell hole, for nothing more than the survival of a bunch of criminals, then we're good enough to have a say in how this country is run. But it can't be done through the political parties. It has to be us, acting together. Only we can bring about change."

"In other broadcasts, I've talked to you about the need to be ready for armed struggle. We need to arm and train because, mark my words, the government will come after us. Remember Waco? The government will come after us, they will try to seize our guns in violation of the Constitution, and if they cannot disarm us, they will kill us. So we are in a race. A race to arm and to train, and we cannot afford to let up that effort.

"But that is not all. The battle won't be won by arms alone. As militia organizations, we must become involved in the communities we care about. We have to build grassroots support, not by making promises, but by delivering the goods. We need to be present in our communities. By helping our neighbours we gain the support of our neighbours.

"So my message to you tonight is to build support by providing what the government refuses to provide. You, militiamen and women of America, must find needs in communities where you live and fill those needs, openly and proudly."

Montpetit pressed stop on the remote and stood up. "Now listen, men. This is where Lieutenant Kerry, and just about all of the US militias go wrong. He sees the militias only in terms of a security force. His vision is limited. Listen."

Montpetit pushed play and sat down.

"Is there a policing problem in your neighbourhood? Then get out into the streets and solve that. Illegal immigrants taking jobs from Americans? Go into those businesses and tell them to stop. Drug problems? Stop the drugs. You have the power. Use it.

"We will be present for good in the neighbourhoods of America, and we will restore security to American streets. But we have to deliver. We have to succeed where the civil authorities have failed. And to do that we need to arm and train for the war that's coming."

They watched for another ten minutes as Paul Kerry delivered his vision of the American Militia movement, an armed police force imposing order. American citizens who would bring America back to what it used to be.

Then the screen switched to pictures of heavily armed men patrolling the Rio Grande border for illegal immigrants, the enemies of the American people.

Montpetit stood up and the lights went back on. He turned off the television with the remote and turned to face the group.

"Much as I admire Lieutenant Kerry, his movement is missing the one ingredient that will take them from the fringe into the heart of society. Before the people will desert the established order and embrace change, we need to show them that we can replace the old order. And we do that, not just by protecting the people from crime and violence, but in providing for them in all the other areas where governments still pretend to be necessary. And that's what we're doing in Hochelaga.

"You don't need force to deliver help to the people. You've seen it every day. The goddamn politicians are stepping back and letting us do all the good we want, because that means they can get away with doing even less. It won't be long before we're an essential presence, both for the people who depend on us and for the politicians who gladly hand over all the obligations of the state. They won't object unless we start touching their perks. And by the time we start to do that, it will be too late for them."

He explained how a grassroots community organization was crucial to wean people off the state and build up loyalty to the *Patriotes*. The ballot boxes could wait, would have to wait, while they built a loyal following that would be invincible.

Every member of the militia had a job to do, and each job was vital. Yes, some would deliver peace and security in the streets, like the US militias dream of doing. Others would organize community efforts to address economic problems, with everything from childcare to helping the aged.

"Before long, when good, honest citizens need help, they will turn to the *Patriotes* before they turn to the government. We will become the people's provider and protector. As the State had replaced the Church, so the *Patriotes* will replace the State. Not by force, but by presence.

"Eventually, those parasites who use the apparatus of the State to steal from the citizens will have to pay for their criminality, but it is better for the moment that they don't feel threatened. Let them rely on the *Patriotes* to fill the gaps where they have failed, until one day the people will realize that the politicians are a cancer that feeds off the common people and give nothing back. And when the time is right, we will cut that cancer out of society."

Montpetit continued, "It's important that you understand our goals. The higher goals. This isn't the Canadian army, where you have to do the bidding of some political fat cat who sends you to die so that he can win points with his friends in the UN or NATO. To belong to the *Patriotes* means that you're investing your brains as well as your heart. We will change society. We will bring Quebec back to where it should be. And we will do it together."

The guys started cheering and popping beer cans.

Mayor Chambord stood behind the bank of microphones that had been set up in the Grand Hall of Montreal's City Hall. A thicket of reporters was waiting for him to start, and he surveyed them over his glasses, his gaunt features stilled in concentration with the intensity of an egret looking for movement in water.

"Ladies and gentlemen. This morning, I gave instructions for the conduct of a citizen-led inquiry into yesterday's events in Hochelaga. I have asked five dedicated and respected citizens to examine these events and to report back to me with recommendations within thirty days. The timeframe is short, but the issue is urgent."

Nobody could have failed to notice the repetition of "citizen."

It had been his Chief of Staff's idea to show that the Mayor was not relying on a discredited political class. After years of corruption scandals, few people had confidence in City Hall's ability to do anything honestly, so the Mayor's office concocted the idea of a citizens' inquiry, one that looked like it had nothing to do with politicians. Of course, the citizens had been carefully chosen. The Mayor began to read the list.

"Colonel Alfonse Montpetit, the Founder and President of *Société des Patriotes de Montréal*, a community organization that is doing remarkable work on so many fronts in the community. Madame Lucy Farand, professor of women's studies at the *Université de Montréal* and resident of Hochelaga for fifteen years. Mr. Ken Brownie, the President of David's Gate Developments, whose company has been revitalizing the neighbourhood and investing millions of dollars in new construction. Svetlana Jette, the current President of the Association of Housing Cooperatives of Hochelaga. And, finally, Robert Savoie, a businessman and President of the Ontario Street Merchants' Association."

"Ladies and gentlemen, this fine group of citizens, all of whom have lived and worked in the neighbourhood for years, have agreed to take on this important job. They will have thirty days to examine the circumstances of the riot and to report back to me with recommendations to deal with the causes of the public anger we have seen.

"Rest assured, there will be no sacred cows in this inquiry. I have made it clear that there is to be nothing but the truth. Blame – or praise – will fall where it may.

"I would also like to advise you that I was informed this morning that two officers of the *Service de police de la Ville de Montréal* have been relieved of all police responsibilities until an internal police inquiry into their actions has been completed. To demonstrate how seriously we and the SPVM take the allegations that have been made against them, the officers will be withdrawn from all police work, effective immediately. They are not simply being transferred to desk duty, as is usually the case. No, we believe this matter is so serious that they must remain outside the police services until all investigations are terminated."

Vanier pushed the mute button on the remote control and looked around the squad room like someone whose house is on fire, trying to decide what to take with him. Every cop knows his career is in trouble when public officials take a personal interest in it, and Vanier had never seen police officers so publicly held out to dry. Everyone is innocent until proven guilty, except cops.

He turned to Saint-Jacques, expecting tears, but what he saw was fury.

"What do you think?" he asked.

"Who the hell does he think he is?"

"He's the Mayor."

"And we're screwed."

"That bad?"

"Totally. That bastard just pitched us in the garbage."

"It was an execution, boss," said DS Laurent. "He just put you two up against the wall. He doesn't want to be seen pulling the trigger, but wants the job done. And just in case there are any doubts, he gets to write the story."

"The committee?" asked Vanier

"Yeah. The so-called citizens' committee. The ones I know are all the Mayor's friends. The other ones are probably tied to him too. It's a joke."

"I know Montpetit. What about the others?"

Laurent leaned forward in his chair. "Ken Brownie, the developer. He's been making a killing buying up distressed properties. Then he puts up condos. He's a major donor to the Mayor's party and basically gets whatever zoning changes he wants. Svetlana Jette is an up-and-comer, she's in charge of the co-op association. She was really important for the grassroots vote. Oh, and in case you didn't know it, the *Patriotes* are big donors to the Mayor's party."

Vanier wasn't surprised. "How do you know this? I thought you lived in NDG."

"I do. But my sister has lived in Hochelaga for the last twenty years. Every time we have supper, I get the full rundown of what's happening in Hochelaga."

"So one of the people we're looking at in a murder investigation is now on a committee investigating us?" said Saint-Jacques.

"Pretty much," said Vanier. "But we're not working any murder investigation. There's no 'we.' We've been sent home, remember?"

"So, one of the people you pissed off is now investigating both of us," said Saint-Jacques.

"Doesn't sound good, does it?"

The door to the squad room opened, and Chief Bedard walked in with the awkward gait of someone carrying too much weight. DS Brisette from Internal was with him, looking pleased with himself.

"Detective Inspector, Detective Sergeant, I assume you heard the announcement?"

"We heard. You're quick to implement," said Vanier.

Bedard grimaced. "Then you know the drill. You're both off duty. Indefinitely. You need to surrender your guns and badges and leave the premises. While off duty," he made a show of looking Vanier in the eye, "there will be no police work of any kind. You are both civilians. Understand?"

"Got it," said Vanier.

The Chief looked at Saint-Jacques for a response.

"Yes, sir," she said, with a trace of sarcasm that had Vanier thinking that she was finally beginning to understand life on the force.

"The only police officers you are to communicate with are me and Sergeants Brisette and Pilon. You are to use Internal Investigations as your primary contact with the force."

He turned and walked out, leaving Brisette the pleasure of collecting guns and badges, and of having Vanier and Saint-Jacques sign off officially on the terms of their suspension.

Saint-Jacques carried two coffees to the table by the window where Vanier was staring out.

"Two cream, no sugar, right?" she said, putting the paper cup in front of him. He was distracted.

"Thanks."

She sat down.

When he turned back from the window, he saw that she was staring at him with that gaze that made most people uncomfortable, it was more effective that a slap on the back of the head at getting your attention. She had pale blue eyes that slipped to grey, depending on her mood, or the light, he could never figure it out. Hard eyes to lie to.

"So you took him from the interview room, down the stairs and let him out the back door."

"Yes."

"Anyone see you?"

Vanier thought for a moment. "No, at least I don't think so. Everyone was either outside or in the front looking out the window, I don't remember seeing anyone on the way out."

"It would be good to have a witness," said Saint-Jacques.

"It doesn't matter. It'll all be on camera. There was one in the interview room, and there must be two or three on the way down."

She put down her coffee. "That's a problem, sir."

"What do you mean?"

"The cameras. There aren't any videos. There was a malfunction. All the cameras in the station were down. No pictures."

"You're kidding, right?"

Saint-Jacques sipped her coffee. "I wish I was." She studied Vanier's reaction.

"Shit."

"That's an understatement."

"The kid's lying, Sylvie. I didn't touch him."

"He's not lying about his injuries. They're real."

"He was fine when I let him go. He was sneering at me, and I thought about wiping the stupid grin off his face. But I didn't, shit, he was a kid. I let him out the back door and went upstairs to join you guys. That was that. If he got beaten up, it was after he left."

"In forty-five minutes?" said Saint-Jacques. "The ambulance picked him up forty-five minutes after he left."

Vanier realized his version was hard to believe. He wondered if Saint-Jacques believed it.

"Can you speak to Barbeau?" he asked.

"I'm not supposed to speak to anyone connected with this."

"Okay," he said. "I'll do it."

"That's not a good idea. You're not supposed to be speaking to anyone either."

"I didn't get the memo."

"That's a terrible idea, sir. First, if he is lying, he's not going to tell the truth just because you ask him to. And, second – ," she hesitated, not wanting to speak the alternative, that Barbeau wasn't lying. "Second, your speaking to Barbeau will only dig this hole deeper."

Vanier said nothing, taking a gulp of coffee. She was right, but it didn't help. Doing nothing had never appealed to Vanier, particularly when his ass was on the line.

He stood up, decided. "I'm going to find out what's going on and finish with this."

"Please, sir. Sit down for a second. We need a plan."

He sat down and said, "I have a plan. I'm going to figure out what's going on. The kid's lying. I know it sounds like bullshit. But it's the truth. So, the question is, Why? And I'm going to find out."

"You're supposed to be off duty."

"Yeah. And I'm supposed to wait around and hope that someone else solves the problem. I can't do that, Sylvie. If this drags on, it gets worse, not better."

"You don't think it will work out? I mean. you have nothing to hide."

"I've got nothing to hide. But who's going to believe me? There's no evidence to support me, and the punk really was beaten. The bosses will do whatever is necessary to make the problem go away. And, right now, I'm the problem."

"We're both the problem. I'm suspended too, remember?"

"Yeah. And we're supposed to sit on our hands and wait. *One day the truth will out.* Like hell it will."

Saint-Jacques knew he was right. Hoping someone else would care enough to spend time coming up with the truth was like buying a lottery ticket. Delusional. Vanier was in deep shit. She was collateral damage. If he couldn't clear himself, the best she could hope for would be a desk job for twenty-five years.

She picked up her coffee, blew on the surface and sipped, looking at him over the rim of the cup, body language for *I'm listening*.

"Let's see what we can find out about the cameras. Are we certain there's no footage? Why did they screw up? Too much of a coincidence that they all went off at the right time."

"You think someone at the station – "

"I'm not thinking anything. Just that I'd like to know for certain there's no footage, and I want to know why the system screwed up. What was the problem? Did someone flip a switch?"

"I know someone in IT. He'll tell me who knows what. It's

somewhere to start."

"And the *Patriotes*. They come out of this shining. Montpetit is a big hero that saved the day. That's bullshit. What's he up to? Who are they? Do they have a grudge against the police?"

Saint-Jacques writing notes. "You think the *Patriotes* might have done Barbeau?"

"Someone did. I know it doesn't make a lot of sense, but someone thinks it's a great idea to make the police look bad. Maybe it's them."

"Or, maybe someone wants to stop you."

"Legault's murder? Is this meant to distract me?"

"There may be a connection, sir."

"Who knows. Who's picking up the Legault case?"

"Laurent. And he promised to keep in touch."

"It's still a live case. It's not gone cold."

"But the *Patriotes*?"

"Who knows. We've got two of their guys from the *Patriotes* persuading Panagopoulos to sign over Legault's apartment, and Legault is kidnapped and killed a few days later. If they hadn't dropped Legault's body from the truck, everything would be fine. Life would go on, with the *Patriotes* running the apartment. Laurent's got lots of leads to track down."

"What about the two guys that visited Panagopoulos?"

"Still no word. They don't answer their phones and they're never at home."

"The Colonel must have sent them on vacation."

"The easy thing would be to put it down to a drug deal gone bad and move on."

"Yeah, but luckily Laurent doesn't like easy any more than I do."

Saint-Jacques was feeling better. She didn't have to stand back and let her life be decided by other people. She could at least do something.

"There's a lot of stuff to look at," said Vanier. "We just need to do the legwork."

"So we have a plan?"

"I don't know if it's a plan. But it's better than sitting at home doing nothing. I'm not going down, Sylvie. Not for this."

"Then we've got work to do, sir."

The inside windows of the black SUV were steamed up with the breath of the two men. They were parked under a leafless tree that did nothing to slow the rain sheeting down the windscreen. It was as though they were sitting in a cave behind a waterfall. They were both wearing leather jackets and blue jeans, but they couldn't have been more unalike. Eddie Pickton was in the passenger seat, a full patch Hells Angel in uniform. The driver could have been a GQ model.

Pickton said, "Louis is pissed. He wants his container back."

The driver said, "He's crazy. We didn't even know he had a container coming through the Port. But he should have told us."

"He doesn't trust you."

"Fuck him. What we did with Legault, it was a group thing. It brought the gangs together. By participating, everyone put something on the line. We organized that to build trust, to show that we can work together."

"Didn't work. He figures nobody's going to risk going to the police with Legault's murder, so it doesn't mean anything."

"He's wrong, there. What happened with Legault was supposed to show we could work together. But if he steps out of line, we've got insurance."

"How so?"

"We got some great pictures of Louis beating the shit out of Mr. Legault. A couple of them show just the two of them, and Louis holding a hammer. He seemed to be having a good time."

"It means nothing. If he's fingered for Legault's murder, first thing he'll do is cut a deal with the cops. He would sell you guys out in a second. Shit, he'd sell me out too if it comes to that. Then we'd all be in shit. We all took turns on Legault."

"Maybe he won't get a chance to cut a deal."

Pickton looked at the driver, waiting for more. The driver said nothing. Pickton said, "So what about the container?"

The driver looked out at the rain. Pickton continued, "I know you've got it. You guys are making it impossible to work in the Port."

"I told Louis. If he has anything moving through the Port, he should tell us. Then we'll make sure nothing happens to it."

"Tell you and pay, you mean."

"No, we'll look after his shipments for free. What the fuck do you think? Things have changed. Louis has to understand. We control the Port, and he needs to get used to that."

"So how much for the container?"

"That's assuming we have it. How much is it worth?"

"If you've got it, you know. If you don't, it doesn't matter. Does it?"

"So tell him to come see me himself."

"He won't. I told you. He doesn't trust you guys. That's why he sent me."

"And you trust us?"

"I do what Louis tells me to do."

Pickton lit a cigarette, and the driver turned on the engine and opened all the windows.

"Fuck," said Pickton, "Do you have to do that? The rain's coming in."

"Do you have to smoke in the car? Why can't you wait?"

"I smoke. What's the big deal?"

"It stinks. I'm going to have to change my clothes when I get home."

Pickton was trying to blow the smoke out the window, but it kept drifting back. He threw the half-finished cigarette out into the rain. "You can close the windows now. I'm getting soaked."

"Give it a minute for the smoke to clear."

"Next time I'll bring an umbrella."

"Listen, Eddie. I like you. Sure, you've got some dirty fucking habits, but I think we can do business together. If Louis doesn't understand that times have changed, maybe it's time he stepped down."

"Louis? Step down? You can't be serious. If he's not in charge, he's dead. There's too many people with a grudge against him. If he lets go for a second, he's finished."

"You got a grudge against him?"

"It's not about me."

"But if he stepped down, somebody would take his place."

"Yeah. There would be a bit of scuffle to see who's in charge. But things would settle down."

"And what if we helped you to be in charge?"

This time it was Pickton's turn to stare out the window. The driver continued. "Let's say we took Louis out of the picture. Nothing to do with you. Nothing to do with us. Just an accident. Then we help you keep control, run interference for you. You know, block the defence and let you run up the field and score. We could work together, Eddie. You know that."

Pickton said nothing.

"Louis's out of touch. It takes more than muscle to keep on top. Some things you can fight, and some things, well you just have to go along. We're here to stay, and Louis has to work with us or he doesn't work. No choice."

Pickton said, "So I tell Louis you know nothing about the container?"

"Tell Louis he can have the container for $500,000 cash. I figure that's about 25% of what he was expecting to make. It's through the Port and ready to go."

"He's not going to like that."

"And maybe his time is over. A war's bad for business, and we both know he can't win." The driver put his hand on Pickton's arm. "Eddie, listen to me. I think you'd be a good man to run things when he's gone."

"I'll get back to you."

Pickton got out of the car, and Corporal Brasso moved out of the shadows to replace him in the passenger seat. They nodded at each other, and Brasso climbed into the car and closed the door.

"So how'd it go?" asked Brasso, as he watched Pickton walk away, trying to light a cigarette in the rain.

"As I thought," said the driver. "We either get paid or Louis's out of the picture."

Eight

Vanier wasn't used to being unemployed. He woke up early, showered, and shaved. He put on his least crumpled suit, a shirt that wasn't too wrinkled, and a tie that didn't look too much like it came from a vintage clothing store. And there he was, sitting on the couch, all dressed up, with nowhere to go.

Alex had come in late and wouldn't stir before the afternoon.

His suspension orders were clear: nothing to do with the investigation, nowhere near Station 23 or any of its officers, and nowhere near Barbeau or his family. He was supposed to wait, quietly and out of sight, while others decided his fate.

He hadn't heard back from Saint-Jacques, who was following up with her IT contact to see what happened with Station 23's video system. He was waiting for Laurent to give him any news on the Legault investigation. And he hadn't quite figured out how to continue looking into the *Patriotes* without violating the suspension rules. He figured he should let at least one day elapse before he did that.

He decided meditation would help, even if he could only manage five minutes. Five minutes today, maybe ten tomorrow. Maybe he could get back to a regular twenty minutes a day. It wasn't easy. He hadn't meditated in weeks, not since Alex came back. He sat down on the couch, loosened his tie, and focussed on his breathing. At first, he could only manage two or three breaths before his attention was pulled away, meandering off like a beagle finding a new scent every three feet. He only got to stillness for seconds at a time. Even so, when he gave up the battle and opened his eyes, he had managed fifteen minutes. Fifteen minutes that had passed like five, and he felt better.

He put on his coat, left the apartment with no direction in mind. Following Dr. Penfield east to the top of McTavish, he went down the steps into the McGill campus. It was crowded with students, faculty, and staff arriving for another day, worlds away from where he was. Trees were budding, and shoots of new growth were breaking through the surface of bare ground. It was a landscape of greys, all the shades of brown, and tiny green spots of new life. He left the campus through the Roddick Gates and continued south, manoeuvering through the tide of commuters released from *métro* stations, buses, and parking lots, flooding the city with nine-to-five effort. He felt detached, like he was watching them from a bubble, the only person without a destination.

The glass doors of Place Ville Marie were disgorging people onto the street, and Vanier struggled through them. He declined the offers of the free newspaper. He'd looked at them before and decided they made him angry, another example of the relentless effort to stop people thinking. They consisted of a few cut-and-paste extracts from newsfeeds giving the stripped-down version of the same news that was broadcast on every newscast, a syndicated Hollywood gossip column, horoscopes, lottery results, the absolute minimum of content on which to hang advertising for cars, televisions, and drugs to relieve the commuter's despair of knowing that the youthful dreams were dead and this was as good as it was going to get.

In Central Station, he ordered a coffee and a croissant from *Première Moisson* and sat down at an empty table where he could watch the shoulder-to-shoulder parade of commuters in the narrow passageway leading out from the concourse. The crowd had a pattern, surging to unmanageable numbers with each arriving train from the suburbs, then slowing to flow like treacle through passageways towards escalators that would take them to buildings and the street. Some people would stop and line up ten deep to buy coffee and a muffin at Tim Hortons.

Vanier had never been part of the daily movement of the herd. Policemen stood apart. But now he felt he wasn't part of anything.

The croissant was good, a crunchy, multi-layered pastry of butter, with sugar and salt hiding in the background. He went back for another. By 8:20, most of the herd had passed, and by 9 a.m., the passageway was back to strolling pedestrians.

It was the first time in years when he was forced to fill an empty space in his day rather than wondering how to fit everything in. He began formulating a plan to go shopping, buy a shirt, or even a new suit, shit, anything new would be an improvement. Then his phone rang. An unknown number. He answered. "Vanier."

"Garguet here."

"Louis Garguet?"

Louis Garguet was the leader of the Hells Angels in Montreal. Vanier knew he'd risen to the top by being a murderous bastard and was staying there by adding diplomacy to his skills. The rumour was he had been responsible for ending the biker wars and getting the Hells back to business in the shadows. The wars had outraged the public. Nobody much cared about bikers killing themselves, but people drew the line at bombs in the streets and civilian casualties. After Garguet, the killing was done in private, and the public stopped caring.

Garguet said, "You're quick."

"You're famous."

"I've got something for you. I want to see you. Two o'clock this afternoon at the Club Gym. I'll be waiting."

"Club Gym? Where's that?"

"Opposite Station 23. You know where that is, don't you?"

Vanier recalled looking out over the crowd of protesters from the second floor. There had been a gym directly opposite, almost the same size as the police station. Then it clicked. Years ago, the gym had been owned by the Hells. At the height of their power someone had the idea of sticking it to the police by buying the building opposite the station as a way of showing the police that the Hells didn't give a shit about them.

"And you're on your own. Or we don't talk."

The line died. Vanier was relieved he didn't have to go shopping.

Vanier was sitting in the Volvo with new tires outside Club Gym on Hochelaga Street. Station 23 was directly opposite. Most of the damage from the riot had been cleaned up. All that was left was the darkened asphalt where police cars had burned. From what he could see through the plate glass, Club Gym was a serious muscle gym, the kind where you're in the wrong place if you're not taking steroids – or selling them. It didn't look like one of the forgiving temples where out-of-shape citizens could pretend to get back in shape.

The Hells had bought the building in the nineties, in retaliation for the constant police surveillance of their own bunker, back when the biker war was in full swing. It was also a message to the rival banditos. Taking over a building opposite a police station said that the Hells were powerful. It was still a Hells' property, but it had been flipped through so many shell companies, it was immune to any proceeds-of-crime seizure.

Vanier pushed open the door and walked in. Two girls who looked like they had just finished their shift at a strip bar were lounging behind the reception desk, along with a steroid-chomper in a T-shirt that was a size too small. He was posing, showing his bulging arms to maximum effect. He gave Vanier a look that said he had him for a cop and then turned away. Vanier got a smile from one of the girls and couldn't help smiling back.

"Help you?"

"I'm looking for Garguet. He's expecting me."

"Oh yeah. He said someone might show up. He's probably in the weight room. You'll have to get changed."

"Changed?" Vanier wasn't thinking about getting into shape. "You're not serious?"

She was still smiling. "It's the rules. He said you probably wouldn't have anything to wear, and to give you this." She lifted a gym bag onto the counter. "The changing rooms are along the hallway. "There's a lock and a key for the locker in the bag."

He looked at her, and she shrugged. There was no choice. He took the bag and went down the hallway to the changing room. The bag had an extra-large pair of running pants, a huge T-shirt, a towel and a pair of red flip-flops. The clothes had a damp, musty smell, like they'd come from the gym's Lost and Found. Underneath the clothes, he found an unmarked DVD in a plastic case. When he put on the pants and T-shirt he knew he looked ridiculous. He weighed 180 pounds, and was in reasonable shape, a little slack, maybe, but nothing that a month or two of weights wouldn't cure. The clothes would have been loose on a 250 pound doughnut addict. He decided against putting his street clothes in the locker, not wanting to give Garguet a chance to make them disappear. So he put everything in the bag and left the changing room, one hand clutching the bag, the other holding up his pants.

Garguet was on the second floor, lying on a bench pressing two manhole covers connected by a steel bar. The Arnold Schwarzenegger guy from reception was behind Garguet, spotting him. Garguet was muscled, but his gut was obvious even when he was lying on his back and straining. Vanier was at a disadvantage, trying to look like he had some authority while holding up his pants. Garguet cradled the weight and nodded to Arnie.

"Take a break for a while. I need to talk to the Inspector."

Then he raised himself up to a sitting position and motioned for Vanier to sit on a bench opposite, about three feet away. Vanier sat down, and their knees were almost touching.

He looked at Vanier and leaned forward.

"You're in trouble."

"What else is new?"

Garguet reached down for two eighty-five pound barbells next to his feet and started curling them while he watched Vanier.

"You don't seem to be in too good shape, Inspector. You should exercise more."

"Or get a new tailor."

"A dangerous occupation, being a cop. You need to be fit."

"Get a lot of cops in here?"

"Some. We let them in. It's against the law to discriminate. You know that, Inspector."

"Yeah. I heard."

"And besides, we're just across the road from the station. You could get a membership. We got a special on at the moment."

"Not like you to be generous."

"Self-interest, my friend. If I can help myself by helping others … Shit, generosity just comes natural."

"I'll take a brochure on the way out," Vanier said. "So what's the deal?"

"Deal? No deal. I'm making an unsolicited donation from the goodness of my heart. Let's say I just signed up for that organization to defend the wrongly convicted."

"I'm not convicted."

"You're being investigated. Just about the same thing for a cop."

"It's bullshit, everyone knows it."

"We're both professionals, Inspector. Since when did truth matter?

You've been dressed up like a lamb at an Easter barbecue. And unless you do something about it, you're finished."

Vanier said nothing. They both knew it was true.

"Take a look out the window, Inspector."

Vanier went over to the window and looked across the street to the station. If it wasn't for the venetian blinds, he'd be able to see what was in the sandwiches they were having for lunch.

"See anything interesting?"

Vanier continued staring out the windows.

"Station 23."

"No. On this side. On the lawn."

There was a flagpole in the middle of the lawn in front of the building. On top, was a camera. "Cameras?"

"Fucking genius. I can see why you made Inspector." Garguet was still pumping the barbells. "Station 23 has cameras pointing at us, and we have the same pointing at them. They went in years ago. I suppose you've checked the videos at the station."

"There's nothing useful on them."

"Bullshit, nothing useful. There's nothing. I know the system was down at the time of your little incident. Or it was made to go down."

Vanier wondered how he knew.

"Either way, there's no video to help you."

Vanier was thinking about the DVD in this gym bag.

"So guess what, Inspector?"

"Your cameras didn't go down. You've got the riot on film?"

"We got it all. Everyone. See the condos back of the station?"

Vanier saw a brick building on the corner that overlooked the back of the station. "And?"

"We've got a camera in one of those, looking at the back door." Garguet put the barbells down. "So look at the DVD. If you're smart, you'll learn something."

123

"That's it?"

"That's it. Except for the brochure. Ask Chantal at reception on the way out."

Vanier picked up the bag and turned to walk away.

"One more thing, Inspector."

"What's that?"

"Don't forget this. I'm doing you a big favour."

"Yeah. Thanks. I'll send you a Christmas card."

"I'll be in touch when I need something."

Vanier didn't respond.

Outside the gym, he kept his head down, wondering if someone from Station 23 would notice him leaving. He had dumped the clothes but kept the gym bag, so he at least looked the part. He was tempted to go straight home and watch the DVD, but there was something else. He put the bag in the trunk and drove the car three blocks down the street and parked, away from the station. Then he started walking. At a good pace, it still took him thirty minutes to reach the alley where Barbeau was found.

It was narrow, only half as wide again as a car, and stinking from food scraps spilling from the slit belly of a garbage bag, a feast for the rats. Someone had written *POLICE = CHIENS* on the wall. There was a pile of cheap bouquets beneath the sign, the flowers already faded. It was easy to see where Barbeau had fallen, a long dark stain traced a rivulet from the spot where blood spilled from his head to where it pooled in the middle of the alley.

He thought about the blood and walked back out of the alley and half way up the street. He couldn't see any blood spots. True, it had rained since the kid had been discovered, but not that much, and it takes a lot to wash bloodstains away. He walked back to the car, scouring the pavement for signs of blood. He had retraced the last steps of enough victims to recognize the trail of someone leaking blood along the street, but there was nothing.

She picked up the phone on the third ring. "Saint-Jacques."

"There's a couple of things."

"Oh, it's you."

Vanier sensed the tension in her voice. "Yes, Sylvie. It's me. I'm not the enemy."

"Sorry, I'm not taking this well. You know this is going to stay with me forever. The outcome doesn't matter. It's the accusation that counts."

"That's why we have to nail this. We can't sit around waiting for someone else to do it. We need to prove it's a pack of lies. That's what it's going to take to make those assholes from Internal cave in and close the file."

"It doesn't matter what we do. It will always be hanging over me."

"Sylvie, we'll beat this. Believe me. But we've got to keep at it. If we do nothing, we're sunk. Did you hear back from your friends about what went wrong with the cameras? They all shut down at just the right time? How does that happen? If they had been working, they'd show the kid walking out the back door without a scratch on him."

"I called him," she said. "He said he'd get back to me." She didn't sound excited, and Vanier noticed that there was nothing in the background. Usually when he called there was pop music playing in the background. Most of the time he had no idea what it was, gym-music he called it.

"Maybe someone played with the cameras. But we need to find out. There's something else."

"What?"

"I went to the alley today. Where he was found. I walked there from the station and it took thirty minutes. I was moving, but it took thirty minutes."

"And?"

"The call came in to the ambulance twenty minutes after he

left."

"That's it?"

"I know it's not much. But it's a piece of the puzzle. The kid says he walked to the alley and collapsed. In the shape he was supposed to be in, he couldn't have walked there in time."

"Maybe he ran. He's younger than you. And adrenaline can do strange things."

"Yeah. Maybe he ran." Vanier knew it was a pretty weak straw to be clutching onto. "But he didn't run home. His mother lives in the opposite direction."

"That's it?" she asked for the second time.

"There were no bloodstains leading to the alley. If he was bleeding in the alley, there should be some spots that dripped on the way."

"Did you have a crime scene guy look?"

"Not yet. But I got someone going out in the morning. Personal favour. Shit Sylvie, I'm trying. I know it's weak, but everything helps."

"And you didn't beat him?"

"Jesus Christ. How many times do I have to tell you? No, I didn't beat the shithead." Vanier clicked disconnect on his phone.

She called back in seconds.

"Okay, I'll see what I can do about the cameras. I'll call you."

"Thanks."

This time it was Saint-Jacques who disconnected.

Vanier thought about what she was going through. Saint-Jacques carried the burden of being beautiful and smart, very smart. She had spent too much time fending off the advances of the preening class who wanted to own the beauty but had only a vague sense of the person. She was a cop for the right reasons, the straightest of straight arrows. And being a cop was her life. She had become Detective Sergeant because she was good, she didn't play politics, and didn't cultivate friends higher up. If she was to go any further on the force, it would have to be on merit alone, and being associated with Vanier's misdeeds wouldn't help. With most people, she had a tropical wood hardness about her, and Vanier felt the defences being lowered into place for him too. He wondered if he was just the latest in a long line of men who had disappointed her.

He wasn't sure why he hadn't told Saint-Jacques about the DVD. He'd looked at it, and it wasn't good enough. It could be helpful, but not much more, like the lack of bloodstains, the distance to the alley, and the kid not going home. Helpful, but not enough by a long shot.

Garguet's DVD had grainy images of the riot spilling around the building, and you could barely make out the kid emerging from the back door. He wasn't limping and didn't look in pain. The kid high-fived a guy in a raincoat and they walked off together. Problem was, you could only see the back of the raincoat. It wasn't enough.

Vanier knew that reasonable doubt wasn't going to cut it. He was going to have to prove that the kid walked out of the station unharmed. And that meant finding the guy he high-fived in the parking lot.

Vanier was at sitting in front of the computer screen researching the *Patriotes*. Alex was wearing a headset and was lost in a video game. Vanier clicked on a YouTube video of Montpetit and listened to the Colonel explain his movement. He started with a litany of the complaints that the disaffected could identify with: politicians who lusted for money and power, lording it over the citizens; governments that took the hard-earned wages of the people and gave nothing back; public services that were strangled with budget cuts; and corporations that bought elections to install compliant hacks in power. The system was breaking down, and the people needed to defend themselves against the excesses of their overlords.

It was all about self-defence, and the potential enemies were legion. Montpetit talked about his pride in the ancestors of the Quebec people. Betrayed by the French and handed over like farm animals to the English, they had still managed to keep their identity as a proud people. The *Patriotes* were going to reawaken that pride, and Quebecers would become masters in their own home. His message was that Quebecers could look after themselves, and the *Patriotes* were going to lead the way.

Halfway through, the audio continued, but the screen switched away from Montpetit behind a desk to show him visiting the *Patriotes*' daycare centres, food banks, and shelters, always surrounded by laughing children or grateful people.

Then the screen images switched to the *Patriotes* playing war games, with real guns and mismatched uniforms, and men and women with berets and green fatigues marching in the annual Saint-Jean-Baptiste parade. There was one five-second clip that showed about twenty green uniformed men marching behind the *Patriotes* flag in a parade. Six men stepped out of the crowd and fell in just behind the flag and then, as if on command, each of them lifted the hems of their green T-shirts and tucked the shirts behind pistols that were shoved into the top of their pants. They walked for two blocks, then covered the guns and left the parade.

Vanier hadn't noticed, but Alex was standing behind him watching the screen.

"Assholes."

"What?" asked Vanier, turning around.

"Those guys. They're all over the place."

"The *Patriotes*?"

"No. Militias. Militias are all over the place." Alex sat down on the couch. "In the US, the rest of Canada. They're guys who can't let go. Maybe they have a point, you know. But most of them just miss the status. Overseas, these guys were more important than they'd ever been in their lives. They carried guns and got respect. Yeah, it was only because people were scared of them, but they loved it. And then they come home and they're nothing. Worse than nothing. Regular people are embarrassed by veterans, and the military brass thinks we're just a burden."

Vanier knew it was true. He'd seen it himself. We can send kids off to get themselves killed, but we treat them like crap when they get home. Shit, most employers won't hire veterans because they think they are unstable.

"We came home broken or mad, mad-angry, that is. There aren't many come home normal. The angry ones join the militias. The broken ones… they just get more broken." His voice trailed off. Then, "So why are you looking at this stuff?"

Vanier explained how he thought the *Patriotes* might have something to do with Legault's murder.

"Good luck to them," said Alex.

"What?"

"You heard. You said it yourself. This Legault was a scumbag, a drug dealer."

"Whatever he was, it's not right. Nobody deserves that. That's why we have laws."

"And we all must obey the law, right? Canadian values, right?"

"Don't mock it."

"Canadian values are a myth, Dad. Why was I in Afghanistan?"

"To help liberate the country from a bunch of barbarians. Build a better place for the people."

As soon as he said it, he realized how ridiculous it sounded. They were sent to Afghanistan to get rid of an unfriendly government and replace it with a friendly one. And if the only friends you could find were a corrupt gang of thieves and killers who would support whoever paid them enough, well, so be it.

"That's bullshit, Dad, and you know it. We lost 160 Canadians. The Americans lost over two thousand. Why? To put that gangster Karzai in power and keep him there."

Vanier didn't have an answer. It wasn't his job to justify Canada's foreign policy. That policy was brewed in the same filthy cauldron that had allowed Canadian governments to decide which corrupt gang could brutalize its people and which would be condemned as outlaw states. You can't have domestic values and foreign values.

"So don't ask me to feel sorry for a drug dealer when I know people who've lost limbs to keep drug dealers in power in Afghanistan. There are too many good people to worry about. Drug dealers get killed. It goes with the territory."

Alex walked off to his bedroom, and Vanier returned to the screen and continued to dig into the *Patriotes*. Montpetit was a baby warlord trying to manoeuvre into a position where the authorities would have to treat him like just another player in society. If the *Patriotes* could get strong enough, the politicians would embrace Montpetit with the usual, compromising flexibility that allows politicians to forgive the past atrocities of the newly powerful.

Vanier understood the strategy, and how the hungry, homeless, or simply poor could ignore the military trappings to receive a handout. The *Patriotes* were digging themselves deeply into the fabric of Hochelaga, becoming as normal and indispensable as garbage pick-up.

He clicked through a series of photos of a *Patriotes*' summer camp. The caption said that each summer the group organized four one-week camps for underprivileged kids. The photos showed kids having fun outdoors, canoeing, swimming, rushing over obstacle courses, and doing target practice with hunting rifles. It was like the Boy Scouts on steroids, and the Colonel was everywhere, surrounded by smiling children.

Midnight's not late when you've nothing to do and nowhere to go in the morning. Vanier was driving east on Sainte-Catherine near Moreau Street, the edge of what Wallach had called the zone of tolerance. Clutches of girls stood every half block watching the traffic for customers. He found a parking spot, got out, and started walking. The only places open were massage parlours, strip clubs, and the occasional *dépanneur*. The gaps in between were boarded-up storefronts. It was the kind of seedy dissipation you might expect in a third-world port.

The massage parlours were all alike, with a small reception area in front, and a door leading to the business cubicles in back. They could have been chiropodists except for the signage; one was running a special: *No Frills Rub and Tug – $35*. Only the strip bars made an effort, with neon signs and high-definition pictures of women who had never been to Canada, never mind Hochelaga. He pulled open the door to a bar called The Gentleman's Club, pushed past heavy velvet curtains, and blinked in the darkness.

A waitress in a skimpy French Maid costume approached, smiling. "Table?"

Vanier looked around. "I'll sit at the bar."

It was a quiet night. There was only one other guy at the bar. He had his back to the stage, but was staring into the giant mirror against the wall to see what he was missing. Vanier sat at the far end, back against the wall, where he could see the whole club. He ordered a Jameson.

The DJ station was against the side wall behind a circular stage that jutted out into the center of the room. The woman on stage was coming to the end of her set piece. Vanier knew the drill, all clothes on for the first song, top off for the second, and naked for the third. She was on the third song, riding a white rug, not even trying to look interested.

On one of the tables near the stage, a bunch of young American students were sharing beer from a pitcher, trying their best to look nonchalant with a naked stripper at eye level grinding to "Pour Some Sugar on Me." At the other table, an old guy in his seventies was nursing a beer, staring hard at the stage, making an effort to commit the image to memory.

As Vanier's eyes became accustomed to the darkness, he could pick out the other patrons scattered around the room in shadows, some paying for waitresses to gyrate on portable pedestals and lean their breasts over them.

The barman was leaning on the bar reading a newspaper. When he finally looked up, Vanier gestured for another. The barman reached for Vanier's glass.

"Don't bother. The Inspector's leaving."

Vanier turned to see Paul Brasso standing beside him with a bouncer.

"Where's your boss, Corporal? It is Corporal, isn't it? Corporal Brasso."

"You're leaving."

"The *Patriotes* running strip clubs, now? Or are you just here to do some of that charitable work your boss was talking about?"

"I said you're leaving."

The bouncer grinned.

"He looks like he's drunk. Drunk and looking for a fight."

"So what's it to be, Inspector? I would really like it if you refused to leave so we could help you out."

The bouncer laughed.

"Yeah. Me too."

Vanier was on his feet.

"One day, Brasso. One day."

Nine

When he got the call from the Colonel to sue the city, Pierre Dufrene started thinking about another press conference. He liked the idea of appearing as the crusading lawyer protecting the weak against the oppressor. All Barbeau would have to do would be to tell his story of police brutality; another citizen subjected to arbitrary abuse by an out-of-control police force. But when he remembered Barbeau's previous outing, he realized he wasn't press conference material. After the first interview, Dufrene had serious doubts about even taking him on as a client. He did it for the Colonel, not Barbeau. Trouble was, the kid thought he was giving the orders, and he expected Dufrene to do what he was told.

However you looked at it, Dufrene knew the kid wasn't appealing. He was a mouthy idiot, revelling in his celebrity status, and Dufrene couldn't change that. Given five minutes alone with Barbeau, most sane people would be tempted to give him a severe beating themselves.

The Colonel agreed. There would be no press conference. They would keep the kid under wraps and just sue the bastards. Dufrene crafted a lawsuit that sought $1.5 million from the *Service de police de la Ville de Montréal*, the City of Montreal, and personally against Detective Inspector Luc Vanier and his partner Detective Sergeant Sylvie Saint-Jacques. He didn't need a press conference with the kid swaggering before the media with an idiot smirk on his face.

Instead, he sent copies of the Statement of Claim to all the media outlets he could think of and waited for calls. His pitch improved with each new call: No, he was sorry, he couldn't talk about the details of the claim because that was before the court, but the allegations were serious, and they pointed to a deplorable lack of oversight, management, and training of police officers. Citizens have the right to a police force that does not brutalize them. And it was every citizen's right to fight back when they were brutalized. And no, his client wasn't available for an interview.

Dufrene knew it was the kind of case that would make his career. With luck, the city would settle, and he wouldn't even have to go to court.

Desportes was watching the computer screen, every now and then making a strangled, almost giggling noise of approval. Kyle was stretched out on the couch in a blanket, reading a graphic novel, a red tuque on his head. Desportes had bought the book for him after Star mentioned he liked comic books. Star was perched on the couch, at Kyle's feet, resting her chin on her knees and watching Desportes's back.

"He doesn't say much, your brother," said Desportes.

"He doesn't say anything. He's autistic."

"So you said." Desportes turned around to look at Kyle. "He never says anything?"

"Nothing. Makes noises sometimes. But no words."

"He likes the book."

"I told you. He'll read it, maybe a hundred, two hundred times, and then he'll stop." She turned to look at Kyle. He was immersed in the book, like he was reading it for the first time.

"I don't think he can read the words," Desportes said, turning back to the screen.

"You never know," said Star. "What do you do? For a living

I mean. You work from home?"

"Sort of. You could say I'm an independent small businessman. I trade stocks and shares and do some consulting."

"You make good money." It wasn't a question. He didn't seem to worry about money. As far as Star was concerned, if you didn't worry about money, you were rich.

"I lead a simple life. I don't need much."

"What do you consult about?"

"This and that. People who have problems come to me and sometimes I can help them. Like two businesses are in competition and want to find a way to work together. Or someone wants to get a good job. Lots of things."

"Is it legal, what you do?"

"I'd like to think so."

"That's not an answer."

"It's the only one you're going to get. Did you know it's illegal to sleep in the street? Or to beg for money? Or to go rooting for food in dumpsters?"

"You're kidding."

"People do illegal things every day. But they can only lock up so many people. So the authorities have to choose what laws to enforce and against whom."

"Sounds like you're making up a story. Like to justify what you do."

"Maybe I am."

She went quiet, and Desportes turned back to the computer.

After a while, she asked, "Could you teach me? I could be your assistant."

"Assistant? I don't need an assistant. I work alone."

"I'm sure you could do with some help. If you thought about it. You could find a lot of things for me to do. I'm cheap, you know."

"How could I hire someone I know nothing about?"

"You know me. And I'm a hard worker."

He turned to look at her. "Do you have a cv?"

"What? You mean the paper that lists all the stuff you've done. Like the jobs and that?"

"Exactly. Do you have one?"

"No. No one ever asked for one."

"So why don't you just tell me about yourself. Start wherever you want and end up with today, or yesterday. Like where is your family?"

Her arms tightened around her legs and she looked over at Kyle. He was deep in the book.

"Kyle's my family."

"But before that?"

She was thinking, and having trouble. Then her arms loosened a bit and she said. "Born in Drummondville, well miles outside actually … On a farm. But they didn't grow anything except some vegetables for us and chickens for eggs and meat … Don't know where money ever came from, but there was never very much. Kyle was born four years after me. When he was two years old, my father left … We never saw him again. Don't remember him too well … I just remember him not being there."

She was having trouble getting the story out, taking deep breaths, and blinking back tears. Kyle was motionless, except for his eyes moving from panel to panel, neither faster nor slower than before.

"My mother was crazy. People in the village thought she was just a weird hippie, but she was nuts. As soon as my father left, Cliff showed up and started acting like he's our father. Mom was just crazy, I told you that. Right? She would forget to feed us, she'd disappear for days, she couldn't cook, couldn't clean. Cliff was crazy too, but violent crazy … He was the angriest person I ever knew. After he showed up … All I remember is being scared … Scared to go home from school … Scared to get up in the morning … Scared to eat … Scared to not eat. Anything would set him off, and he exploded all the time … Two or three times a day."

Desportes said nothing. He sat still and listened.

"He was always beating us. All the time. But he beat Kyle worst of all. I think because it didn't seem to have any effect on him. Sure he'd bleed and he'd bruise, but he wouldn't cry out. First time me and Kyle ran away, I was thirteen. Mom and Cliff had been gone for two days on a party … I spent the first day scared they would come back. We went to a neighbour, but as soon as Cliff and my Mom came back, the neighbour brought us back … When I was fifteen, me and Kyle left for good. We hitched a ride to Drummondville and took the bus to Montreal." She took a long pause. "I'm still looking for our father."

"What for," Desportes asked. It seemed like such a forlorn hope.

"I'm going to kill him."

Desportes didn't answer. He just turned back to the screen and started typing again.

An old lady in a housecoat was standing in the doorway staring at Vanier suspiciously.

"Yes?"

"Inspector Vanier. For Father Harris. Is he at home?"

"Do you have a card?"

Vanier pulled one out of his pocket and handed it to her. She squinted at it.

"I'll see. Wait here." She closed the door. When she came back, she said, "Father will see you in his office. Come in."

She let him into a carpeted hallway that would have been dark in the middle of summer. The only light came from a window over the door made opaque by street grime. She pointed him to a chair in a small study and told him to wait. The only colours in the room were brown and black, and a splash of blood red from a picture of the Sacred Heart of Jesus. The place was worn with age, like the church itself.

He didn't have to wait long. There was a shuffling in the hallway, and Father Harris walked in slowly, bent in an impossible stoop, as though God was forcing his frail body down with an invisible finger. He swivelled his neck to look up at Vanier. Vanier stood up, towering over him.

"No. Stay sitting."

The priest moved behind the desk and lowered himself into the seat. Then he swivelled his neck again to face Vanier.

"Thanks for seeing me, Father. I'm here because I thought you could give me some background. You've been in Hochelaga for longer than most, and I am trying to learn about the place.

"You're the policeman who was involved in the riot. I heard you were suspended."

There wasn't anything wrong with his mind, thought Vanier. "You're right, but this isn't really police business."

"Isn't really?"

"Maybe not at all. As you said, I'm suspended."

"As long as that's understood. What is it you want to know?"

"I'm trying to understand this place. Consider me an ignorant stranger. I was investigating a murder, and then a riot that exploded out of nowhere. Now I'm under investigation for something I didn't do, but someone did. I'm trying to understand."

"Surely that's for this new committee to look into."

"The committee will do what it wants. I'm just trying to understand the neighbourhood. I thought I did. It's like, shit's happening ... Excuse me, like bad things are happening, and they're connected, or they may be, and I don't know enough to get the connections. And, if I don't get them, I'm in trouble. Big trouble."

"You're feeling under threat?"

"That's not the point."

"On the contrary, I think it is. This community, no, the people of this community, have been feeling under threat for generations. The old people fear crime and being abandoned. The young are facing a future with no hope. There are too many people surviving on welfare or punishing dead-end jobs. Pessimism, fear, and despair have been pervasive in this community for years."

"What about the changes that are happening? Things are improving, no? New condominiums going up all over the place, new homes and businesses."

"That's outsiders. All that development just puts more pressure on the people who have been here all their lives. All this so-called progress is not helping the people who have always lived here. There's no new jobs for them. It's just new people moving in and displacing the ones who are here. And it's not just a question of housing. Sure, apartments disappear and become condos for newcomers. But it's deeper than that. When everyone's in the same boat, when your neighbours are having as tough a time as you are, poverty is bearable. But these days the poor are forced to rub shoulders with the young professionals who have moved into the new condo development, and they realize how bad their own situation is. They become ashamed of their poverty, as though they could have done anything about it. Then there's a sort of sullen envy that sets in. There are upmarket restaurants opening every week, but most people can only look in the window."

"What about the *Patriotes*. Where do they fit in?"

"I wondered how long it would take you to get to them."

"They seem to be very active here. I'm surprised. I'd never heard of them before."

"They fill a gap, a large gap. They're local, from here, and they're doing what any good Christian does, helping others. The government has become almost invisible. Sure, it still hands out money, but these days, it's always from a distance. It used to be that you would go down to the local office and fill out unemployment forms or welfare applications and then go back the following week to collect your cheque. Now everything is done online, or by telephone, and there's a direct deposit to your account. Government is anonymous to most people."

"And the *Patriotes* are in the community."

"They're everywhere. Running programs, classes, providing security, everywhere you turn. They're a big part of Hochelaga."

"Security?" That was the first Vanier heard of security.

"Just like they have in the rich communities. The *Patriotes* provide the local public security force."

"I haven't seen them."

"Oh, you have. You just haven't noticed. They don't have the uniforms and marked cars, like they have in Outremont and Westmount. But the *Patriotes* have a contract to provide local security here. The police can't do everything. And believe me, the *Patriotes* take a keen interest in keeping crime under control. It's their neighbourhood, you understand."

"You make it sound like they've taken over the place."

"You make it sound like a bad thing. I like to think of it as the community providing for itself. The church has long since given up on earthly politics ... Well, mostly. But it wasn't that long ago that we staffed the hospitals and the schools ourselves and had an influence on every important political question. But since we withdrew from daily life, nobody has been able to fill the gap."

"The government?"

"Certainly not the government. They've always been too far away from the people, and anyway, there's never enough money to fill all the needs. So people work with what they have. And right now, Colonel Montpetit, with all his idiosyncrasies, is all the people have. He's doing wonderful things for the community. And, most importantly, he's part of the community. People know where he is, and if you have a problem you can go and see him. No need to go to City Hall or Quebec City or even Ottawa. You don't need to talk to bureaucrats or politicians."

Vanier wondered how much of the priest's equanimity was a show.

"Even our church benefits. We get rent from the daycare in the basement and all kinds of other meetings. The wrestling pays virtually all of the maintenance costs of the Church."

"Wrestling?

"Yes. Every Friday and Saturday night, there's wrestling in the basement. The *Patriotes* organize it, they run the league. It's very popular and it brings people to the church. Even if they're not praying, at least they know where we are."

Vanier was surprised, but not for the first time.

Ten

Vanier was walking east on Sainte-Catherine Street in the heart of the Gay Village. A canopy of strings of pink balls waved over his head, and it wasn't hard for him to see he was in a different world. A world where gays were safely in the majority and tolerance seemed to be the motto. That's why it felt different from most other places.

He took a window seat in *Le Planète*, ordered a coffee, and stared out onto the street. It didn't take long for her to show up. He recognized her from television and raised his hand in greeting. Melanie Trudel co-anchored the evening news on CTV. Vanier had called her because he knew her reputation, a tough-as-nails professional with a heart, sometimes.

She gave him a noncommittal wave through the window, no smile.

He was already standing when she reached his table. "Inspector Vanier, I recognized you from the newspaper."

He smiled, and they shook hands.

"Please. Sit down, Madame Trudel. And thanks for seeing me."

She did, taking out a notebook at the same time.

"Call me Melanie. Are we on or off the record?"

"Hadn't thought about it." He said. He hadn't realized there was a choice. "Better be off."

"Okay. If there's a quote I need, I'll ask you to go on the record."

"Fine."

"I hear you're in trouble." A journalist's opening, leaving room for him to talk about anything he wanted.

"Things could be better. I'm suspended. You know that."

"Who doesn't?" she said. Then, "I'm sorry." She sounded like she meant it.

"Don't worry. I'm working on it. It's not true, what I'm accused of. Things are going to work out."

She didn't ask the question, but he answered anyway. "Melanie, I didn't beat that kid. I don't know who did, but it wasn't me. I'm trying to find out."

The waiter appeared, and she ordered a latte without looking at the menu. There was still time for a late lunch, but she wasn't going to eat. She wanted him to know this was business.

"You said on the phone that you thought I could help you."

"I said we could help each other."

"How so?"

"I've seen a video taken just as I let the kid out the back door of Station 23."

Her eyes lit up at the mention of the back door. Journalists prefer back doors because they imply shady dealings and intrigue.

"It's not what you think. The doors in front were locked because of the riot. It was safer to send him out the back way. Anyway, in the video, the kid appears unhurt, and he was met by a guy in a raincoat."

"Doesn't that solve your problem? If you have an image of the kid leaving, and he's okay, isn't that the end of the story?"

"The picture's not that good. It's grimy, black and white, and it was getting dark. You know how it is with bad videos, you see what you want to see. The other problem is there's only a back of the head of the guy who met him."

"And?"

"And here's where you can help. The camera shows your cameraman was filming from the other side. He would have got a better picture of the kid, and a face shot of the guy who met him."

"Inspector, you know the procedure. Your guys have already asked for our footage, and we refused. It's a question of freedom of the press. The lawyers will fight it out in court, and eventually a judge will decide. So, if what you say is true, it's just a question of time."

"I know. And all that will take us to September. And we probably won't even get the film. Besides, I don't think anyone on our side is really keen to get the video footage."

"They made a request."

"Yeah. They made a request. But they don't seem that enthusiastic about pushing it."

"Just how many people have you pissed off in the force?"

Vanier ignored the question. Said, "The way things are going, there won't be any proof of anything and they'll close the investigation saying there isn't enough evidence to make a conclusion. You know what that means?"

"Not enough evidence? It means you're guilty, but they can't prove it. The public will suspect a cover-up, and you'll be on a short walk to early retirement."

"It's not just me. My partner will be smeared too. So I need to prove I didn't do it." He knew he was asking a big favour. "Help me. If there's footage showing the kid walking away without a mark on him, I'd like to know. You will be helping to save the career of two police officers." He didn't know if she cared.

Trudel brought the latte to her lips and stared at him. She was calculating, testing the angles to see how she could benefit from the situation. He continued,

"We could take it one step at a time. You don't need to decide yet. Just take a look at what you've got and see if there's anything there."

"I don't even know what the kid looks like."

"You do. He held a press conference. When I let him out the back door, he was wearing an oversized white parka jacket, a white baseball cap at a stupid angle, gold chains around his neck, and a pair of jeans that looked like they would fall off if he ran."

"A fashion maven."

"And he had fluorescent green sneakers."

"Hard to miss in a crowd."

"Depends on the crowd, I suppose. But you'll be able to pick him out. He walked out from behind the station and high-fived a guy at the edge of the crowd, and then they both walked off. Your cameraman was filming about four feet away and would have got a good shot of both of them."

She considered for a moment, stirring the foam into her coffee.

"All you have to do is to take a look to see if there's anything there that might help. Then it's up to you."

She let him wait, probably counting the seconds off in her head.

"Okay. I'll take a look at the footage. If there is something interesting, then I'll decide if I want to help you."

"That's all I'm asking." He knew that she would give the second step serious thought. "I need help."

"I know. But it's not that easy. I'm a journalist, not a good Samaritan."

She stared into his eyes for a few moments, and he knew it wasn't going to be easy. She finished the latte and stood up. "Let me think about it. I'll get back to you."

"So you'll review the footage?"

"I'll get back to you," she said, and left.

He watched her in the street, but she didn't look back. He ordered a beer.

Louis Garguet was handing out weapons from a concealed storage locker in the basement of the Club Gym. He was excited and had five guys, pumped with adrenaline, hanging on his every word. The guys were stowing shotguns and pistols into their gym bags.

Most humans have a desperate need to belong, and the guys in the basement had found their tribe. They were as disparate as any other group of guys, but united by their common fate to have been out of the room when impulse control was being doled out. A sad bunch of losers who had found an occupation where a taste for violence was a job requirement, and having nothing to lose an asset. The air was fetid with sweat, and they liked it that way.

"Where's Eddie?" asked Garguet. Somebody try him on the phone again and tell him to get his ass in here. Pronto. Don't tell him what it's about. You never know who's listening."

Then he grabbed a huge sheet of white paper and held it up against the wall. He pumped staples into it from a staple gun to keep it there.

A tall guy with long hair and a beard started dialling on his cell phone, and this time it seemed to work. When he finished talking, he announced, "Eddie says he'll be here in twenty minutes."

"Thanks, Tony. The bastard's probably been whoring all afternoon," said Garguet. "Okay, the rest of you listen up. Eduardo finally gave me access to the GPS he put in the container, and we've tracked it down. It's sitting in a warehouse at the bottom of Jeanne d'Arc near Notre-Dame. We're going to take it back at 4 a.m. tomorrow." He looked at his watch. "That's in nine hours."

He traced lines on the paper with a red felt-tip to show the intersection.

"We'll use three cars." Garguet pointed with the market. "Pierre, you and Nick in your truck. George, you and Tony in Tony's SUV. Then me, Eddie and Rico in my SUV. And Nick, you're going to be driving the baby home."

He went back to the sheet of paper and drew a rectangle.

"That's the building. You've probably seen it. Green and red. A brick warehouse."

"Yeah, I pass it all the time. It's shut down, no?" said Pierre. "I never seen anybody there."

"According to the GPS, our container is sitting in there waiting for us."

"What about a truck? We need a truck," said Tony.

"The container should be on a truck. Would have been a waste of time to take it off. But if there's no truck, I have a guy if we need him. I'll call, and he'll be there in two minutes with a truck we can use."

"Who are we going after boss? Who's guarding it?"

"*Patriotes*. That's who. But I don't know how many are going to be guarding the place. I figure at four in the morning, if they're there, they'll be asleep, or close to it." He began drawing doors on the rectangle. "There are three doors. No, four. Two on one side, one at the back, and the garage door. That's for the truck."

"You've been over to see the place?" asked Rico.

"Yeah. I drove by a couple of times. And I checked it out on Google Street View. Modern tools," Garguet continued. "So we pull quietly into the lot. Then we blow the two doors at the front and go in fast. George and Nick on this one, and me, Eddie, and Rico on this one." He marked initials on the paper. "Like I said, we blow the doors. And then go in shooting. Anybody inside moves, shoot them. Shit, if they don't move, shoot them anyway. No survivors. Understood?"

"What about me and Pierre?" asked Tony. "I don't want nobody saying we weren't part of the action."

"I was getting to you, Tony. You two go round back, to this door." Garguet was writing initials on the back door.

"We blow it and go in?"

"Fucking brilliant, Tony. Yeah, you blow the door, run in and start shooting. Just when we're coming in on the other side. We can all shoot each other."

It got a laugh.

"No. You don't blow it. You two stay outside and watch the door. Anyone tries to leave, you shoot them. Got it?"

"Yeah, Louis. I got it."

"And don't stand in front of the door in case you catch a stray bullet. Let the wall block you."

"Got it."

"Once inside, we secure the place. Like I said, anybody moves, shoot them. Nick, you get the truck going. You'll probably have to jack the electricals."

"Sure, Louis." Nick looked almost normal, with short hair and a long sleeved shirt. If he had brown shorts he could have passed for the UPS man. "I can get any truck going in five minutes, max."

"Good," said Garguet. "As soon as the motor starts running, we open the garage door, and Nick takes off."

"Where do I take it to, Louis?"

"Ontario. I'll give you the location later. Guys, as soon as Nick's out the door, we close the place up and leave. Got it?"

The guys were excited.

Garguet went through the plan, such as it was, again, and again. They were to meet at 3:45 a.m. in the parking lot of LaFleur's, an all-night hamburger stand on Notre-Dame. Then they would take Notre-Dame for the five-minute drive west. They were to cut the engines as soon as they turned into the lot and cruise to a stop as close to the doors as possible. On the third run-through, Eddie came down the stairs.

"Where the fuck you been?" Garguet said.

Eddie shrugged his shoulders and smiled.

"You whore-master. Can't you keep it in your pants?"

A few of the guys laughed, and Eddie shrugged.

Garguet went through the plan again. Eddie was hearing it for the first time. By ten o'clock, everyone had things fixed in their heads.

"Okay. So you all take off. Walk out of here like after a hard workout at the gym. One by one. Nothing strange. And stay quiet. No drinking and no dope till we're finished. At three-fifteen, you join up and head towards LaFleur's. At three forty-five, we leave LaFleur's. Got it?"

The guys nodded

"Okay. I want all cell phones here. No calls. No leaks. Understood?"

Eddie was first to surrender his phone. He figured there was no choice, but he made sure to lift the battery. He didn't want any incoming calls when he wasn't there. He dropped the phone in a cardboard box and wondered where he could go to find a payphone.

As the guys were getting ready to leave, Garguet said, "We're going to have fun, tonight. And we're going to kick some serious ass."

As they filed out, he added, "Eddie. I want you to stay. We'll work out together."

"Sure, Louis. I don't have nothing to do anyway."

Desportes was sitting in Bar 3687 on Sainte-Catherine Street. The owner named it after its street address and used as much imagination in decorating it. Desportes was sitting alone at one of the formica-topped tables. Two tables down, a woman sat in a pink fake fur jacket and a tight short skirt, nursing a glass of wine. It was her third. It wasn't unusual. People often had to get their bearings before they talked to Desportes. When she came inside from yet another cigarette break, she seemed to have made up her mind. She sat down, gulped down the last of the wine and carried the glass to the bar for a refill. Then she walked over to Desportes's table. In the tight skirt and high heels, she couldn't stop her ass swinging back and forth like she was trolling for business.

"I was wondering when you'd come over."

"Are you Hugo?"

"That's my name."

"Can I sit down?"

He pushed the chair away from the table with his hand and gestured for her to sit.

She sat and made a hopeless effort to pull the hem of the skirt down. "I don't know where to start. People said you might be able to help."

"Maybe. What's the problem?" He waved to signal another beer.

"It's my son. Serge. He's disappeared."

"I'm sorry to hear that. How old is he?"

"Fifteen."

"Kids leave home at fifteen."

"No. He had it too good at home. He has no reason to leave. But the things that have happened, I think he's in trouble."

"Tell me."

As soon as she started, he realized he knew most of the story. It had been hard to miss.

"You're Serge Barbeau's mother?"

"Yes. The last time I saw him was about eight o'clock on Tuesday. the day after he was beaten up, when they had his press conference on TV. You know, they shouldn't have made Serge do that. He's not good at speaking in public. I had to go to a friend's to see it because my cable's cut off. Those bastards. I owe them about $60 and they cut me off. Anyway, Serge came in for dinner, and I started talking about it, asking him about what happened at the police station, and he goes crazy. He started shouting, like *why don't I believe him*? He said I was calling him a liar. It's not that I didn't believe him. I just wanted to know what happened. Anyway, he still ate dinner. See, that's what I mean, he wouldn't run away. Even when he's mad at me, he stays around for dinner.

"So, right after dinner he gets a call and tells me he's going out. And that's the last I saw of him."

"He hasn't called since then?"

"No. At about one o'clock I got a text." She pulled out her phone and pushed buttons. Then held the screen up so he could see.

Have to go away for a few days. Will be in touch.

"I've called his cell phone, left messages. And nothing. Now the phone's dead – ." She began to choke at the word dead. "And – I don't know. I've got a really bad feeling ... "

"It makes sense for him to lie low, doesn't it? I mean, from what I read, the cop he accused said he lied about the beating. Maybe he was scared the cops would do something."

"Serge isn't that smart. He wouldn't even think about ... What was it you said? Lying low. But that's the point. If he did lie about the police, someone else did it to him ... Beat him up, I mean."

Desportes looked her in the eyes. "You think he lied?"

"No. Well, I don't know now. He was so defensive when I even asked about it. Like he didn't expect me to believe it."

"So where might he have gone?"

"I tried to find out. I tried to find out what he'd been doing, like who he's been hanging with. But you know this place, nobody says nothing. It's tough to raise kids around here. I don't know where he is most of the time, I don't know who his friends are. It's easy for a kid to get into trouble here."

"But what can I do for you?"

"Maybe you could find out what happened to him. Maybe you can ask around and find out. Anything. I want to know."

Desportes was intrigued. He had followed Barbeau's story, mainly because he was surprised by the *Patriotes*' ability to organize a riot at short notice, and puzzled about why they would even want to. He didn't understand the kid's disappearance, and trying to figure out what happened might be interesting.

"If I ask around, where can I reach you?"

Madame Barbeau gave him her phone number and then told him where they lived. He knew the street, a low rent area where people clung on by their fingernails. The last stop before moving on to rooming houses with shared toilets.

"Okay, Madame Barbeau. I'll see what I can do. I'll call you."

"Anything you can do. I'll pay."

"Let's see how things go first."

She slugged the remnants of the wine and stood up, unsteadily. Her heels were too high for walking, but she tried her best to leave with dignity, not looking back.

Sylvie Saint-Jacques knew where she was going, and Vanier followed. They walked up Emery Street, past a second-hand bookseller, and Saint-Jacques pulled open the door and held it for Vanier. Inside, it was quiet, only the gentle murmur of conversation. Several of the tables were taken, but nobody looked up. Vanier glanced back through the window as though to make sure that the cacophony of street noise still existed. It did, but outside. Then he picked up the low sound of Miles Davis rippling through the room from excellent speakers. "It Never Entered My Mind" always stopped him in his tracks.

A tall bearded man in jeans and a T-shirt approached them. He ignored Vanier, and said, "Sylvie, it's been way too long."

Saint-Jacques gave him the obligatory double-cheek kiss. "Good to see you, Nelson, and you're right. It's been too long. We're supposed to meet someone."

Nelson swivelled, letting her take in the long room.

"I think .... " Saint-Jacques gestured to a woman with a bright purple streak in her dark hair sitting alone in a booth, staring into her tea. Vanier was already on his way. Saint-Jacques followed.

The woman didn't look up when they approached.

"Madame Lavigeur?" said Saint-Jacques.

She jumped a little and then gave a weak smile. "Yes, that's me. But call me Melissa."

"And you should call me Sylvie," said Saint-Jacques, sliding into the bench opposite her. "And this is Luc Vanier. We work together."

"I know. I saw you both, remember?"

Lavigeur took Vanier's outstretched hand and gave it a limp shake. Nelson placed two menus on the table as Vanier slid in beside Saint-Jacques. Vanier looked around, taking in the wooden ceiling fans that turned slowly over their heads, the dark wood of the tables, and the enclosed serving section where plumes of steam rose from several kettles of boiling water. An aroma of tea hung throughout the room, clean and comforting. He gave Lavigeur a smile.

"First, we need to order," said Saint-Jacques. "Then we can talk."

Vanier opened the menu and knew immediately he was lost. It was more information than he had expected, and he realized he couldn't just order a cup of tea. He flipped through ten pages to get an idea. Tea was organized by type and region, with small photos of the estates they came from, or the pots and cups used for brewing or drinking. He looked at the pictures, beaten by the choices.

"What do you think?" he asked, turning to Saint-Jacques.

"What do you like? Green, white, black, or maybe fermented?"

"Fermented?" He'd never heard of fermented tea, but he had great respect for fermented beverages in general.

"Saint-Jacques saw his reaction. "It's not alcoholic, just a way of preparing the leaves. They're fermented for a couple of years. It gives the tea a much different taste. You might like it."

"I suppose a bag of Tetley's is out of the question."

The two women laughed, and Saint-Jacques took charge.

"Not on the menu. Why don't I order for you? You like black tea, right?"

"Sure." Vanier guessed that he might like a black tea, and as traditional as possible.

Nelson reappeared, and Saint-Jacques ordered Wulong for Vanier and a Rosée du Gyokuro for herself.

Nelson said to Vanier, "You'll enjoy that. Wulong teas are some of my favourites."

Vanier smiled as though he had passed some test.

Lavigeur picked up her pot and refilled her cup.

"So, Melissa, what did you want to talk about?"

"It's probably nothing, but when I saw you the other day, I thought, what's to lose? If I don't say anything, maybe I'll regret it."

"You were at one of the desks," said Vanier.

"Yeah. I've worked there for six months, about."

"What do you do at the *Patriotes*?" asked Saint-Jacques.

"A little bit of everything, but, mostly, I write grant proposals. And I supervise a bunch of programs, you know, hire the staff, get the location, that sort of thing. Oh, and I write the reports on the programs."

"What does that mean?" asked Vanier. "Like you ask for the money and then you report how it was spent."

"More or less. Writing a grant application is a skill, and I'm good at it. The way it works is that a Department will get a budget to, say, promote early childcare. They don't have the people to actually do it, so they give it to someone else to do. Usually, you have to develop a proposal and ask for funding. If they accept the proposal, you get some of the money. When it's finished, you report how great the program was and then you get the rest of the money."

"That's a full time job?"

"Almost. There's a lot of money in the charity sector. It's how organizations survive. Say there's a need for after-school programs.

We put together a proposal and ask for $100,000. If it's approved, we hire someone to do it for $25,000 and pocket the rest. At the end, I write a report showing how the $100,000 was well spent and what the results were."

"But you didn't spend $100,000?" asked Saint-Jacques.

"Not even close. But that's how the community charity sector works."

"Not just the *Patriotes*?"

"Hell, no." She laughed at their ignorance. "You can always find people who will do the actual work. They get a fixed rate, doesn't matter how many hours they put in, that's all they get. But you need administration, that's where the money is. It happens all the time. In the charities, the only areas making money are the administration. The people who actually deliver the services get screwed. It's a scam."

"If everyone's doing it, why did you want to talk to us about the *Patriotes*?" asked Saint-Jacques.

"I'm worried I might be involved in something illegal. There's so many strange things going on there. Something's not right."

"Like what, Melissa?"

She pulled back from the table and lost the slouch. She was thinking. Then she leaned forward.

"Well, the big thing is the money."

"Money?"

"I have to pay tons of people in my work. And it's always cash. The contract workers, church halls for meetings, cafés for sandwiches, printing, that sort of thing. It's all small stuff, but it adds up. It's always cash. And everyone else has to do it too. We fill out requisition forms and we always get cash back. Never a cheque. Even though the form says to fill in who to make the cheque payable to. It always comes back as cash and we have to get a receipt."

"But it's just petty cash," said Saint-Jacques.

"It adds up. And they have an accountant. They could use cheques."

"But it's not a lot."

"Not for me. It's not a lot for me. Maybe four or five thousand a month. But it's the same for all the programs. After I called you," she looked at Saint-Jacques, "I tried to figure out how much it might be, if all those kinds of payments were in cash. It's $50,000 to $60,000 a month. And that got me thinking about how much money was coming in. I went back over all the grant applications I filled in, and so for this year, I've applied for one and a half million dollars. And it's only April."

"Melissa, there's nothing illegal about getting government grants to do programs," said Saint-Jacques. "And, I suppose, if the actual programs cost less than the grant, they soak up the rest in administration charges. That's okay too. As for the cash, it's strange, but, again, nothing illegal."

Vanier put down his teacup. "What about the security? I heard the *Patriotes* have a public security contract. What do you know about that?"

"Not much. It's run from upstairs. I think it's just for the zone. They have guys there all the time. We don't get involved with that. The charity is called *Société des Patriotes de Montréal*. Security is a separate company, HSS – Hochelaga Security Services. They're both run from upstairs."

Lavigeur looked at her watch. "I've got to go. I have to pick up my kids."

"Thanks, Melissa," said Saint-Jacques.

"But you don't think …," she said, as though she was looking for confirmation that there was a problem.

"We're still looking at things," said Vanier. "Maybe things will begin to make sense when we know more. But like Sylvie said, thanks for talking to us."

She looked at Vanier. "And that incident with the kid. I believe you. And what you're doing, it's important. There's something bad happening here."

Vanier got up as she left and shook her hand again. He slipped into her spot and pulled his cup across the table.

"So what do you think, Sylvie?"

"It's strange. But we don't have a clue what's going on. And we aren't supposed to be doing anything."

"It stinks, Sylvie. And I'm not letting these bastards get away with screwing with us."

It was Wednesday night, and traffic was slow in the zone. Vanier was in his Volvo, cruising slowly along Sainte-Catherine Street like a john. He was also getting the same hand-waving invitations. He pulled over and nodded to a green woolly top and black pants that were tighter than paint. She leaned in the window and smiled.

"Hi. You looking for something?"

"Yeah," he said. "How much?"

"Depends what you want, honey, and where you want it." She was all smiles, but her eyes were alert, taking in Vanier and everything in the car. She was cautious, but eager. Business was slow.

"BJ. In the car?"

She opened the car and got in, reaching across to put her hand on his thigh. He enjoyed it.

"Sixty." She held her hand out. "We can drive into the alley off Moreau."

"I could arrest you right now."

"Shit. A fucking cop. You've no right, you know. There's no arrests, not anymore. What's the matter with you?"

"I didn't get the memo."

"Well you'd better look it up. We don't work up on Ontario. And you stay away from us down here. That's the deal."

"Who made the deal?"

"Prime Minister Harper. How the fuck should I know. I just know that's the deal."

"I'm looking for someone. She may be working here."

She was interested again. "You've got a crush? It's good to play the field. For you, I'll do an introductory special. Fifty bucks. And you'll be smiling all night." She put her hand back on his thigh.

He let her hand stay where it was. "You help me find her, and you can go back to work."

She removed her hand. "Who is she?"

"Maude. Maude Roberge. Émile Legault's girlfriend, till he got killed. I heard she's back working."

"She never gave up working. Just now, she's back on the street."

"So you know her?"

"It's not a big place." She pulled out a cigarette and lit it. He pushed the button for the window. "Suppose I know her. How much if I help you?"

"I told you. You don't get arrested."

"Come on, I'm supposed to be earning money. What's it to you?"

Vanier knew she'd take what she could get. The sixty for a blow job was her opening offer, she'd dropped to fifty in a heartbeat.

"Twenty."

"Forty." She gave him a smile and put her hand back on his thigh. "For forty, I'll show you where she is, and give you a hand job."

"Thirty. Without the hand job." He pulled out a ten and a twenty and handed it to her.

"Drive three blocks down. That's where she usually works."

Vanier followed the instructions.

"That's her," she said. "In the red coat." She was pointing to a woman standing at the curb on the next block. The red coat was

Little Red Riding Hood loud. She had a huge white shoulder bag in case you missed the red.

"I'll get out here," she said, taking the thirty dollars.

He stopped the car and the woman got out, struggling on her heels. She closed the door and leaned in the window. "Don't tell her it was me."

"Sure."

Vanier drove to the next block and stopped in front of Maude, sliding the window down. Maude leaned in. She looked wrecked. Her make-up was heavy, looked like it was put on in the dark. Some of it was almost in the right place.

"Hey darling. What you thinking about?"

"What's on offer?"

At the sound of a serious customer, she pulled open the door and climbed in.

"Whatever you want, Mister. Anything special in mind?" For the second time in minutes he felt the hand on his thigh. He pushed the door lock and removed her hand.

"Just some information, Maude."

At the sound of her name, she looked at his face. She hadn't bothered before. She was trying to remember.

"Sometimes, I'm so bad with faces. We've been together before?"

He returned her gaze. Up close, she looked worse than wrecked. "You don't recognize me?"

"It doesn't matter, love. What do you want me to call you?"

Then finally she got it. Almost. "You're a cop. Oh, shit."

She sat back in her seat, resigned.

"Maude, we've met. I'm investigating Émile's murder."

Her hand went for the door handle, but the door was locked. Vanier pulled away from the curb.

"I want to leave ... Right now."

"Just a chat, Maude. You and me. It won't take long."

She sat back. She was used to doing what she was told. "I've got nothing to say."

"I'll buy you a coffee."

Maude lit a cigarette, and Vanier punched the window down again. He drove her to a Tim Hortons, its thousand-watt interior looking bright but not warm. She wanted a coffee, a chicken sandwich, and a muffin. When they sat down, she put the chicken sandwich in her bag and began picking at the muffin. She looked at him across the plastic table.

"I've got to get back."

"Émile's father said you know a lot more than you told me."

"I told you. I don't know who it was. Émile pissed off so many people, it could have been anyone."

"Was Émile having trouble?"

She looked up at him like it was a stupid question.

"Émile was always in trouble. His whole life was a bag of shit. He was paranoid. With reason."

"How so?"

"Payments. He was always behind. He was his own best customer, and when he did sell stuff, he'd piss it off gambling or buying guns or some shit. He didn't pay the suppliers. Then he got crazy when guys would come around to collect. Like they were disrespecting him."

"Who was he buying drugs from?"

"He went through different guys. Mostly unaffiliated. He thought it didn't matter if he stiffed them because they didn't have enough muscle to collect. He was an idiot."

"And?"

"It's just like any other business. My dad used to have an import business."

Vanier raised an eyebrow

160

"It's not what you're thinking. It was legitimate. He used to import food. If someone stiffed him, he'd sell the debt to people who were better at collecting. Same thing. The Hells started showing up to collect debts he owed to other dealers. I figured they bought the debts."

"And Émile couldn't pay?"

She gave him the look again. Another stupid question. "There's no can't pay with the Hells. He found money, but never enough. And he was getting worse every day. He was smoking heroine all day and walking around with a gun stuffed in his pants. Fucking wind would blow and he'd pull out the gun. He was always looking out the window."

"So you think the Hells took him?"

"Yeah. That's it."

"That's it?"

"Yeah, it must have been the Hells."

"Why would they kill him if he owed them money?"

"How do I know? Maybe as an example, to show people what happens if you don't pay." She turned to look at the clock on the wall, studying it carefully, like she was counting. "I have to go. I told you."

"So who are you working for now?"

"No one. I work for myself."

"Émile's father said you used to take notes, you used to write everything down."

She brightened up.

"Yeah. You know like in that film. You know, where the guy, like can't remember anything, so he writes everything down."

"*Memento*?"

"Maybe, I'm not sure. I loved that film."

She drifted away, maybe remembering the film.

"So where are the notes?"

161

"I lost them. They gave me a green garbage bag with my clothes and put me in the car. That was it. Nothing else in the bag. I looked."

Vanier knew he was wasting his time. He drove her back to her spot. She turned to him. "I need money. I've been gone too long and I need something to show for it."

"I thought you said you worked for yourself."

"Sixty bucks. For this long, I need sixty."

He reached into his pocket. "Here's forty."

She reached out for the two bills, but Vanier pulled back. "Who do you work for, Maude?

"Same as everyone else around here."

"Who's that?"

"Ask around, it's not a big secret." She grabbed the money, got out of the car, spun around to get her bearings, and then took up her post at the curb.

Vanier drove off, parked at the next block, and adjusted the rear-view mirror. There were more women than cars, and every time a car stopped the women jockeyed for position at the passenger window. Even so, within minutes Maude got into another car and was gone.

He continued watching the street and thinking, until a truck pulled up behind him and lit up the inside of the Volvo with its high-beams. Then the beams flashed, and Vanier was again aware of his lack of status. He could still get out and act like a cop, but he didn't have a badge or a gun to protect him. He thought about leaving, but the high-beams flashed again. Fuck you, he thought, and decided to stay.

In the side mirror he watched a buzz-cut guy in his twenties get out of the truck and walk towards the Volvo. Vanier slid the window down and shifted his weight to be ready to smash the door into the guy's knees.

"You're going to have to move along, sir."

"Says who?"

"Don't make things difficult, just move on."

"Why don't you call the police?"

"Sir, I'm public security. And I have the right to ask you to move on. You don't really want me to call the police, do you?"

"A *Patriote?*"

"Everyone's a patriot. I love this country. Now move on."

Vanier started the car and drove slowly away.

At 3:45 a.m., the third car pulled into the parking lot at LaFleur's and joined the other two. Garguet was leaning into an SUV, giving last-minute instructions. Five minutes later, the three-car motorcade pulled out for the short drive along Notre-Dame to the warehouse. They turned right, up Jeanne d'Arc, then left into the parking lot. They shut the engines and cruised silently to a stop. The parking lot was empty, and the building looked deserted.

Nick and Tony were cradling sawn-off shotguns and disappeared around to the back. Rico had served his apprenticeship making pipe bombs, and he was looking after the explosives. It didn't take him long to fix small charges to each door. The others sheltered along the walls and watched while Rico pushed some numbers on a cell phone. The first door blew off its hinges and fell to the floor with a crash. The second door didn't move until Garguet kicked it. Then it swung open. They went inside quickly, through the smoke that filled the doorways. Garguet flicked the light switch as he passed, and everyone was screaming at once: *Police. On your feet. Hands in the air. Now.*

All of them had all been on the receiving end of enough police raids to know how it was done and how it sounded. And they knew that if it really was a police raid, you shouldn't be reaching for a gun unless you had a death wish. But there was no response. The place was silent except for their own screaming. The truck, with the container sitting on its bed, was in the centre of the long room.

"Jesus. Looks like they left it alone, boss. Fucking idiots," said Pierre, smiling.

"Better search the place, spread out," Garguet said.

Before they could move, they heard the door on the other side of the truck scraping on the stone floor. Garguet leaned down to look under the truck and saw feet running out the door. The shots came seconds later; two blasts in quick succession.

"Rico, go outside by this door," said Garguet, gesturing to the one he had just came through. "See what's happening."

Rico disappeared out the door. "Okay, the rest of you spread out and search the place."

On the other side of the truck, Tony and Nick were dragging the body of Serge Barbeau into the building, his blood making skid marks on the floor.

"He's dead. He was trying to escape," said Nick.

"Too bad, he should have stayed here."

"The place is empty," said Pierre. "Christ, you're brilliant, Louis. They must all be up at the zone."

"Damn right," said Garguet. Then he turned to Nick in the truck. "Let me know when you're ready to go."

Nick jumped up into the cab and started fiddling with the wiring under the dashboard. The motor started in seconds, and Nick gave a wave. Eddie pushed the button at the side of the garage door, and it opened slowly. They stood there watching as Nick drove out and turned down to Notre-Dame. In ten minutes he'd be on the highway, heading for Ontario.

Eddie pushed another button, and the garage door closed. They went back out to the parking lot through the blasted doors and were gone in seconds.

Serge Barbeau lay dead on the concrete floor.

Eleven

Saint-Jacques had received her copy of the Statement of Claim, freshly stamped by the Superior Court and served on her by a bailiff. She'd never been sued before. She scanned it to make a copy and put the original in an envelope. Then she spent three hours reading and re-reading it, using a yellow marker to highlight whole passages, and writing notes in the margin. She felt like she knew it by heart, word for word. Then she called Vanier.

"Yeah, I got it this morning. But I haven't read it yet."

"You haven't read it?" She didn't understand how he could not have read it.

"What's to read? It's not true, and I'm going to show them it's not true. There's nothing to worry about."

"They say I was complicit. That I knew or should reasonably have known that you were assaulting Barbeau," said Saint-Jacques.

"Don't worry, Sylvie, it's bullshit, it's not true," said Vanier.

"Oh. That's it. The truth will out. What if it doesn't?"

He didn't have an answer. They both knew of the tenuous connection between truth and justice. The justice system was as unpredictable as a horse race, and there was no such thing as a sure thing.

"I'm sorry. Maybe I'm overreacting," she said, trying to ignore the nagging doubts. She hadn't seen Barbeau leave the station, and she knew Vanier was capable of getting rough.

"No. Don't apologize. I'll read the damn thing and then we can talk about it."

"Okay. Call me." Saint-Jacques hung up the phone.

Sitting in his Volvo in the driveway of Anjili's apartment build-ing, Vanier checked the time. He had promised to be on time, and he was five minutes early. A miracle. He had even remembered to make the reservation, a table for two at *Le Sel de mer*. He was trying to make amends, trying not to screw things up. He punched her number in his cell phone.

"Hey."

"It's me. I'm downstairs."

"Already? Wonders never cease. I'm running late. Luc, can you come up? I'll buzz you in, and you can let yourself into the apart-ment. I'll be in the shower."

"Sure." He grabbed the flowers, another peace offering. She didn't say anything when he rang the intercom, just buzzed the door open.

He could hear the shower as he walked in, slipping off his shoes. He put the flowers on the table and dumped his coat over the couch. Then he sat down. He got up again to put the coat in the closet, poured himself a whiskey, and relaxed into the couch. The bathroom door opened and the flowery shampoo and soap smell wafted down the hallway. He was tempted to follow the scent, but didn't; he was walking a tightrope and didn't want to fall. It was 6:30, and the dinner reservation was for 7 p.m.

"Luc," she called from the back bedroom. "Don't worry about the time. I called and they said as long as we get there before nine, they'd feed us."

"Okay," he called back. Too loudly, because she was walking towards him down the hallway in a white lacy bra and panty set, the kind that felt as good as they looked. She leaned down, took his glass, and put it on the table. Then she took his hand and pulled him up.

"They'll feed us as long as we're there by nine."

"I heard."

"Nice flowers by the way."

"Thanks."

She led him back down the hallway into the bedroom, then let go his hand and turned towards him. Slowly, she unclasped the front hooks on her bra, and Vanier watched, ready to accept anything she had in mind. Her panties followed. Then she walked into Vanier and kissed him, but not for long. She stepped back and started undressing him with determination. There was no question, no hesitation, just get the damn clothes off as quick as possible, and Vanier wasn't arguing.

The sex was rough. She wanted to fight and he let her, he wasn't even close to resisting. He let her hit and scratch and claw and grab handfuls of him, and squeeze like she wanted to cause him pain. Vanier kind of understood what she was doing. She was in a hurry and quickly started climbing those women's peaks, the kind where you think okay, this is it, but it's not, and he just kept climbing with her. All the time, she said nothing, moaning to herself while punching him, solid punches, one after the other into his ribs, while she played with his tongue in her mouth. Then, out of nowhere, she started to laugh. Without losing the rhythm, she burst through the anger into the kind of laughter you never hear from adults. An innocent laughter that means nothing but having fun. And Vanier realized that making love to a woman who's laughing because she's having fun is the greatest; you can pretend a lot of things but you can't pretend you're having fun. Then the laughter stopped and she held on tight and continued climbing. To Vanier, it felt like they were completely naked for the first time.

She was slick with sweat and his hands glided into slippery crevasses as she pushed into him. When she was ready they made eye contact. It wasn't one of those rest on the shoulder, dig your head into the pillow, and explode kind of things. They stared at each other for the final moments and connected. It was the most personal sex he'd had in years. Then she hit the top, and he followed into the fireworks and overloaded circuits as best he could.

They lay there, and he could feel her heart pounding, quickly, and then slowly settling down.

"Holy shit," she said finally, with a smile.

"Yeah," he said, feeling her heartbeat against his chest.

He was almost dozing off in the afterglow when she said, "I wanted you to know."

"Hmm."

"That I want you in my bed, Luc. If you know that, the rest is manageable."

Vanier knew enough to continue with the non-verbal. "Hmm."

"I know it's hard on you. You drive me home and we sit outside in the car while you try to decide: do I come in and leave after a few hours, or just not come in, and avoid the pain."

"It's hard."

"I'm not saying I like it when you wake up at one o'clock and go home. But I understand. And if that's the way it has to be for a while, I can live with it. We just need to be honest. And I want you in my bed as often as I can."

He rolled up on his arm and leaned forward to kiss her, his hand roaming over her stomach, caressing the undersides of her breasts.

"No time, Mister. I'm starving," she said, breaking the kiss and rolling away. "And you're going to buy me a big hunk of meat. Rare."

Then she disappeared into the bathroom.

The only light in the Botanical Gardens came from a pale moon that disappeared behind scattered clouds for minutes at a time. The Alpine Garden section was being expanded, and huge boulders from Saint-François-de-Salle were dumped around the site, waiting to be arranged into place by cranes. The workers had finished putting in the soil, a mixture of clinker and fill to provide good drainage. After the heavy rain, it was damp and muddy, tough going for the two men digging a grave.

"You really think they had to kill him? He was only a kid. He was a stupid shit with only half a brain. But still, he was only a kid."

The other guy didn't answer. Conversation was becoming too much work. They'd been digging for almost an hour and were over four feet down. They were both sweating.

"We're going to have to retaliate, right?"

"Assuming we know who did it."

"Come on, man. We all know who did it. It was Garguet. The container was his."

"I thought he was under control. You know, being cooperative."

"Joe, you can't trust scum like that. But shit, if we have to take out the Hells, that's going to be messy."

"Well it's not our problem. We just follow orders. That's the way I like it. Not complicated."

"It's not complicated. But it could get very ugly."

"Nah. If you ask me, Denis, the Hells are a bunch of pussies. If it comes to a fight, it's no contest."

"You know, personally, I couldn't stand the little fuck. This deep enough, you think?" said Denis.

"I guess so. Once they put the boulders in, that will be the end of Serge Barbeau. He'll be pushing up daisies."

"Edelweiss, you mean. It's an alpine garden."

"Edelweiss?"

"Yeah, they grow in the Alps. Didn't you see *The Sound of Music*?"

They both laughed and began singing about blossoms of snow blooming and growing forever.

After another half hour of digging, Joe grabbed the makeshift ladder at the top of the grave, propped it against the wall of the grave, and climbed out. His partner followed, and they both walked to the truck and let down the flatbed hatch. They dragged the dark blue body bag to the edge and grabbed the handles at each end. Then they carried it over to the hole.

"Skinny bastard. Hardly weighs anything," said Joe.

"All mouth. That was him. Fuck all else."

They dropped the bag into the hole with a wet thud and began shovelling the earth back in. It took half an hour. When they were finished, you couldn't tell the soil had been disturbed, and Serge Barbeau lay peacefully under five feet of soil. Soon to be five feet of soil and a six ton granite boulder.

"A beer would go down well."

"I'd kill for a beer."

They threw their mud-caked overalls and rubber boots into the bed of the truck and took off, remembering to replace the padlock on the gate as they left.

Vanier was driving home, listening to Etta James and feeling good, like he was going to be able to hold it all together. Like there was hope. He thought of stopping off at the Blue Angel for a nightcap. Then he thought of Alex and decided against it.

He pulled out his keys as he walked down the hallway. He looked down to check the shoes outside the door. It was a habit now, checking the shoes. Alex had two pairs, and unless he had bought new ones, he was at home. Vanier turned the key and pushed. The door moved two inches before it was stopped dead by the chain.

"Shit," he cursed, under his breath. Then he yelled through the crack, "Alex. Come and open the door. The chain's on."

He put his ear to the crack and listened. Only silence. No television, no music, and the lights were off. He reached into his pocket for his cell phone and punched in Alex's number. The call went straight to voicemail. He yelled again through the crack in the door, "Alex. Come on, open the door." Then he fist-pounded the wood. There was only silence from inside.

Vanier stood back and then leapt forward, shoulder first into the door. The chain remained in place. He tried twice more and realized that it wasn't going to work, so he turned and ran back down the hallway and took the elevator to the basement garage. The janitor had a plywood workroom in the garage where he kept tools and paint. It was locked, but one kick was enough to open it. He scanned the small room and saw a crowbar on a hook. Vanier grabbed it and rushed back to the elevator, cursing it for taking so long to get back to his floor. Then he ran down the hallway and used the crowbar to force the door. This time the chain gave with the sound of screws being pulled out of wood. He was inside and went through the apartment, flicking the light switches to bathe the place in light. In seconds, he had checked every room. Alex wasn't there. But you can't put a chain on the door from the outside. Then he thought of the balcony. He crossed the living room, pulled open the balcony door, and stepped out. Security lights along the building illuminated every spot where Alex would have landed. Vanier walked the length of the balcony peering down to the ground. There was nothing.

He went back into the apartment and started opening closets. In Alex's bedroom he pushed back the sliding doors of the built-in closet and saw him, sitting on the floor with his knees pulled up tight to his chest and his arms wrapped around his legs.

Vanier got down on his knees and reached for him. Alex didn't react. He was shaking, as though he was cold, and his teeth were chattering, but there were beads of sweat on his face and his T-shirt was dark, stained with damp at the armpits and on his chest. Vanier crept closer and put an arm around his shoulder, pulling himself into the closet to sit beside him.

"Hey Alex, it's okay. Don't worry. Things are fine."

He put his hand on Alex's neck and felt the pulse racing. His body was tense, as though he could spring up at any second, and Vanier knew there was nothing to do but wait, so he mumbled the meaningless platitudes, a familiar noise to convey his presence, and he squeezed Alex's shoulder from time to time. After half an hour, Alex rested his head on Vanier's shoulder and seemed to relax. Later still he said, "I'm sorry".

"Don't be …. It was a panic attack, that's all. I've read about them. They seem real, Alex, but they're not."

"I don't want to talk about it, Dad."

"Okay."

They sat in the dark in silence. Vanier looked down at his son's face and saw tears caught in the light of the moon. He squeezed his arm around the boy again.

Twelve

Star was ushered into the office of the lawyer Pierre Dufrene by a young girl in heavy makeup. Star didn't use makeup, she wouldn't know where to start, and she looked pale by comparison. She was wearing an outfit that Desportes had helped her choose from *Village des Valeurs*. He had said it made her look like a poor student trying to look professional. Until she saw the receptionist, she had thought the outfit made her look good.

"Clara Furlow," the girl said to Dufrene, as she ushered Star into the office. Star had chosen the name herself and was enjoying the change of identity. She reached out to shake Dufrene's hand, but he looked at his watch instead. He gestured for her to sit on one of the chairs in front of the desk. "I understand this isn't for a consultation."

"No, sir. I'm with the *Commission scolaire de Montréal*. Well, actually I'm doing a three-month work-placement with them. I'm a student in social work at UQAM, and work-placement is part of the program." She handed him a card that Desportes had made up yesterday. Dufrene barely glanced at it before dropping it among the piles of paper already on his desk.

"What can I do for you?"

"I was given three kids to work with. Kids who were slipping in school and in danger of dropping out. I'm supposed to work with them, one-on-one, to get them back on track."

"And?"

"One of the kids is Serge Barbeau. He seems to have gone missing. I was wondering if you could help me track him down."

"And why do you think I can help you?"

"Mr. Frechette at the school told me you were his lawyer. He recognized you at the press conference after the incident at the police station."

"You're not the only one looking for him. The police would love to talk to him, too."

"I suppose." She pulled her chair closer to the desk and rested her notebook on top of a pile of folders. "You don't mind, do you? It's easier to write on a flat surface." Star gripped the notebook tightly in an effort to stop her hands from shaking.

"You're nervous."

"I'm not used to this. I'm supposed to act professional. Maybe that's why they give us work-placement."

"Anyway, there's nothing to write. I can't help you. I have no idea where he is. Even if I did, it's confidential," he said, getting up.

"Okay. But I thought, he's your client, maybe you could get a message to him."

"Was my client. If I can't find him, I guess he's no longer my client. Tell you what, if you find him, tell him he still needs a lawyer. Tell him he should call me."

As he finished his sentence, Star leaned her chair forward to write in the notebook, balancing it on a pile of file folders. They began to lean.

"Watch out." Dufrene jumped up as the folders slipped to the floor, emptying themselves on the way. He reached out to try to stem the flow of paper and then bent to stuff them back into folders and pile them back on the desk. He didn't notice Star place a small plastic box on the underside of the desk's lip.

"I'm sorry. Oh, I'm so sorry." Star didn't bend down to help him.

"You should go now. Practice is over."

She stood up. "I'm really sorry."

"You should be more careful. Don't they teach that in university?"

Star had no idea what they taught in university. She backed herself to the door with a final, "I'm sorry. Listen, if he wants to call me, my number is on the card." She looked at the mess on his desk and handed him another. "I'll give you two. If you lose one, you'll have another."

Three blocks from Dufrene's office, Star walked into Atomic Café and ordered an espresso. Desportes was working on his laptop at a small table wearing headphones. She carried the espresso over.

"Wonderful, Star," he said as he handed her the headphones and set up the audio again. "Listen."

She put on the headphones and heard a crash of papers and her mumbled apologies. Then a static and a slap, which she assumed was the device being attached. She heard more of her muttered apologies and wondered why she sounded so stupid. Desportes pushed some buttons, and she listened to the fast-forward noise for a few seconds and then the sound of a telephone keyboard being punched.

Desportes lifted the left ear pad cushion and leaned over. "This is about two minutes after you left."

"Colonel. It's Dufrene."

There was a silence.

"I thought I should call you. I just had a visit from Barbeau's school, they're looking for him."

. . .

"No, I didn't tell her anything. Just that I had no idea where he was."

. . .

"Yeah, the same as I told the police."

...

"But I was thinking. Maybe it would be a good idea to get his mother to send a note to the school. You know, to say he went to visit someone. Just something to reassure them."

...

"No sir. Like you say, I know nothing. That's all I'm saying to anyone. He was my client but I haven't heard from him. End of story."

...

"Yes, sir."

Star heard the phone being cradled and smiled at Desportes. She was excited. Pleased that she accomplished something.

"So what do you think?" Desportes asked

"Me?" She was surprised. She hadn't thought anything; she had just listened to the tape. Desportes waited for a response.

"He was speaking to someone called Colonel. He was reporting that someone from the school was looking for Barbeau and suggesting that the Colonel get Barbeau's mother to send a note to the school." Star looked up. "Why would he do that? And who is he calling?"

"Good questions. Let's deal with the second one right now. Watch."

He went back to the beginning of the recording, to the keypad beeps of the telephone, and opened another program on the screen. He played the beeps again and numbers appeared on the screen. Then he typed the number into Canada 411 but came up empty. So he clicked into a pay service and entered the numbers. A box on the screen showed a name and an address.

"Amazing, that's close by. Who is he?" said Star.

"Colonel Alfonse Montpetit, leader of the *Patriotes*."

"What's the *Patriotes*?"

"A mix between a community organization and a pretend army.

They run social programs, and some of them like to dress up like soldiers."

"Strange."

"Indeed."

"Why would Dufrene … ?"

"That was your first question. And to answer that we need more information."

Montreal's *Palais de Justice* is an imposing block of granite and black metal that sits on the edge of the old town, a modernistic fist in the air for authority. It's where all fights are finally ended, and the people who wander its hallways reflect the fact that fighting knows no barriers: husbands and wives with lifetimes of accumulated grievances, business partners fighting over the scraps of failed ideas, relatives dragging out promises made by the deceased but not kept, and, of course, the criminal accused, more dark-skinned than white, more uneducated than not, more poor than rich. Every player has their coterie of witnesses with selective memories as pliable as putty.

It's a machine with steel-hard parts that grinds down everyone that enters, and the machinery needs its mechanics; the black-clad lawyers in flowing gowns for spectacle, the uniformed security men and women prowling for trouble, the journalist looking for sensation, and the people who push the coffee trolleys through the hallways dispensing the sugar and caffeine-laden fuel that keeps everything going. The only people who enjoy the place are the spectators with nothing better to do than watch blood sport, seeking out the juiciest combats.

And then there are the judges, invisible except when presiding over combat, who enter and leave through back entrances and private elevators out of sight of the public, living behind the walls like an infestation.

In the bowels of the *Palais* are interview rooms, where lawyers examine the other side's witnesses before trial, and everything is transcribed, so that two years later, when the case eventually comes to trial, the witness can be challenged on slight difference in his story: *Were you lying then or are you lying now?*

Vanier and Saint-Jacques were waiting for the lawyers that had been appointed by the Detectives Association. Barbeau's lawyer, Pierre Dufrene, was supposed to produce the kid for an examination before anyone had to file a defence to his action. They were getting two kicks at the Barbeau can. Vanier's lawyer was going to examine Barbeau before they filed their defence; Saint-Jacques's lawyer, and the city's lawyer would examine him later. The lawyers were late.

Saint-Jacques and Vanier had hardly said a word to each other since they arrived. Every time he tried to start a conversation, she would give a clipped, one- or two-word response, and go silent again. She was used to being a witness, waiting to be called, and then simply telling what she knew with no embellishment. She wasn't used to being the accused, and she was battling her doubts about what Vanier was capable of doing.

An impossibly young girl, like a student playing dress-up, approached.

"Inspector Vanier?"

Vanier looked down at her. "Yes?"

"I'm *Maître* Lavoie. *Maître* Metzler has a motion this morning, so he can't make it. He asked me to do the examination."

Saint-Jacques rolled her eyes.

"But he knows the case," said Vanier.

"Don't worry. I've read the file." She wasn't giving him a choice. She was all he was going to get, and she seemed used to handling *Maître* Metzler's disappointed clients.

"So we just wait for *Maître* Dufrene and Barbeau?" asked Vanier.

"Yes." She looked at her watch. "They should be here by now.

I've got to be somewhere else in an hour."

"That's all it's going to take?"

"Forty-five minutes, one hour max. I've got questions, but that's as long as it should take."

"What if it takes longer?"

"It won't," she said with a smile. She looked at her watch again. "The stenographer is setting up. We'll be ready to go as soon as Barbeau shows up."

Saint-Jacques was on the phone, leaving her name and number. She looked at Vanier. "My guy's not answering."

"Don't worry. He'll show up soon," said Lavoie, sure of something she knew nothing about.

Vanier was getting tired of standing around. "Can we see the room?"

"Sure."

Lavoie led them into a small partitioned cubicle with a desk and little else. Two seats on each side and a fifth at the end for the stenographer. The stenographer was fiddling with a tape machine and smiled at them as they came in. She asked for all their business cards. "It's for the transcript. I need to spell the names correctly."

Lavoie had her card on the table before the stenographer finished speaking. Vanier was searching his pockets. He eventually borrowed a pen and wrote his name and address on the stenographer's notepad.

Saint-Jacques put her card on the table. "We need another seat," she said to no one in particular. "I'll go find one."

Vanier checked the time on his cell phone, they were half an hour late getting started. Lavoie's phone rang. She put it to her ear and listened, looking at Vanier with a shrug of her shoulders and a *what can I do expression* on her face.

"Okay. We'll be in touch."

She put her phone back in her bag and turned to the stenographer.

"We won't be needing you today, Madame. *Maître* Dufrene just cancelled. She turned to Vanier. Saint-Jacques was coming back with a chair.

"The plaintiff's lawyer just called. He apologizes, but his client's a no-show. He needs to reschedule."

"So what can we do?" asked Vanier.

"Not much. We have to give them a chance to produce Barbeau. Maybe ten days. If Barbeau doesn't submit to an examination, we file a motion to dismiss."

"That's it?"

"That's it. If he cannot produce the Plaintiff, he can't go forward. End of story."

Saint-Jacques didn't look pleased.

"That's good news, isn't it?" Lavoie asked, fishing her Black-Berry out of her bag.

"The best," said Vanier.

"Maybe," said Saint-Jacques. "Did he say why Barbeau didn't show up?"

"He just said that he tried to locate him but hasn't been able to. That's all he knows."

Lavoie was already leaving, reaching out to shake hands as she checked emails on her phone.

"*Maître* Meltzer will be in touch. If we don't have the witness in ten days, we'll move to dismiss." They followed her out into the hallway and let her run ahead for the elevator.

Saint-Jacques said, "Where do you think he is?"

"No idea. He didn't strike me as reliable."

She looked at Vanier as if she had more questions but decided against them.

"Plans?" Vanier asked

"Today? Not really. But I've got to find something. This sitting around is killing me." She saw it hurt him, as though he was responsible.

Vanier wanted to tell her again that he didn't beat the kid, but didn't see the point.

"I'm going to the psychiatrist this afternoon."

Saint-Jacques raised an eyebrow.

"Alex's psychiatrist. He asked me to come with Alex."

"How's it going?"

"I think he's broken. Like he can't be fixed. It's tough, Sylvie."

The ground in the park was sodden from melted snow and spring rain. Star was sitting on an A-frame picnic table, her feet planted on the bench, picking at paint chips peeling off the surface, trying to see how big a chip could peel before it broke off. It had been somebody's job to put the picnic tables into storage for the winter, but nobody did it, and they spent the winter under snow.

She didn't need a disguise to look like just another disaffected kid who didn't give a shit about anything. But just in case, she had a half-empty bottle of cheap vodka between her feet.

Two boys approached in hoodies and jackets. A girl followed at a distance. Star had been watching them since they started to meander across the grass. She figured they had been heading for the picnic table before they saw it was occupied. Now they were trying to decide. The boys stopped just short of the table, the girl, still trailing behind them, stared up at the sky, like she was looking for something.

Star finally acknowledged them. Said, "Hey."

The older boy said, "Hey. We usually hang here."

"It's a public park," said Star, trying not to sound too aggressive.

The boys sat on the table, the same side as Star. The girl approached cautiously.

"You're not from here," said the older of the two boys.

"No," said Star.

"Where you from?"

"Montreal."

The younger boy leaned forward and turned his head to get a look at Star.

"Hochelaga's in Montreal," he said.

"But I'm not from here."

Star reached for the bottle and took a swig of vodka. She screwed the top back on and then, almost as an afterthought, offered it to the older boy.

"Thanks." He took the bottle and put it to his mouth, gulped, winced, and passed it on. "That's good. My name's Gaston."

He offered his fist to Star and they touched knuckles. "Star," she said.

The younger boy took a slug and handed the bottle back. "Theo," he said, leaning across to brush knuckles.

"That's Zoë," said Gaston. "She doesn't drink."

Zoë moved her hand in a kind of wave and smiled at Star. "It smells like spring," she said.

"That's all the dog shit," Theo said. "Look."

They all looked down. The ground was covered in decomposing dog turds that had survived the winter covered in snow.

"That's a lot of shit," said Star.

"Nobody picks it up in the winter. Figure it'll disappear under the snow." said Theo. "Imagine, maybe thirty dogs a day taking a crap and nobody picking it up for three months. That's … "

He hesitated for a second.

"That's two thousand, seven hundred shits. Let's say an average of two turds a shit, that's five thousand, four hundred individual turds."

"Like I said, a lot of shit," said Star.

They all started laughing, and Star passed the bottle around. Then they let Theo calculate how much shit was generated every day by all the people living in Montreal. It took him a few minutes

182

to do the math, but it was a lot.

After a while, Star said, "I've been looking for Serge Barbeau. He lives around here somewhere. You know him?"

The laughing stopped.

"You a friend of his?" asked Gaston.

"Yeah."

Star felt the chill. Wrong answer. She picked up the bottle took another swig. Passed it around.

"He's a friend until I find him and get my money back. The fuck stole my money."

"Sounds like Barbeau," said Theo.

"I met him outside the Berri *métro*. I was panhandling. I'd saved $200. Shithead hung around with me all day. I couldn't get rid of him. He was trying to make out."

"Eugh," said Zoë.

"No kidding," said Star. "Anyway, I couldn't get rid of him. There was a bunch of us sleeping in an empty building below Sainte-Catherine, and we let him stay. But I heard him leave in the middle of the night. I guess he couldn't take the cold. In the morning, I noticed my stash was gone. He had taken my money. I remember he said he came from Hochelaga, so I came to look for him. I want my money."

"He's a shit. I knew him in school. The fucker doesn't have a single friend, he burns everyone," said Gaston.

Star started asking questions, and they answered. She did what Desportes had said, testing them with easy ones, where he lived, his mother's name and the like. Then where he hung out. She asked all the questions she could think of, but they couldn't help with the big one.

"We all saw him on TV when he was beaten up. But since then, nothing," said Gaston. "Strange. You'd think now that he's famous, he'd be everywhere."

"But you'll ask around?"

"Sure thing. We'll ask around."

It was a forty-minute drive back to Montreal from the psychiatrist at the Veterans Hospital in Sainte-Anne-de-Bellevue. Alex had said almost nothing on the drive out. Vanier had put it down to nervousness before meeting the shrink. Now, it was Vanier's mind that was chewing through unanswerable questions. He was disappointed that the diagnosis of Post Traumatic Stress Disorder was confirmed, but almost relieved to be able to identify what was wrong. The biggest unknown was how Alex would take it, he had said the strict minimum in the psychiatrist's office.

Vanier opened with, "So what do you think, Alex?"

Alex held up a fistful of paper – prescriptions for sleeping pills and anti-depressants and reading material on PTSD. "I got pills and brochures. But she hasn't got a clue, does she?"

Vanier glanced over. "She knows enough to admit it. That's something."

"I suppose. They've got a list of symptoms as long as your arm, but not everyone has the same symptoms. And it's not something you can cure, like a broken leg or a disease, but you're supposed to have hope. Drugs to make you sleep, and drugs to calm you down, they won't fix the problem, but you might feel better, maybe. Basically, she said 'we know nothing, so here are some drugs that might work, and here's a list of therapy groups, and here's some reading material. Feel free, mix and match. If something works, good luck!'"

Vanier didn't say anything. He wasn't surprised there was no magic bullet. He had already watched psychiatry at work as his mother spiralled down into the black hole of Alzheimer's. Nobody had a clue what was going on inside her brain, so the psychiatrist ended up as an experimental drug-pusher, hoping something might work and measuring success in docility. In the psychiatric world, agitation is always a bad thing, so docility must be good. He turned to Alex. "And don't forget the meditation."

"I was wondering when you'd bring up the Hare Krishna stuff."

"Don't knock it till you've tried it. And it's not Hare Krishna."

"If meditation works, why aren't you wandering around, grinning like the Dalai Lama?"

Vanier smiled.

"I don't practice enough. I'm a dilettante." He made a mental note to practice more, the same mental note he had been making for five years. "I'll give you the name of the woman who taught me. She's a good teacher. She helped me through a tough time."

Alex held the index finger and thumb of each hand together, closed his eyes, and let out a long Om sound.

"She teaches prisoners. Real hard bastards, in maximum security. So I wouldn't mock it when you're around her. I'll give you her coordinates."

"Sure," said Alex.

"And the groups. The doctor wouldn't have suggested groups if she thought they were a waste of time."

"Sure, Dad. I'll try a group, too." Alex slumped back in his seat and stared out the window, as though agreeing to the meditation lady and group therapy just confirmed how screwed up he was.

Thirteen

Dufrene knew he had a problem. Barbeau's failure to show up was just another of his idiot client's mistakes, and from what he had heard, Barbeau had been making mistakes all his life, one of the many drawbacks of being Serge Barbeau. But if he couldn't find his client, he had a decision to make. Vanier's lawyer had filed a motion to dismiss the action, and the other defendants were piling on in support. He had hoped the City and the *Service de Police* would cut a side deal, and hang the two cops out to dry, but it hadn't happened yet. He called the Colonel and explained the problem.

"So if we don't produce the kid for examination, the case gets thrown? Is that what you're telling me?"

"Yes. Maybe I can get a delay, but the chances of that are slim. The court will probably say I should just file again if my client decides to cooperate. Do you have any idea where he is?"

"If I knew, we wouldn't be having this conversation. Wait a second, what if someone disappeared the kid? The court wouldn't like that, would it?"

"Disappeared the kid? You mean like deliberately made him disappear?"

"Yeah. The judge wouldn't be pleased with that, would he?"

"I can't do that. I can't even suggest it without evidence."

"No, but you don't have to actually say it. I know lawyers. They're good with words. You can plant the seed can't you?"

"What do you mean?"

"Make it clear that you have your suspicions, but because you're a lawyer, you can't speak your mind."

"You mean, like ethically."

"Yeah. You've got ethics, so you can't do it. But you've got suspicions too."

Dufrene thought about, it wouldn't be hard to do. "Maybe."

"Then do it. I'll help you."

The *Journal de Montréal* had received a ten-second video clip and released four screenshots in the morning edition, one on the front page and three more inside. One would have been enough.

The front page was dominated with a photograph of Louis Garguet standing over a man tied to a chair. The banner headline said: *The Final Hours of Émile Legault*. The guy in the chair looked like he'd fallen face down onto concrete from the third floor. His head was drooping and his face was covered in blood that streaked down his chest and arms. The newspaper identified the guy in the chair as Émile Legault. Garguet was standing over him holding a hammer and smiling. The pictures inside were similar, Legault being beaten to death and Garguet looking like it was all in a day's work. The *Journal*'s chief crime reporter, Norman Tessier, wrote that the DVD had arrived in a brown envelope with a handwritten note. He had immediately turned them both over to the police, but not before making copies for his exclusive use.

Vanier had heard the story on the radio and had gone out to buy a copy of the newspaper. Now he was struggling to understand the photo. It reminded him of the photos from Abu Ghraib of kid soldiers posing for photographs while torturing prisoners, or the photo essay of Canadian soldiers beating a 15-year-old to death over twelve hours in Somalia for stealing food. He didn't understand the urge to record the brutal horror of what sons, daughters, and next-door neighbours are capable of doing in the right circumstances.

And Garguet didn't need photographs to prove what he was capable of. The opportunity to beat a man to death wasn't a once-in-a-lifetime meeting with fate for Garguet, it was his life, the real and constant world. And posing for photographs like a trophy hunter made no sense. Yet there it was. Vanier let the pictures sink in and wondered if Garguet was really posing. He didn't seem to be aware of the camera. He looked more like a pool player reading the table after a good break, except there was no pool table, and the cue was a hammer hanging casually from his hand, its business end dark with blood.

At 11 a.m., Saint-Jacques called and told Vanier to look at the television news on TVA. He tried to explain that he had already seen the story in the *Journal*, but she cut him off.

"Just watch the latest and call me back."

It took a few minutes but he found it, footage of Garguet arriving at Headquarters. The screen showed the usual march of a handcuffed suspect into the front entrance of the building. Flood and Laurent were flanking Garguet. The prisoner was holding his head up in a show of unconcerned confidence for the cameras. Journalists were milling around, shouting questions and flashing photographs, and being ignored by the three men. As the three of them went up the steps to the main entrance, Garguet hesitated for a second, seeming to have trouble balancing himself with his hands cuffed behind his back. Flood took his right arm, as if to help him, and reached out for the door. Then Garguet seemed to leap forward, his head exploding against the plate glass door. The glass shattered, and Garguet's fall was broken by the handrail that stretched across the door, so he didn't hit the ground, he balanced bent over the handle like an overcoat on a railing. Then Laurent and Flood manhandled Garguet off the door handle and dragged him inside the station.

Vanier speed-dialled Saint-Jacques, his cell phone cradled between his shoulder and ear while he tried to bring the clip up on the TVA website.

"Laurent and Flood?"

"Fine, I called. Garguet's dead."

"It looked like his head exploded. When was it?"

"About half an hour ago."

"Wait. I got it. On the computer."

Vanier pressed the play button on the screen and watched again as the three men approached the door. He pressed stop as Flood moved to open the door, and then moved the video forward as slowly as he could. Then he saw the light, a bead of red on the back of Garguet's skull just a second before he pitched forward through the plate glass.

"What have you heard?"

"Not much. They told me that Laurent and Flood were unhurt, but that's all. We're pariah, remember? We don't exist."

"Sylvie, take it easy."

"Take it easy? Things are out of control. Garguet was trying to tell you something with his video, and now he's dead. Shit's happening and we're involved. I need to do something. I can't just sit and watch all this happening."

"Why don't you come by? We can talk this thing through."

"I'll be there in twenty minutes."

It took a while, but Vanier finally got Laurent on the phone.

"So, how are you feeling?" asked Vanier.

"Like shit. I heard the bullet blow through his head. Shit, it was six inches from my own."

"It looked like a clean shot."

"Clean. The experts said it was sniper clean. They found the shooting site, on the third floor opposite the parking. But there was nothing there, no prints, no hair, no spent case, nothing. Like the shooter was dressed in a forensics suit. Small powder burn on the window ledge, that's it."

"Someone knew you were bringing Garguet in."

"It wasn't a big secret. The place was full of reporters waiting for us. Everyone who wanted to know could have figured it out from the radio chatter."

"And somebody set him up?"

"Set him up good. He wasn't walking away from this."

"How was he on the drive down?"

"Like he was mad as hell. Not at us. Just mad. He kept saying that he wanted his lawyer and then he would talk to us. You know, the way everyone's rushing to make the first deal with Crown when the shit hits the fan. It was like he knew that he was nailed, and it's only the first deal that counts."

"He didn't take the pictures himself, and someone sent them to the papers."

"Yeah. I guess he was going to nark the others out and hope for a lighter sentence."

"And he would have succeeded."

"Listen, boss, I have to go. It's a madhouse down here."

"OK. Appreciate the call."

"Sure."

The image was replaying in Vanier's head like one of the six or seven television moments burned into the subconscious of generations; the close-up, pistol execution on a Saigon street, Lee Harvey, his face scrunched up, taking one in the stomach, or the broken Saddam Hussein, surprised until the end as the floor gave way beneath him. Vanier was used to seeing death in repose, desecrated bodies that only gave clues to the final moments, and no matter how he imagined, he could never fully recreate those moments. He carried around too many still-photo memories of the dead, but they faded with time. But he knew that the shot to the back of Garguet's head and his pitch forward through the glass door would be with him forever.

Kids relaxing on park benches in Hochelaga are magnets for police with nothing better to do. So the kids always sit well back into the park to get some advance warning. By the time the cruiser has parked and the uniforms have slogged across the grass fondling their gear, there's always plenty of time to ditch the joints and booze.

Star and her new buddy Gaston were sitting on one table facing two boys on the other. The benches were close enough, so they only had to lean slightly to pass the joint. Gaston had introduced the others as Claude and Jacques. It was 4:30 in the afternoon, and the park was deserted except for two mothers watching a gang of six-year-olds climbing on the pretend fort.

"This is good stuff, fuck," said Jacques, taking one last pull and passing the joint on.

"Crazy," said Star. "Makes the world livable."

Claude pulled on the joint and passed it to Gaston, holding the smoke in his lungs.

Star was waiting for the questions. She felt like she was some kind of world traveller who just arrived in town.

"So where in Montreal you from?" asked Claude.

"South Shore, at first," said Star. She didn't see any need to tell the truth. "It's the worst place on earth. Full of families and nothing to do."

"What about the malls? I've seen them. Huge ones. Like a million stores inside."

Star vaguely remembered malls, and what she remembered wasn't great. Without money, looking at window displays gets depressing. Just a reminder of what you don't have.

Gaston had set up the meeting. He passed her the joint, and she took a deep pull. Handed it back to Jacques.

She had been hanging out with Gaston all afternoon, showing off her talents as a shoplifter. They had spent an hour in *Village des Valeurs*, America's gift to Hochelaga's poor, an American multinational retailer designed to look like a charity store so that it can compete with the Salvation Army. As though the Salvation Army needed competition.

Star was good at shoplifting. She had given it thought and she had rules; don't waste your time with crap, just because it's small and fits in your pocket doesn't mean it belongs there, and just because it doesn't fit in your pocket doesn't mean you shouldn't steal it. The highlight of the day's lesson was Star walking out of the Village with a three-by-four framed poster of a lavender garden she'd lifted from the home décor section. They tried to sell it to passersby on the street. Then they tried to give it away. At three o'clock, they carried it into Le Roi d'Ontario and ordered hot dogs. After they finished, they walked out and left the lavender garden leaning against a wall.

Gaston had a cell phone, and Star listened every time he was on a call, trying to figure out what was happening, but it was nearly impossible. All the calls were the same, a telegraphic series of Yeahs and Nos, or quick-fire sentences that she couldn't follow. If someone happened to be nearby, they'd meet. That's how they were now sitting in the park with these two kids.

"So you're looking for shithead?" asked Jacques.

"Barbeau? Yeah, he stole my money. You know where I can find him?"

"If you've got a shovel," he said. "He went to the Alpine Gardens, up in the park. But he ain't coming back, poor bastard." Jacques laughed.

"The Alpine Gardens? What are you talking about?"

"It's a section of the Botanical Gardens. We go there when it's closed. Great place to chill. Couple of nights ago, we were up there having a few beers and we heard a truck. Nobody's supposed to be there at night. We all dove into the bushes to hide. Anyway, this truck pulls up right where they're fixing up the Alpine Gardens.

They're putting in new boulders, and I was, like, fifteen feet away. Two guys get out of the truck and start digging. Man, they were at it forever. We could hear them talking, and it didn't take long to figure out they were digging a grave for Barbeau."

"Shit," said Gaston.

"We were scared shirtless, man."

"How did you know it was for Barbeau?"

"They said his name, maybe three times. When they dug the hole, they pulled this long bag out of the back of the truck. You could tell there was a body in it, the way it sagged down in the middle. Then they dropped it in the hole and covered it up. Shit, I still hear the sound it made when they dropped it in. Imagine, fuck."

"You know the guys?" asked Starr.

"Sure. They're with the *Patriotes*. I've seen them around. They called each other Joe and Denis. I remember that. And I got the plate number from the truck. Crazy Assed Shit 286."

"What?"

"Crazy Assed Shit. CAS 286. It's how I remembered the plate. Man I was scared. It took them forever before they finished and drove off. And I was kneeling in the bushes all the time. My legs were killing me, but I couldn't move."

"Where'd they go?"

"Same way they came in, I suppose. The maintenance gate on Pie-IX."

"I thought you said the place was closed."

"Yeah. They must have had a key, I suppose."

"You didn't go to the police?" said Star. She knew it was a stupid question as soon as she asked it.

"Are you kidding, they'd probably lock me up for it. Seriously. Anyway, it's not my problem. I never liked Barbeau."

"So you're not getting your money back," said Gaston.

"I guess not. Unless you want to help me dig him up and check his pockets."

They laughed. Star lit another joint.

"Eddie Pickton," the voice boomed over his cell phone. "The boy becomes a man."

Pickton was on his way to the gym. After Garguet's killing, he didn't know what to expect.

"You're the man, Eddie. You're in charge. All you have to do is make it happen. I said we'd help you."

"I've gotta think. It's not going to be easy."

"Eddie. You and I. We can work together. We just need to get you installed as number one."

Eddie wasn't sure he wanted to be number one. Number one is a target. He said, "Listen. I'm on my way to meet the guys. Decide the response. There has to be a response, or we look like pussies."

"You've got to keep things under control, Eddie."

"It's not that easy. Tony is looking for the top job. And he's out for blood."

"Tony's not smart like you, Eddie. He'll get you all killed."

"But the guys are going to want to fight back. They all know it was you guys. They can't take that."

"I'm not asking you to give up the fight. I'm asking you to stay alive."

"Yeah?"

"The way I figure it, Tony will want to come after us. Encourage him. Tell the guys you're up for it. But just tell us when you're coming. We'll take Tony out of the picture and you're in charge."

"You're crazy."

"Eddie. Do you really want a war? You guys can't win. I'm offering you to stay in business and cooperate."

"I'll think about it." Eddie didn't like his options.

"Nobody wants a war. And you guys are finished if you start

one. You've got a chance to keep things nice and quiet."

"I said I'll think about it."

"Just let me know what's happening. If shit happens and you haven't told me ..."

"What?"

"It's goodbye, Eddie."

The phone clicked dead just as Pickton pulled into the Club Gym's parking lot.

The mood was somber in the basement of Club Gym. They had all seen the images of Louis being blasted through the plate glass window at police headquarters. They knew who had set him up and who had killed him, but Louis hadn't been the only one who had taken a piece of Legault. The *Patriotes* had invited people from all the gangs, and they'd all taken turns with Legault, proving how tough they were. One guy was pissed that Legault was already dead when his turn came. It was supposed to have been some kind of bonding exercise.

Eddie Pickton and Tony Esposito were the obvious candidates to take over from Garguet, but it wasn't clear which one. Pickton had a reputation for thinking things through, weighing the odds. Esposito believed in force. Esposito wanted quick retaliation against the *Patriotes*, and staked out his ground, while Pickton held back, giving Esposito room to talk his way to his own execution.

Esposito said, "I say we borrow six of the guys from the Laval chapter and take on the *Patriotes* head to head."

"Tony. We can't do another war," said Pickton. "If the fighting gets too public, everyone loses. The police will be all over us, and the business will be under pressure for years."

"We can't do nothing. We'll look like pussies. We gotta hit back."

"You're right, Tony," Pickton said. "But tit for tat. They took out our boss, we pop Montpetit."

"You scared of taking them on?"

"Don't start with that shit," Pickton said. "I'm not fucking scared. I'm thinking of the business. We can hit back. But this doesn't have to escalate."

The other guys began to chime in.

"Eddie's right," said Nick. "I know you're mad, Tony. We're all mad. But we don't have to start a war."

The debate continued, and Tony realized there was no appetite for escalating. Business was tough enough without getting distracted into a blood feud. They needed to keep the business going and do what they had to do to maintain respect. But they could be smart about it.

"Yeah," said Tony, finally. "We retaliate but we don't go further. Our boss. Their boss. There's just one thing."

"What's that, Tony?" asked Pickton.

"I want to do this myself. I want to take out the fucker."

Pickton was only too happy to agree. He went up to Esposito and gave him a massive bear hug.

"You're the man, Tony."

At 10:30, Eddie Pickton was on his balcony looking down into the street. He pushed the call button on his cell phone.

"Yeah?"

"It's me," he said.

"Eddie. Good to hear from you. What's the word?"

"The target's Montpetit. Tomorrow morning on Sherbrooke, on his way to work. Tony and Nick are going to follow him on motorcycles. When he stops at a light, Tony will pull alongside and pop him. Not very sophisticated, but it's Tony's gig."

"How will they know when he's on his way?"

"Someone will be looking out for Montpetit leaving his house. When he's about to hit Sherbrooke, Tony will get a call and be on him from there."

"Thanks, Eddie."

"Make sure you get the right guy. Tony is the shooter. Don't shoot Nick. Don't shoot the guy with short hair. Remember, Tony's got long hair and a beard."

"We'll do what we can, Eddie."

"It's going to be hard to keep things under control after it happens. You guys better offer a deal right away."

"We'll make you look good, Eddie. Don't worry."

Pickton clicked disconnect and walked back inside his apartment.

Fourteen

Vanier hadn't seen his original lawyer since their first interview. Isabelle Lavoie had become his lawyer, and he didn't have any say in it. Saint-Jacques had also been demoted to a junior lawyer. Lavoie was on her feet before Justice Otis arguing for a dismissal of the case. Unfortunately, she had been distracted from her argument plan by a copy of the *Journal de Montréal* that featured an interview with Colonel Montpetit, who was, in the words of the journalist, "incensed" that the Barbeau case was in danger of being dismissed. The Colonel noted that those allegedly responsible for beating him up would have a serious motive for making him disappear. He all but accused Vanier of killing Barbeau to save his career. Now Lavoie was digging the hole deeper, making sure that, if the idea hadn't crossed the judge's mind before, it was now front and center.

"*Maître* Lavoie. What exactly is your point?" asked Judge Otis.

"My point, Judge, is that the court should not be influenced by such ill-informed speculation as this," she said, holding up the *Journal de Montréal*.

"But you're the one who brought it to my attention. Are you asking me to look at it so that I can ignore it?"

"What I'm saying is that this Court shouldn't be influenced by sensationalism. My client has been sued, and if the plaintiff will not appear for examination, the claim must be dismissed."

Vanier was clenching his fists, struggling to maintain control.

Judges had never warmed to him, but he figured even he could have done a better job. Lavoie was circling the sinkhole, about to disappear.

"My client has the right to go on with his life. *Maître* Dufrene has failed to produce his client for examination and he has failed to provide any explanation whatsoever."

Dufrene jumped to his feet. "It's grotesque to suggest that I should be providing an explanation when my client has disappeared off the face of the earth in the most suspicious circumstances."

The judge wasn't impressed. "Sit down, *Maître*, you'll get your chance." He turned his attention back to Lavoie. "Anything else, *Maître*?"

"Only this, Judge. This pending lawsuit, which has no merit whatsoever, is, by its very existence, ruining my client's life."

"You've already said that. But let's not exaggerate. He's suspended with pay while the case is pending. There are lots of people who would appreciate an extended paid holiday."

"Not my client, sir."

"So you say. Maybe he should take up fishing." The Judge was careful not to look in Vanier's direction. He turned to Dufrene. "Do you have any idea where your client is?"

"If I did, Judge, I would have produced him. All I am asking for is a ninety-day delay to investigate what happened to him."

"Investigate is a loaded term, counsel," said the Judge.

"I'm sure that the Court is also interested in finding out what happened to Serge Barbeau. All I'm asking for is a short delay to produce him." He made a theatrical pause. "If he's alive."

The Judge turned back to Lavoie. "Last words?"

"Briefly, Judge. This court's role is not to speculate on what might happen. It must simply deal with the matters brought before. If *Maître* Dufrene wants an investigation, he can bring his suspicions … "

"To the police?"

She knew a judicial smack-down when she heard one. She stood her ground. "Yes, Judge. To the police."

Judge Otis looked down at his notes and then back to Lavoie. "I'm suspending the action for sixty days to give *Maître* Dufrene time to, ah, locate his client. I understand that this will cause a prejudice to the police officers involved, but I consider the broader interests of justice demand a continuation."

He didn't even glance in the direction of Vanier and Saint-Jacques, just picked up his file, wheeled back his chair, and disappeared through the door behind the bench.

Show over. Vanier and Saint-Jacques were contemplating the struggle through the journalists that were waiting outside.

It was 8:30 in the morning, and Tony Esposito and Nick Delisle had their motorcycles backed to the curb on Sherbrooke Street. Esposito was cradling his cell phone in one hand and watching traffic. It was heavy in both directions, and he was beginning to wonder if it was such a good place for a hit, but it was too late for him to back out. Delisle was yawning next to him. He had only slept two hours and was feeling a hangover coming on.

"Where the fuck is he?" said Esposito.

"He'll be here, Tony. Just wait for the call. Soon as he leaves the house, Rico's gonna call, and then it's four or five minutes until he gets to Sherbrooke."

Esposito was staring at the corner where the Colonel's car was supposed to turn onto Sherebrooke. Traffic was backed up at the light, and they'd have no problem picking him up.

"He'd better get here soon. This waiting is killing me," Esposito said as his phone rang. He put it to his ear and listened for a couple of seconds. Then he turned to Delisle. "He's on his way. He's alone in the car."

They both watched the intersection until the Colonel's minivan came into view and stopped at the red light.

"The fuck he's driving a minivan for?" asked Esposito.

"He's got kids. I guess he drives them to hockey."

"They'll be orphans in five minutes. You ready?"

Esposito was clipping on his helmet. He felt for the gun stuck into his pants and revved the engine. The minivan pulled out onto Sherbrooke Street. They let it pass and pulled out into traffic three cars behind.

The Colonel was a careful driver, indicating lane changes and pumping the brakes well before he had any reason to stop. The light ahead turned orange, and he slowed to a stop before it turned red.

Esposito held up his hand to indicate to Delisle and pulled out of traffic, slowly rolling along the centre lane past three cars. He reached into his jacket and down for the gun. When he got to the minivan, he had one hand steadying the bike, the other holding the gun. Then he saw in the driver's mirror, and it wasn't the Colonel in the car. He was approaching the driver's door when it swung open forcefully into his front wheel, tipping the bike to the ground. It fell on his leg, and he lost his grip on the gun. He tried frantically to free it and grab for the gun at the same time. Delisle swung out into the oncoming traffic to avoid crashing into him. He made a quick turn in the middle of the intersection and stopped the bike. He reached for his gun, but it was too late. The driver was already pumping three shots into Esposito's chest, the explosions muffled by a silencer. Esposito's body jumped at each shot, and Delisle knew he couldn't do anything without getting shot himself. He wheeled the bike around and sped off. The minivan did a U-turn and took off in the opposite direction. Esposito lay motionless on the ground.

Hugo Desportes didn't seem surprised to hear of Barbeau's death and burial, but he had Star repeat what she knew three times to make sure he got every detail.

"So what do you think we should do, Star?"

"Tell his mother? That's what she hired you to do, no?"

"Maybe. And if we do that?"

Star was thinking. "She'd go to the police. She would want the body."

"I guess. Then she would tell the police where she's heard it and they'd come looking for you. That brings me into it. And to the kids who watched the burial."

"And Barbeau would still be dead."

She was beginning to see it wasn't a good idea.

"Plus, I don't want the police here. Especially not over a dead body."

"So someone gets away with murder?" she asked.

"It happens all the time."

"But that's not right."

"You're beginning to learn, Star."

"But we have to do something. Even if Barbeau was a shit, killing him was wrong. And why did they kill him?"

"Good question. Who knows?"

"Maybe we can call in the information anonymously."

"I suppose. Assuming they would even bother to dig up the garden, what then? The guys who did it would start wondering how the police found out. If your buddies go to the park often enough, it probably isn't a secret. Maybe they find them. So they're in danger. And the guy you talked to leads to you."

"Or they do nothing. Maybe they just sit tight and hope the police do nothing."

"Possibly. Want to take the chance?"

Kyle was asleep on the couch. Star removed the book on his chest and placed a blanket over him. "If I wake him up, he won't go back to sleep again."

"I'm going to bed, and you should too. Maybe we'll have a better idea in the morning."

Star wasn't sure there were any good ideas. The idea of getting away with murder wasn't something she had ever thought about. And then she thought about her father. She had spent the last ten years thinking about killing him. Now she thought about getting away with it.

Fifteen

Desportes had called in a favour from someone at the *Société de l'assurance automobile du Québec*, and by 11 a.m. he had the name and address that went with the plates Star had given him: Crazy Assed Shit 286. He sat down at the table and wrote a short note:

I know who you buried in the Alpine Gardens.

Call me.

Underneath the message, he wrote the telephone number of a pay-as-you-go cell phone he kept for untraceable calls. He folded the note and gave it to Star to deliver.

Star had no problem finding the truck. It was parked just up the street from the address Hugo had given her. She approached it from behind and stepped off the curb as though she was crossing the street. She kept walking next to the parked cars until she was alongside the truck. Then she reached over, slipped the envelope underneath the wiper blade, and kept walking. Her heart was pounding, but she waited until she got to the corner before she started to run.

Back at Desportes's place, they had nothing to do but wait. Desportes was at the computer, and she was in her usual place, perched on the couch at Kyle's feet. It took her an hour before she calmed down. Then she said, "So, Hugo, do you have a cv?"

"What do you mean?"

"You know. You asked me for a cv before I could be your assistant. I told you my story. What's yours?"

Desportes swivelled around in his chair to face her. His eyes would catch hers momentarily and then look away, like he was pondering. Then he swung back to the computer.

"Too bad, is it?" asked Star.

He swivelled around again. Another long pause, and Star waited.

"I used to have dreams, Star. Now I'm just a rat swimming around in the sewer with all the other rats.

"Years ago, when I was young, I worked my way out of a shit neighbourhood and a crappy family and graduated law school in the top third of the class. I had dreams of how I could do good. I didn't expect a job at one of the big law firms, and they didn't disappoint me. They didn't even respond to my letters. The only choice for me, and all the others who weren't in the club, was to start out on the fringes of the establishment and try to work your way in slowly. So, I opened my own practice, sharing space with a bunch of other lawyers. We were all struggling for any business that came along. The only clients we could get were those without money.

"I did a lot of criminal cases, legal aid, and I began to see how the justice system worked. Back then, it was efficient, but it had nothing to do with justice. Don't know if it's changed that much. Policemen lied, prosecutors hid whatever didn't suit their case, judges snickered, and poor bastards went to jail. The system worked on deals cut between the prosecutor and the defence. If you didn't make a deal, your client got shafted anyway, so you held your nose and made a deal. And the judges blessed all of the deals – especially the deals that stank."

Star sensed that he wasn't going to stop, so she put the kettle on to boil.

"Back then, I thought that all you had to do was put forward your best defence, and the Court, in its wisdom, would decide. That wasn't the case. The courts had to lock up enough people to show people there were consequences to breaking the law. And if you weren't greasing the judge or the prosecutor, your client was going to jail. Guilt and innocence were incidental; the system ran on money and power. A Mohawk who shoplifted a can of beer would get three months, but a call centre operator who fleeced widows and orphans wouldn't even be charged.

"Freddy Bellville was my last client, a nasty, stupid piece of shit with the IQ of a weasel. The kind of guy that no one would miss if he fell under a truck.

"Freddy spent his last night of freedom in bed in his shithole apartment. He was woken up at five o'clock in the morning by a swat team; four of them standing around the bed with shotguns pointed at his head. Freddy sits up and puts his arms in the air. He doesn't have a clue what's going on. Then one of the swat team gives a signal, and the other three leave. According to Freddy, the guy who stayed behind took a gun out of a plastic bag and dropped it on the bed. Then he put the shotgun to Freddy's head and told him to pick up the gun. He made Freddy handle it for a while, then told him to put it under the bed. Then he called for the other guys to come back in, and told Freddy to get dressed.

"While the kid was pulling on his jeans, the cop looks under the bed and acts all surprised when he sees the gun. They cuffed Freddy and brought him to the station. Freddy doesn't have a clue and he's sitting in a cell, scared shitless. Then, like a gift from heaven, Tony Paletto, a hotshot criminal lawyer shows up to represent Freddy. Back then, Paletto was the lawyer of choice for half the criminals in Montreal. He told Freddy how lucky he is that someone cares for him, cares enough to pay for a fancy lawyer. Then he drops it on Freddy that he's being charged with murder and that normally he'd be fucked, except Paletto has a plan; the kid should cop a plea and hope the prosecutor will buy it. Paletto just happens to have a statement all ready to be signed. He says that Freddy might get off with self-defence. At worst, it would be manslaughter, which was no big deal. With time off for good behaviour, Freddy could be out in two years. If he fought it, it could be up to fifteen. So the kid signed."

Star spooned tea into a pot and poured boiling water into it. She took three cups from the cupboard and put them on the counter. Then she sat down again. Desportes barely noticed.

"The kid's statement says something along the lines of: I, asshole kid, was minding my own business around lunchtime in O'Shea's Hot Dog Emporium and Pool Room when some guy walked in and asks to play a game of pool. The guy wanted to bet fifty dollars he could beat me. Sure, I say. And I beat his ass. When I asked him for the fifty bucks, he got pissed and pulled a gun on me. We struggled, and the gun went off. The guy dropped to the floor, and I got scared and ran out with the gun.

"So everyone's happy, case solved in record time and another punk off the streets. Well, everyone's happy except Nick Coluso. Back then it wasn't a good idea to make Coluso unhappy. If you crossed Coluso you were dead, simple as that. And he wasn't shy about letting people know. Anyway, it seems that the guy who got shot in O'Shea's was Coluso's brother Gino. Whoever killed Gino was up shit's creek. So whoever really did it, stitched up Freddy as the shooter in record time.

"Now Freddy wasn't smart by a long stretch, but he eventually realized that he was screwed, and that maybe Paletto wasn't working for him. Freddy's mother came to see me. She decided that if Freddy could prove his innocence, he'd be off the hook with the court and, more importantly, with Nick Coluso. And I was stupid enough to take the case and have the kid plead not guilty."

Star poured three cups of tea. She put one into Kyle's hand and placed another next to Desportes. He was off in another world. She took her own cup and sat down again, facing Desportes. He barely broke stride in his story.

"We were a dangerous combination: an idealistic kid pretending to be a lawyer with a stupid punk for a client. We didn't have much to go on. Freddy said that he hadn't been to O'Shea's, he'd spent the afternoon in his apartment. I believed him, but credibility wasn't going to be Freddy's strongest suit. Paletto's statement had 'fix' written all over it, and I figured we could get it thrown out by arguing that the kid's constitutional rights had been violated. The fingerprints on the gun were a real problem, I figured all I could do was cross-examine the cops and try to shake them off their story, and then put the kid on the stand to explain what really happened. Even with the best of luck, I knew the kid would probably be convicted. But we didn't have a choice. The kid was dead unless he could prove to Coluso that he'd been framed.

"The trial was a disaster. Tony Paletto got on the stand and lied as only a trained lawyer can lie. He said that Freddy had called him after his arrest and begged him to take the case. It didn't matter that Paletto was one of the most expensive defence lawyers in the city, and the kid didn't have a pot to piss in. Paletto made a speech about every lawyer's duty to do pro-bono work, like he was some kind of defender of the downtrodden. The swat-team stuck together like a Greek chorus. The Sergeant said they showed up at the kid's house after a tip from a concerned member of the public. The judge freaked out when I started to cross-examine one of them about how the gun ended up in the kid's room. He threatened me with contempt if I was too energetic in suggesting that upstanding police officers were not telling the truth. Then the Crown led in a parade of witnesses from the pool-hall, each one telling the same story: Freddy was the shooter. The Crown had given me notice of the witnesses a month before the trial, and I had a file on every one of them. They were all the typical pool hall clients, dealers, small-time crooks, and pimps. The jury would never have believed those bastards if they knew their background, but the judge said the witnesses weren't on trial and refused to let me cross-examine them on their previous convictions, or how they earned their living. Not only did they point the finger at the kid, but they destroyed his self-defence argument. They all said it was the kid that pulled the gun after he lost the pool game. So Freddy was convicted.

"Five days later I heard on the morning news that Freddy was killed. They found his body in a locked cell with his stomach sliced open. The authorities tried to say that it was suicide, like Freddy did hara-kiri to atone for his sins. Bullshit. Coluso got the job done. He had got the guards to look the other way, maybe even supply a key, and he had got some ambitious punk to do him a favour. We could have had the conviction overturned on appeal, maybe. I still believe we could have. The trial was a farce. The kid was stitched up and delivered to Coluso because it was in everyone's interest.

"The morning I heard the news, I was ambushed by a news crew outside my office, and I got carried away. I said things on camera that I really believed, that the kid had been set up, that the court and the police all had a hand in doing it, and that the system was dirtier than a Bombay sewer. And guess what? Two days later, I got a letter from the Bar saying that I had been accused of conduct unbecoming of a member of the profession. They decided to make an example of me, a young punk lawyer that doesn't follow the rules. I went through three lawyers, all good ones, some even honest, and they all said the same thing. I should apologize. I should get down on my hands and knees and beg for forgiveness. And maybe, they said, maybe, if I was to grovel enough, I would only be suspended for six months. I fired each of them in turn and defended myself.

"Big surprise. I got a registered letter in the mail. My case has been considered: gross misconduct showing a character wholly unsuited to the practice of law. I was permanently disbarred. End of story."

It was dark outside, and Star got up to turn on lights. As she walked by Desportes, she touched his shoulder, the same way she did with Kyle all the time.

"So now you know," he said. "That's my cv."

Star didn't know what to say. She settled on, "I'll get some food going."

Desportes got up from his chair and dropped into the armchair.

"Food would be good," he said.

Vanier checked the display on his cell phone and pushed answer. Then he pulled the car to the curb, killed the engine, and listened.

"Inspector Vanier, it's Melanie Trudel." She sounded business-like, not the television personality.

"Hi."

"I did what you asked. I reviewed all our footage from the riot."

"And?"

"He's on it. There's a couple of clear shots of Mr. Barbeau and of the man who met him. The boy looks fine. He doesn't look hurt."

"I told you he wasn't. Can I get a copy?"

"Inspector, I told you I would think about it. I did. There's an important issue at play here. Journalists can't take sides. I can't become an arm of the police."

"Madame Trudel." They were back to formal. "It's my life were talking about. They're going to hang me out to dry unless I come up with something. And not just me. My partner. She doesn't deserve that. If you saw Barbeau, you know that he wasn't harmed at the station. Can't you just drop a DVD in a brown envelope, and I'll pick it up? Or a print of the guy who met him? One face shot, that's all."

"No, Inspector. You're going to have to do what everyone else has to do."

"A search warrant? You know that's impossible"

"Not a search warrant. Just watch the six o'clock news. And have a DVD ready to hit record."

"You're running the story?"

"It's news, Inspector. That's what we do."

"Thanks."

"No thanks. It's my job. Don't forget to record it."

The phone clicked dead. It was four o'clock. He punched 1 on the speed dial, and Alex answered on the first ring.

"Yo!"

Alex had good days and bad ones, and Vanier could tell them just from the tone of his voice. Today was a good·day.

"Hi Alex. You at home?"

"Yeah. Just chilling."

"I need you to do me a favour? Can you set up the DVD to record? I'll be home shortly, and there's a story on the six o'clock news I want to record."

"Cool."

"You can do that?"

"Sure thing. See you later."

"And can you stick around in case there's a problem?"

"It's a DVD, Dad. I told you before, it's simple."

"Stick around."

Then he called Saint-Jacques and told her to watch the news and record it. He was going to call the Chief, and the guys from internal, but decided against it. He'd watch it first. If it was good, there would be plenty of time to spread the news. He felt hopeful for the first time in a week.

What should have been a twenty-minute drive took well over an hour. Another water main had burst with the spring thaw, and downtown traffic was gridlocked.

When he got home, Alex was kneeling in front of the television playing with wires. Since Alex had moved in, the closest Vanier had got to the television set was six feet away waving the remote. The area in front of the screen was littered with video game consoles and wires, spare consoles, and game cartridges. Alex sat back on his ankles in the middle of the chaos and used the remote to do a trial run. It worked.

Vanier poured himself a whiskey and sat down facing the television.

Alex asked, "So you want the whole thing?"

"Sure."

At six o'clock, Vanier got up for a refill. They watched as the titles played and the camera focused in on Melanie Trudel reading off the headlines: riots in Egypt, tensions in the Gaza, another suicide bombing in Pakistan, more bad economic news from Europe, and then: "In a CTV News exclusive, there is a major development in the Hochelaga police brutality investigation."

Vanier and Alex had to wait through ten minutes of news and five of commercials until Trudel came back to the story.

"CTV News has uncovered footage that casts serious doubt on allegations of police brutality made by Serge Barbeau, a Hochelaga resident who was found barely conscious in an alleyway after a riot to demand his release. Mr. Barbeau later alleged that he had been beaten by police officers from Station 23 while he was under detention. He had been released from detention shortly before being found in the alley. CTV News has now discovered video footage that appears to show Mr. Barbeau leaving Station 23 with no visible signs of a beating. Anthony Haltern has this report."

The screen cut to a reporter standing outside Station 23 looking directly into the camera. "Melanie, we all remember the riot that occurred just over a week ago in Hochelaga. The central figure in that riot was Serge Barbeau, who was later found unconscious and bleeding in an alleyway just two kilometres from the station. Mr. Barbeau claimed that he had been severely beaten while in police custody and only released because of the pressure from the protesters who had gathered outside the station. He said that he was dazed and walked away, before collapsing from his injuries in an alley just south of Sainte-Catherine Street. We've reviewed the footage taken by our video-photographers outside the station and found what appears to be Barbeau emerging from the back of Station 23 and looking, frankly, fairly good. Not like someone who had just undergone a severe beating. Let's watch the footage."

The screen switched to footage of the station parking lot. Barbeau walked into the picture from the left and, in case anyone missed him, an animator had drawn a large white circle around him.

Vanier watched as Barbeau walked in the direction of the camera with the same grin on his face that Vanier had wanted to change. Then Barbeau saw someone he recognized, walked up to him and gave him a high five. The other man reached out and threw a bear hug around the kid. Then the camera caught a two second shot of the man's face.

The image on the screen cut to the studio, where Haltern was sitting around a desk with Trudel.

"Anthony, based on what we see in the clip, is it realistic to think that Mr. Barbeau's injuries were the result of a beating he received in police custody?"

"I have to say no, Melanie. I don't know what happened while he was in custody. But this much seems very clear. The beating that put Barbeau in hospital most likely happened after he was released. Even if we can't see broken bones, we know that Barbeau's nose was broken, and that causes a lot of bleeding. As you saw yourself, he wasn't bleeding. We've been trying to reach Mr. Barbeau all day for his comments, but neither he nor his lawyer have returned our calls."

"Thanks, Anthony." Trudel looked into the camera. "Now it's time for a look at the weather."

Vanier pushed mute on the remote and jumped to his feet. "Shit …. Ha!" he said, over and over, advancing on the Jameson bottle.

"Dad, that's great. You're off the hook."

"I'm off the hook, my lad!"

Vanier pulled out his phone to call Saint-Jacques, but her call came in first.

"It's fantastic, boss! That does it ... doesn't it?"

He sensed the doubt, in her voice. "What the hell else do they need? The kid was fine when I let him go."

"It proves you didn't .... " She stopped herself, as though to admit that proof was needed would acknowledge that she had had doubts. "What do you think happened?"

"I'm going to find out. We need to talk to the guy that gave him the bear hug. The kid was set up to make us look bad. Someone wanted to screw me over. So we start with the guy in the crowd. Who is he?"

"We can tour the photo around Hochelaga. Someone's bound to recognize him."

"We've got work to do, Sylvie." It felt good saying that. "But first we've got to get our jobs back. I'll call the Chief and get back to you."

"But I was just packing to leave. A week in the sun."

"You're kidding right?"

"I'm kidding. Call me back."

He reached Chief Bedard at his office.

"Sir. Did you see the six o'clock news on CTV?"

"You think I have time to watch television? I'm working."

Vanier explained the story. Then he said, "We need to identify the guy who met Barbeau. Saint-Jacques and I can start tomorrow. And someone needs to question the kid before he comes up with another bullshit story."

"Luc, wait. Not so fast. There is an internal investigation going on, and you're suspended until it's complete. If what you say is true, they should be able to wrap it up quickly. But it's going to take a day or two. And I can't reinstate you before it's completed. That wouldn't look good. I can't pre-judge the outcome of the investigation."

"You're not pre-judging the outcome. It's clear. The kid walked out of the station without a mark on him, wrapping his supposedly broken arm around his handler. We need to speak to both of them."

"I'll have internal bring Barbeau in for questioning tomorrow. And we can start looking for the other guy. Luc, you need to be patient. You're not back on the job until the investigation is over. Got that? Take it easy for a day or two, that's all."

It was no use arguing. He hung up before the Chief could say anything else.

Alex had disappeared into his room, and Vanier had to play with two remotes to get back to the start of the clip. He played it back five times, but didn't learn much more. He ejected the DVD and replaced it with the one Garguet had given him. Now that he knew what he was looking for, it made some sense. He watched from the beginning, scanning the gathering crowd, and there he saw the man with the raincoat appear. He was in the crowd, but apart, not yelling chants but just surveying things. He kept his back to the Hells' camera most of the time, but then put his phone to his ear and relaxed into a chatting on the phone stance while the crowd got thicker around him. When the call finished, he turned and moved out of sight of the camera and only reappeared for a few seconds just before the kid came out. It was as though he knew Barbeau was on his way.

Vanier watched and re-watched Garguet's video, trying to figure out what it meant. Garguet was identifying who had picked up Barbeau. Vanier wondered why he hadn't given him more. Maybe that's all there was, or maybe Garguet just didn't like helping the police. In any event, all he had to do was to identify the guy in the raincoat.

Vanier ejected the DVD and put it back into its plastic case, then called Saint-Jacques. She picked up on the first ring.

"We're not back on the job yet, are we?"

"He called you?"

"No. I'm not that important. When you hung up I started thinking. There's no way the Chief would reinstate us unless he's bulletproof on it."

"Christ. You'll go far, Sylvie. You're already thinking like a boss. He wants Internal to close their investigation first, and that's going to take a day or two. You still have time to get to the airport."

"I wish.".

"Sylvie, if you want a break, take it." He could sense the fatigue in her voice. False hopes are exhausting. "Nobody will blame you."

"I'll blame myself." She sounded like she was close to tears and wanted off the phone before she lost it.

"Sleep on it. I'll call you tomorrow."

There was only one occupied table inside The Gentleman's Club, the rest had chairs standing on them while a frail Hispanic woman pushed a vacuum around with less enthusiasm than a guy checking phone booths for spare change. Joe Lacroix, Denis Savard, and Paul Brasso were sitting at the table.

"Go clean somewhere else, fuck," Brasso yelled as the woman pushed the vacuum in their direction. "We're working here."

She changed direction without acknowledging him. Brasso was fingering the note Joe had found on his windshield. He'd read it four times already.

"Like I said, Paul, I didn't call yet."

"Good. Who the hell wrote this?" said Brasso, picking it up, as though squinting at it more closely would reveal something different.

"We're the only ones know it was at the Alpine Gardens," said Denis.

"Obviously someone else knows. The question is who?" said Brasso.

"Who else is looking for Barbeau?" asked Joe.

"The police? His mother? Journalists? Shit, everyone's looking for the bastard," said Denis.

"It's none of them," said Brasso. "This letter is blackmail. Someone is trying to shake us down. Shit, I need to talk to the boss."

Brasso fished his cell phone out of his pocket and punched numbers. "And tell her to shut that goddamn machine off," he said, pointing to the cleaning woman. Joe got up and walked over to the woman.

On the phone Brasso explained the letter and listened. Then he put the phone back in his pocket. Joe and Denis were waiting.

"The boss says we've got to find the guy who left this and bring him in. And we have to do it pretty damn quick."

"Jesus," said Denis. "Where do we start?"

"I've got an idea," said Brasso. "Someone else was looking for Barbeau. Some girl showed up at the lawyer's place the other day looking for him. We should talk to her."

"How do you know?" asked Joe.

"Dufrene called the Colonel right after her visit. I was there when he took the call."

"So who's the girl?"

"Don't know." He pulled out his own phone. "Maybe Dufrene knows."

Brasso spoke to Dufrene for less than two minutes and wrote down a name and a number. Then he put the phone down and picked up Joe's letter.

"It's the same fucking number," he said. "The girl who visited Dufrene left a business card, her name is Clara Furlow, and she has the same phone number as the note you got, Joe. Jackpot!" Brasso smiled.

"So how are we going to find them?"

"Watch me," said Brasso as he punched redial on his phone. Dufrene answered.

They had eaten supper mostly in silence. Desportes seemed lost in his memories, and Star didn't know how to make small talk. Kyle just ate and read. The phone rang when Star was clearing dishes, and she jumped. Desportes picked it up.

"Yeah?"

"Oh, hello. Can I speak to Clara Furlow?"

Desportes was puzzled. "Who's calling?"

"She asked me to call her. Is she there?"

"How did you get the number?"

"It was on the business card she gave me. Can I speak to her or not?"

Desportes handed the phone to Star.

"Hello?"

"Ms. Furlow? It's *Maître* Dufrene. Remember me? You're working with the school board, right?"

Then it clicked, and Star went into her role.

"Oh yes. Of course. I'm sorry. I couldn't place you at first."

"Not to worry. It was a short meeting."

"What can I do for you?"

"Not much, really. But I've had some news about Serge and I wanted to discuss it with you."

"Okay."

"No, not on the phone. Could you come by? Say about two o'clock tomorrow?" She looked at Desportes, but he couldn't hear the conversation. He shrugged to say he couldn't guide her.

"Of course. Yes. Two o'clock tomorrow."

"Great. See you then," he said and disconnected.

Desportes wasn't happy. He shouldn't have used the number for the fake business card for Clara Furlow. Dufrene's call could be a coincidence, or it could be connected to the note Star had left under the windshield. They talked it through. How dangerous could it be to meet a lawyer in his offices? What could go wrong? In the end, Star agreed to the meeting. Desportes would wait for her in the Atomic Café.

The phone rang again at 11:00 p.m. Desportes pushed the connect button and listened.

"I got your note. What the fuck is this about?"

"I assume this is Joe Lacroix."

"If you know my truck, it's not hard to figure out who it's registered to."

"I'm glad you got my note. Here's the deal. I don't give a shit about you, or what you did. Maybe you had a reason. Who cares? But you have to make amends. Madame Barbeau won't have Serge to look after her in her old age, and that's your fault. You need to put $50,000 into her account. Think of it as compensation."

"I don't know what you're talking about."

"Fifty thousand. Direct deposit into her account. Write down these numbers."

Desportes began to recite the numbers for Madame Barbeau's bank account.

"I need a pen."

Desportes waited, then recited the numbers again while the caller wrote them down. "You have five days to make the deposit, and twenty-four hours to confirm that you'll do it. If you don't call back by this time tomorrow, I'll see who else wants to buy the information."

He pushed disconnect on the phone.

"It was him?" Star asked.

"He wrote the numbers down. We've got the right guy."

"So, I should still go to see Dufrene?"

"I don't think the calls were connected. I was just stupid to use the same number. So, yes. We'll see what Dufrene has to say. It's probably nothing." Desportes wasn't entirely convinced.

"And who is this Joe Lacroix? All we've got is a name and an address."

"So let's see what else we can find out about Joseph Lacroix."

Desportes sat down at his computer.

Sixteen

At 1:45 p.m. Star left the Atomic Café to walk to Dufrene's office, and Desportes worked the computer. He put on the headphones and picked up noises around Dufrene's desk. The bug was still working.

Five minutes later Star reached for the door handle to Dufrene's office. She didn't see the two men approaching from behind until they each had a hold of one of her arms. They held her for a few inches off the ground and walked her to the waiting truck before she even had time to think about screaming.

Desportes waited to hear her walk into Dufrene's office. He heard nothing. At 2:10 p.m., he left the café and hurried up the street and burst into Dufrene's office. Dufrene said he knew nothing, that he had been expecting a Ms. Furlow at two o'clock but she hadn't shown up. When Desportes asked what it was he wanted to tell Furlow, Dufrene said he just wanted to close the file. He had withdrawn as Barbeau's lawyer, and she should change her records accordingly.

Outside in the street Desportes looked up and down, as if expecting to see Star.

The hearing into the riot was being held in the basement of the Saint-Nom-de-Jésus Church. Mayor Chambord knew city politics, where power was more often wielded by graft and manipulation rather than by law. He didn't have the legal authority to give the committee anything near the trappings of an official inquiry, so he had given it nothing. Nothing but a request, as though the simplicity of the task gave it all the authority it needed. He had, as he told anyone who would listen, asked five respected citizens to look into the causes of the riot and write a report. He was betting that the absence of any of the usual official trappings would give the committee legitimacy. And the first thing the committee members did, seasoned activists that they were, was to come up with an unofficial title: *The Root Causes Inquiry*. Before the committee had even started, the riot itself had been pushed into the background. It became an inquiry into the conditions in Hochelaga that would make people want to take to the streets and throw rocks and petrol bombs.

The first days of the public hearings had been taken up with carefully chosen individuals and groups complaining about every aspect of life in the neighbourhood. Hour after hour, witnesses talked of poverty, unemployment, hopelessness, isolation, the absence of government services, crime, drugs, prostitution, and the eagerness of the police to harass law-abiding citizens. It was a platform for the disgruntled, and there was no shortage of them in Hochelaga.

It made for great television. A home-grown reality show that left journalists who'd covered municipal politics for years reacting with shock and outrage at how the authorities had been sticking it to the people, as though they'd been on a bathroom break for ten years.

By the time the committee got to the riot itself, it was Thursday morning. Vanier and Saint-Jacques had been invited to come and tell their stories. Neither would have shown up if the Chief hadn't ordered them to, and the Chief was delivering the message from the Mayor. The Police Service had nothing to lose. If Vanier and Saint-Jacques screwed up, the Service would cut them loose and claim it was cleaning house. If they did okay, they might survive. There was no question of them doing well. They were scheduled to follow a slate of carefully chosen witnesses who would tell things from the people's side.

Simple citizen after citizen told the committee how they had heard about Barbeau's arrest and decided to vent their anger peacefully by walking to the police station. They had no idea how things got out of hand. Nobody had seen anyone throwing rocks or bottles, and each one of them had gone home as soon as Colonel Montpetit addressed the crowd and asked them to.

Then it was Vanier's turn. He could feel the hostility as he took his seat at a table in front of the committee. He wasn't sworn in. It wasn't that kind of hearing.

Vanier waited for someone to give him the go-ahead. The Colonel was looking at his fingernails, and the other members of the committee were scribbling notes. The silence eventually forced them to look up.

"I have a prepared statement to read and then I will answer any questions the committee might have."

"Fine. Carry on," said the Colonel.

Vanier started reading from a handwritten statement he had put together. He started with his visit to the *Patriotes'* office in the course of a murder investigation and seeing his tires slashed. He explained about the video camera above the entrance, and how it had captured an image of Barbeau sticking a knife into his tires.

After reading the first couple of paragraphs, he looked up and realized that nobody was paying much attention, they seemed to be waiting it out until he finished. He looked down and continued reading, explaining how his partner had identified Serge Barbeau as the person who slashed the tires and how they went to his apartment and arrested him. They brought him to Station 23 and questioned him for a time. Then he was allowed to leave. Vanier ended by reminding everyone of the television news stories that confirmed that Barbeau had been in perfectly good health when he was released.

"Thank you, Inspector Vanier," said Colonel Montpetit. "I have a few questions. Before I get to them, I want to make it clear that this committee is not looking at the issue of whether Mr. Barbeau was beaten while in police custody."

"He wasn't."

"So you said. Our job is to look at why the riot happened. The question of whether Mr. Barbeau was beaten while in custody is for someone else to decide."

"He wasn't. There is no question to decide."

"Perhaps. Now, I do have some questions."

Vanier clasped his hands in front of him. "I'm sure you do."

"Remind me again, Inspector. Why did you choose to arrest Serge Barbeau?"

"As I said, I had reasonable grounds to believe that he had slashed the tires of a police vehicle."

"A police vehicle? Was it marked as a police vehicle?"

"No. It wasn't."

"Did the vehicle belong to the *Service de Police*?

"No."

"Whose car was it, then?"

"Mine."

"So you suspected he had slashed the tires of your car, not a police vehicle?"

"It was my own car, but it was police business."

"I just wanted to clarify. It was not a police vehicle." Montpetit smiled and looked at the other committee members.

"What unit are you attached to, Inspector?"

"Serious crimes."

"Do you usually investigate offences that involve property damage?"

Vanier felt like he was on a downward spiral. "That depends."

"On how serious the property damage is, I suppose?"

"Among other things, yes."

"Tire slashing. Do you often investigate tire slashing complaints?"

"No."

"But this was personal. Is that it? It was because it was your car?"

Vanier tried to head him off. "If I see something illegal, I can't ignore it. Are you suggesting I should have ignored it?"

"I'm asking the questions, Mr. Vanier." The Colonel had already demoted him to civilian.

"What I'm getting at is that tire slashing is not part of your normal duties. Isn't that true?"

"I don't normally investigate tire slashing. That's true."

"Tell me. For these kinds of property offenses, what are the normal options available to a police officer?"

"I don't understand what you mean."

"I'm sure that the police don't arrest everyone suspected of property offences. Don't put them in detention and subject them to interrogation."

"It depends ...."

"Because if they did, I'm sure you wouldn't have time to deal with serious crime. And that's your real job, isn't it?"

"Not every suspect is arrested. You're right." Vanier's hands had curled into fists.

"So my question is, what were the options?"

"I could have ignored it. I could have just let him go. That happens a lot with property crimes, you know. Just ignore it and wait until the person does something more serious. People are always complaining that the police don't do enough to stop property crimes."

"I suppose you could have just checked his identity and issued him a summons, couldn't you?"

"That would have been an option, yes."

"What I'm trying to understand, Inspector, is why Mr. Barbeau was arrested and detained. I'm sure you had better things to do with your time."

"I wanted to ask him some questions."

"And you couldn't ask them when you met him at his apartment?"

"No. He was in the course of fleeing out the back door." There was a round of subdued guffaws from the audience.

"Perhaps the police intimidated him. We've heard enough here this week to see that the police in Hochelaga are very intimidating."

"Mr. Barbeau did not seem to be intimidated by policemen."

"Isn't it true that there was no good reason to arrest him? Isn't it true that everything you wanted to do could have been done without arresting him? Everything, that is, besides intimidating him, threatening him, or worse."

"Is that a question?"

"No. An observation."

"I didn't beat him. The film of him leaving the police station proves that. I was in the middle of a murder investigation, and my tires were slashed while I was visiting you, Mr. Montpetit. I wanted to know why he did it. Did he pick my car specifically? Why not some other car? Did someone ask them to do it? Pay him, maybe? I was investigating a brutal murder and wondered why my car, alone, was targeted."

"Are you suggesting he was connected to the murder?"

"I'm not suggesting anything. But now that you mention it, Mr. Barbeau's arrest led to a riot. Then he was beaten, and now he's disappeared. Why don't you tell me if there's a connection?"

Colonel Montpetit was irritated. He turned to the crowd, "I think we've heard enough from this witness." And then back to Vanier. "You're excused, Inspector."

"Because when I'm reinstated, that's a lead that I will be following."

"Thank you, Inspector." Montpetit stood up to show that the committee was finished with him. "We'll take a break for fifteen minutes." The other members followed his lead, and they all left the room.

Vanier sat at the table and watched them walk out.

Desportes was desperate. He thought he would never call the police for anything, but he called the police. They all but laughed at him for trying to report the possible kidnapping of a street kid he barely knew. Then he called Barbeau's mother to see if anyone else was trying to track him down. She said no, but she'd heard that the cop that arrested him was still looking for him.

"Do you have his name?"

"Don't remember."

"It's important, try."

"Just a second. I remember he left his business card here when they took Serge. Maybe it's still there."

"I'll wait. Can you go look?"

It took about five minutes, and she was back on the phone.

"Imagine that. It was stuck on the railing where he left it. All that time."

Desportes had her read out the name and telephone numbers. One was a cell phone. He dialled the number and left a message. He asked Vanier to call him. He left the phone number and the address and said it was important.

Star was sitting in a folding metal chair facing a huge man with a shaven head. He was leaning towards her over the back of another chair, so close that she could feel the warmth of his breath. She wasn't tied down, but every time she moved, another man standing over her would move, as though he was ready to grab her again. The bald man was smiling like an undertaker, no humour, a show

226

of teeth without humour.

"Star, tell me again, one more time. Why were you looking for Serge Barbeau?"

"I told you, fuck. I told you already."

She didn't have time to flinch before the back-hand slap caught her full in the face. Getting hit wasn't new, and she wasn't going to cry.

"Language. Please. No swearing, understand?"

"I told you already."

"Answer my question."

"I did, I said ... " Another slap to the face. She tasted blood in her mouth.

"I asked if you understood?"

"Oh ... yes. I understand."

"Say it, then."

"I understand ... no more swearing."

"Good. Now, tell me why you were looking for Serge Barbeau."

"I said. He stole my money. $200. I wanted to get it back."

"But your story keeps changing, Star. Every time it's different. What's the truth?"

"It's not different. It's the same. It's the truth?"

"For example, first you said that somebody told you his lawyer's name. Then you said you got it from the newspaper."

"That was a mistake, I was scared. I got his name from the newspaper."

"But you see my point? Your story keeps changing. How can I believe anything you say?"

"I was confused, that's all. I wasn't lying. Please, I just want to leave."

"Don't you mean you want to go home?"

"Yes. I want to go home."

"And where is home?"

"I told you. I'm living on the street."

"So when you said you wanted to go home, you were lying, right?"

"No. I said I want to leave. You talked about home."

"And where is that?"

"What?"

"Home."

"I said I don't have a home. I'm living on the street. Sometimes I stay with friends, on a couch or something."

Again a lightning backhander across her face. The blows were getting harder.

"Liar! You're lying to me every time you open your mouth. First you want to go home. Then you don't have a home, you're sleeping on the streets. Then you're sleeping on a couch with friends. Why don't you tell the truth?"

The bald man was acting enraged. He stood up, his bulk dwarfing Star.

"I just want to leave. Please"

He reached for the hem of her T-shirt and pulled it up over her head, lifting it half off. Then he anchored it behind her neck, exposing her sports bra.

She jumped from the chair, making a dash for the door, half crawling, half running across the floor. The other man grabbed her before she was three feet away and dumped her back on the chair. As soon as he let go of her she was off again, running for the door.

"Let her go," the bald man shouted, and Star's heart lifted. She reached out for the handle and pulled. The door was locked.

"You can't escape, Star. So let's finish our conversation, and then you can go home. Come." He gestured with both hands for her to come back and sit down and she obeyed. Only then did she notice her T-shirt. She reached up to put it back in place.

"Leave it," he said.

And she did.

The bald man sat down again facing her. He reached into his pocket, and pulled out a plastic sandwich bag and offered it to her. "Take it. You'll need it soon."

She didn't understand, but she took the bag and stuffed it into her pocket.

Then, he turned to the other man. "Joe, I think now would be a good time to restrain Star.

The guy called Joe pulled Star's hands behind her back and slipped plastic cuffs around her wrists, pulling the lead tight. Then the bald man went over to a tall workbench against the wall and came back with a pair of red pruning shears. He sat back in his chair facing Star and leaned over with the shears. He hooked the blade under the fabric of her bra and cut. Then he used the shears to move the fabric away, exposing each breast.

Star vomited onto her pants and began crying. "No. Please. I'm telling you the truth."

The bald man ignored her while he took some paper napkins from his pocket and wiped at the vomits splashes that had landed on his pants. Then he reached over again with the shears, this time he used them to force her chin up so she would look him in the eyes.

"Listen, Star. And believe this. You will give me the truth today. It could be right now, or a few hours from now. Either way, you will tell me the truth. I really hope it will be sooner rather than later. But you're the only one can decide that."

Star was dry heaving, shivering with fright. But she heard him and couldn't see a way out.

"The sandwich bag I just gave you? That's for your nipples. We'll start there," he said, flexing the pruning shears.

Star involuntarily looked down at her breasts. Her nipples were flat against the skin.

"Some cold water will bring them out for cutting. We do have some water don't we, Joe?"

"Yes, sir," said Joe. "I'll get some."

Joe got up and walked across the room.

"Hugo Desportes," Star mumbled.

"What? I couldn't ..."

"Hugo Desportes," she repeated. And once the tap was opened, there was no reason to stop.

They were parked outside the Mega Bus Terminal on Saint-Antoine Street. The driver had said nothing on the ride to the terminal and now sat, half swivelled in his seat, watching Star in the back seat. The guy they called Joe emerged from the terminal building and climbed back into the passenger seat. He turned around to face Star.

"Remember. You are not to come back to Montreal. Ever. And you're to keep your mouth shut about what happened. You understand?"

She nodded, sniffling tears and shaking every now and then. Joe had repeated the same instructions six or seven times already. She hadn't told them about Kyle and, right now, he was all she could think about.

"Say it," he said.

"I'm not coming back. Ever. And I won't tell anybody about what happened."

"Good." Joe leaned over and handed her a bus ticket and what looked like a couple of hundred dollars in cash.

"This is a one-way ticket on the Express to Toronto, and some money to get started. That's your bus in front."

A Van Hool bus was already receiving passengers up the block.

"Let's go."

The driver stayed where he was, and Star and Joe joined the line of passengers, the usual mix of young and old, students going home to visit their parents, and grandparents going to visit their kids. Star was the only passenger without a bag.

Joe waited on the sidewalk and watched as she climbed up into the bus and found a seat towards the back. He was still there when the driver killed the internal lights and eased the bus slowly into traffic. Star looked behind her, but the back window of the bus was blacked out, and she couldn't see if they were following her. Then she relaxed for the first time in hours and tried to pull herself together. The old Asian woman next to her stared out into the night as the bus weaved through traffic for two blocks and slipped onto the highway for the five-and-a-half hour trip to Toronto.

She was about to ask to try to borrow someone's cell phone until she noticed the sign with a cell phone barred with a red line. It would have been too late anyway, she thought, it was almost three hours since she gave them Desportes's address, and if they were going after him, they would already have done it. She thought about Kyle. He was defenceless, and she had abandoned him, no betrayed him. Then she remembered the ankle bracelet. They said they would track her to Toronto, and they would know if she got off before Toronto.

She was the first person into the bathroom. She sat down on the closed toilet and started fiddling with the ankle bracelet. It was fastened up high, and when she moved it down, it was loose on her thin ankle. Someone started knocking on the bathroom door. She took off her boot and sock and wiped soap from the dispenser around her ankle and the inside of the bracelet, all the time cursing the frantic knocking on the door. In a few minutes she had the bracelet slipped off, and she tossed it into the garbage container. She wiped the soap off with paper towels, put her sock and boot back on, and left the toilet. The woman waiting outside flashed her a dirty look and said, "I hope you didn't stink it up."

Star sat back in her seat, ignored by her Asian seatmate. She took the roll of twenties and removed two; the rest she slipped into her sock and deep into the boot. Then she walked to the front of the bus and bent down to put her mouth close to the driver's ear.

"I feel funny, I need to get off the bus."

"What? This is an express. No stops." The driver turned to look at her, "What's the problem? You don't look sick."

"I haven't taken my pills in three days. I thought I was okay." She gave him a demented smile. "Most times I can feel it coming on. I thought I should warn you."

"Why don't you sit down and relax. Maybe sleep. We'll be in Toronto in five hours." He wasn't going to stop just because someone asked him to.

Star went back to her seat, matching the Asian woman's scowl with the same off-centered smile she gave the driver. After a few minutes, she started singing in a little-girl-lost voice.

> *My Mommy lies over the ocean,*
> *My Mommy lies over the sea,*
> *My Mommy lies over the ocean,*
> *So bring back my Mommy to me.*
> *Bring back,*
> *Bring back,*
> *Oh bring back my Mommy to me.*
> *Last night as I lay on my pillow,*
> *Last night as I lay on my bed,*
> *Last night as I lay on my pillow,*
> *I dreamed that my Mommy was dead.*

When she reached the end, she started over. She had their attention. No question. She wasn't making eye contact, but she could see heads turning in her direction. Then, in a voice that would have carried across a battlefield, she screamed,

"Mommy. Where are you?"

She repeated it, loudly, with a plaintive turn at the end. Then she stood up and started walking up the aisle to the front of the bus, putting her head down between each seat as though looking for someone.

"You know I don't like hide and seek, Mommy. You know I don't like it."

She ignored the passengers, but they had given up trying to ignore her.

"Mommy. Please don't do this. Where are you?"

It's odd how words can stir your emotions. You see it with actors who shed real tears on stage, and Star was getting sucked into the little-girl-lost character. She was feeling the girl's anguish.

When she reached the front of the bus, she turned and ran towards the back, bumping seats as she passed. She stopped in front of the toilet and banged on the door.

"Mommy, are you in there?"

Then she pulled the door open, looked inside, slammed it closed, and then turned back up the aisle, looking in each seat as she passed. A lady stood up as she approached and made soothing noises. Star gave her a two-handed push back into her seat.

"Kyle? Stop this. Where are you?" If pretending to look for her mother felt real, calling out for Kyle hit her like a blow, and she started screaming, "I've got to find Kyle. Let me off this fucking bus now."

The driver was getting frantic. He was trying to keep an eye on the highway, talking on his phone, while watching Star in the mirror. He put his phone back into his jacket pocket and said over his shoulder,

"It's going to be okay, kid. We're going to stop." Then he reached forward, uncradled the speaker handset and brought it to his mouth.

"Ladies and gentlemen. We will be making an unscheduled stop in approximately five minutes. If everyone can just remain calm for a few minutes things are going to be fine."

A heavy-set Haitian woman stood up and approached Star, her arms out in a welcome, and Star allowed herself be pulled into the hug. "There darling. Things will be all right. Come sit with me."

Star didn't struggle as the woman guided her down to a seat, putting a fat arm across her shoulder and pulling Star into her soft body.

"We're almost there, darling. Relax. Things will be okay."

Star rested into the unfamiliar comfort of the hug. Minutes later the bus turned off the highway and eventually into the bright courtyard of an Ultramar service station. It pulled to a stop next to a police cruiser and an ambulance.

The door of the bus opened with a hiss, and a uniformed policeman climbed the stairs. He immediately picked out Star. It wasn't hard. Passengers were staring in her direction and, just to be sure, the Haitian woman raised her arm. The policeman moved down the aisle, followed by an ambulance technician, and leaned over to Star. He ignored the Haitian woman.

"Hi, Miss," he said. "I'm Charles. We're going to help you. This is Tony," he said, gesturing to the technician.

"She's having bad thoughts," the Haitian woman said. "Calling for her mother."

Star began to sing again, this time quietly, almost to herself.

The Haitian woman reached over to brush Star's loose hair out of her face. "The child needs help."

"What's your name?"

Star didn't answer. The Haitian woman removed her arm from around Star and raised herself out of the seat. The technician moved into her place, balancing himself with a knee on the seat. He arranged a thick blanket around Star's shoulders.

"Can you walk?"

Star stopped singing and allowed the technician to help her up and lead her off the bus. In the blazing light of the ambulance, he got her short coat off and noticed the bus ticket: Louise Trainor. Then he got her to lie down and began collecting the vital signs: pulse, blood pressure, temperature, breathing rate. She was quiet, and he didn't seem in any hurry to leave. Finally the policemen stood at the door to the ambulance. "You guys ready to go?"

"Sure"

"How is she?"

"Seems fine." He turned to Star, "Don't you, Louise?" Then he turned to the policeman. "According to the ticket, her name is Louise Trainor."

Star said nothing. She heard the ambulance door close, leaving her and the technician inside.

She hadn't thought past getting off the bus. But now that she was off the bus, she had other problems; she was a psychiatric patient having a meltdown. She was surprised how short the drive was, she expected to be taken back to Montreal. Instead, they brought her to the Lakeshore General in Pointe-Claire, about forty-five minutes west of Montreal. She looked up at the clock as they led her into Emergency. It was five-thirty in the afternoon, almost three and a half hours since they'd snatched her.

The emergency room was crowded. In a system where health-care is free, emergency rooms are the bottlenecked entries into the system, and the triage nurse is the gatekeeper. Her job is to predict how long you will survive without seeing a doctor. If you look like you're good for a few hours, you'll probably wait ten. If you look like you won't last more than an hour or two, you'll still wait, but near the front of the line. You need lots of bleeding to get seen immediately.

The triage nurse at the Lakeshore was working the last few hours of a double shift and was stressed and exhausted. She needed details from Star, but Star wasn't giving them. Star had seen enough crazy people on the street to know how many different ways there were to look crazy. She chose a non-threatening, living-on-another-planet look, and ignored the nurse's questions. From time to time she mumbled, "St. Mary's, that's the place."

The nurse took the bait and called the psychiatric ward at St. Mary's in Montreal. In the emergency room, sending people somewhere else is always a good idea, it improves the statistics, and nobody would criticize her for that.

It took some convincing, but St. Mary's agreed to accept her. Star was back in the ambulance heading for Montreal within fifteen minutes of arriving at Lakeshore.

There are thirteen psychiatric emergency institutions on the island of Montreal. St. Mary's Hospital has one of them. Its emergency room is painted a calming blue, but it's hard to notice décor in bedlam. It's an emergency room without inhibitions, where anything is normal, even the security guard at the door. People in crisis wait for a doctor's decision to load them up with chemicals and send them back on the street, or hold them for ten days while their brain chemicals are adjusted with drugs. Those who haven't yet been drugged into docility wander around in comforting circles, wearing humiliation gowns split down the back, while friends and families, if they're lucky enough to have any, try to cope. Nurses and doctors rush from one patient to the next, trying to deal with the never-ending flood of the inconsolable.

The ambulance technician led Star into the room that was dominated by a circular staff pen where nurses and white-coated doctors were sheltered like pioneers who had circled the wagons against attack. Doorless rooms lined the edge of the large space, each with a single bed and a plastic curtain for privacy. Clusters of metal chairs were scattered around in no apparent order. The ambulance technician grabbed one of the chairs and motioned for Star to sit in it while he went to find a nurse.

He walked up to the counter, and a nurse who was listening to someone on the phone cupped her hand over the mouthpiece.

"Louise from Lakeshore?" she asked.

The technician nodded, and they exchanged clipboards. He wanted a confirmation of delivery, and she wanted confirmation of where the latest arrival had come from. With her hand still over the mouthpiece of the telephone, she said, "We don't have a room just yet, but tell Louise I'll be over to see her in a second."

He walked back to Star and relayed the message. Then he took his blanket back and replaced it with one marked St. Mary's Hospital, thin and worn after innumerable cycles from patients to laundry and back again.

"You're in good hands now. Take care of yourself, Louise."

Star watched him leave and realized it was her chance. She stood up and took a step towards the exit, but there was a hand on her shoulder. She spun around. It was the nurse.

"Louise? Hi. My name's Verna. I'm a nurse. I'm here to help you."

Star sat down again, and the nurse pulled up a chair facing her.

"We're going to have to fill in a form, and then the doctor will see you. Let's start with name and date of birth. It's Louise Trainor, isn't it? They told me that's what it said on the bus ticket."

Star looked up. "Louise Trainor. April 16, 1994." She waited for the nurse to finish writing.

"And do you have a hospital card, Louise?"

Star shook her head.

The nurse looked disappointed. Without a card, there was no easy access to a file, which meant a lot more questions. Star's mind was racing, trying to figure out how she would get out, worried that they would drug her into sleep. She didn't know how she was going to get Kyle back.

The nurse continued with questions, and Star made up answers. But she couldn't remember all the important stuff, the name of her psychiatrist, what drugs she had been prescribed, and no, she couldn't remember when her last appointment had been.

The nurse stood up. "Louise, I'm going to order up your chart. That's the best place to start. The doctor will be over in a few minutes. In the meantime, go into the dressing room over there and put this on."

She handed Star a gown and led her to a small cubicle no bigger than the changing room in a low-end clothing store. Star went in and pulled the curtain closed. She didn't undress. She looked out at the room through a crack at the edge of the curtain. The nurse, Verna, was on the phone again, with her back turned to the dressing cubicle. She knew she couldn't make a run for it. All the staff were busy, but they seemed attuned to anything unusual; they spent their working lives looking over their shoulders. Making a dash for the exit would be the sort of thing that gets noticed. Then she saw a cleaner pushing a trolley towards her. He parked it in front of the changing room and went into the toilet with two huge rolls of paper for the dispenser.

Star slipped off her jacket and left the cubicle. Dumping the jacket into the garbage bag on the trolley, she started to push the trolley slowly across the room, like she was putting in a long, eight hour shift.

As she approached the double doors, she stared at the guard and dared him to open them for her. He did, leaning into the door and making room for her to pass.

"Louise. Come back."

It was Verna, but Star wasn't about to turn around. She grabbed her jacket from the garbage and tipped the trolley sideways onto the floor, spilling water, brushes and bottles onto the hallway tiles.

Then she was off, running down the corridor. The upturned trolley slowed down the security guard, but once he cleared it, he started gaining on her. That's when she started shouting.

"He's got a gun! Gun! He's got a gun!"

She rounded a corner and crashed into a big man with a walker, sending the walker clattering to the ground. She screamed and pointed back behind her. "He's got a gun!"

The security man turned the corner and tried to leap over the walker lying across the hallway, but his foot caught, and he went face down. When you're a minimum wage security guard, it doesn't take much convincing to give up the chase.

Star kept running, retracing her steps through the hospital's labyrinth of corridors until she knew she was close to the main exit. Then she slipped her jacket back on and walked slowly, trying to blend in. It worked. Two security guards came running towards her, forcing everyone to move out of the way. She did the same, backing up against the wall, and they kept running.

Seconds later she was outside, looking for a taxi. Taking one from the stand would be too obvious, so she walked half a block and hailed one on Côte-des-Neiges.

Seventeen

Vanier had got Desportes's message late. His phone was shut off most of the day when he was in the committee hearing, and later, trying to forget the hearings at the Blue Angel. When he remembered to switch the phone back on, he had called back, but kept going straight to voicemail. So he decided to pay a visit.

He was about to lean on the buzzer when he noticed the thin space between the door and the jam. He went back to the car to get his gun, the unofficial one he kept hidden in the trunk. Then he pushed the door lightly and it swung open, revealing a dark hallway with a light coming from a room at the end. Two doors gave off the hallway, and both were closed. He tried the handle of the first door, a laundry and storage room, neat and tidy. He pulled the door closed and continued down the hallway. Then he heard the click of cutlery against crockery coming from the room at the end and moved towards the noise, the gun pointing to the floor.

The room was a brightly-lit kitchen. A black and white cat was sitting on the counter, licking a dinner plate. It looked at him but made no move to jump down. The computer on the kitchen table was lit up as though it had just been in use. Vanier heard a click behind him and turned to see a girl sneaking towards the front door.

"Police. Stop."

She didn't. She ran and was pulling the door open when he caught up with her. He kicked it closed with his foot, and she turned into him. That's when he saw the knife and backed off, pointing the gun at her.

"Jesus, I hate knives. Put it down. I'm a police officer. I won't hurt you."

"Fuck you."

"Who are you?"

"None of your fucking business."

"It is. I was looking for Desportes. He called me. Where is he?" She looked at him. "Why?"

"He said there was a problem and he needed my help. He said it would help me with my own problem."

"You have a problem?"

"It's me should be asking the questions."

"Okay," Star said. "Walk backwards into the kitchen and sit at the table. Put the gun on the table."

They walked together. Vanier walked backwards, glancing over his shoulder from time to time. He lowered his gun, but she kept the knife pointing at him. When he sat at the table and put the gun down, she sat down opposite him.

"You have a badge?"

"Actually, no … "

"What kind of a cop doesn't have a badge?"

"A suspended cop."

Then it clicked. "Oh, you're the cop that was supposed to have beaten Barbeau."

"Yes. And I've been looking for him."

"And we found him."

"How so."

Star explained, how she had discovered Barbeau had been murdered and how they were trying to get $50,000 for his mother. Then she explained how she had been lifted and forced to give him Desportes's address. Then she told him about Kyle.

"Do you know where they held you?"

"No. But I think I know where they took them. They took them both. They're not going to kill them, are they? Not for $50,000."

Vanier knew people that got killed for a pack of cigarettes, but he said, "Probably not. It wouldn't make sense. They let you go, didn't they? Scared you, but let you go."

Vanier and Star agreed to a truce of sorts: she kept her knife, and he kept the gun. Now they were driving to an industrial park in Anjou. He was taking directions from Star, and she was reading them off the laptop.

They were homing in on the GPS tracking device that Desportes had set up for Kyle when Star worried that he would wander off and get lost. Star had braided string and hung it around Kyle's neck like a necklace. Now it was a blinking light on a map on the laptop, but it hadn't moved since she had checked it last at the apartment.

"Can't we go any faster?"

"Not if we want to get there."

Speed and avoiding the springtime harvest of potholes were mutually exclusive. The constant freezing and thawing buckles the ground and creates deep holes in the asphalt, turning roads into obstacle courses of water-filled traps that can swallow a tire or smash an axle. You can't see them at a distance, and when you do see them, you have to gauge size and depth and decide if it's more dangerous to swerve around the trap and risk getting hit by a truck in the other lane or just wait for the shudder of a wheel dropping into the unknown. Sometimes they weren't that deep. It was the other times you had to worry about, when the wheel stays in the hole, and the axel snaps like a dry stick.

Vanier had decided that all he needed to do was to confirm that Desportes and Kyle were being held, and he could call it in.

"We'll be there in about five minutes. Anything changed?"

"No. It's still blinking on Rue de l'Innovation."

He dialled Saint-Jacques again. She still didn't pick up, so he left another message.

"Sylvie, I got a lead. I'm on my way to a building, I think it's an industrial site, on Rue de l'Innovation. Call me back."

He checked again to make sure his phone was on vibrate.

"So what's the plan?"

"No plan. I look around, and if they're in the building, I'll call the police. You'll stay in the car."

"Yeah."

Vanier knew he was going to have problems even with the simplest of plans. The girl didn't seem to take orders well.

He turned left onto l'Innovation, and Star jabbed at the window with her finger.

"That's it."

She held the notebook up so he could see the blinking light on the map. They cruised slowly by a one-floor industrial building that was pretty much the same as all the others in the neighbourhood, and the same as millions of other warehouses in industrial parks across Canada. A box with doors, a garage door for trucks in front, and a small door for people on the side. Three pick-up trucks were parked side by side near the back of the parking.

Except for the three trucks, the place was deserted. If he parked on the street, the car would stand out like an ice cream truck, so he pulled into the next lot and parked on the far side of the building, shielded from sightlines.

He told Star to stay put, but she got out and followed him, both of them trying to accustom their eyes to the shadows. The three trucks were off to the side in relative darkness, but a window set high in the wall of the building threw a pool of light on the asphalt. They moved towards it. Underneath the window, Vanier bent slightly and laced his fingers together, offering Star a step up. She grabbed his shoulders, put one foot in his hands, and hauled herself up the wall to peer into the window.

"What do you see?"

"Hugo's there," she whispered. "He's tied up to a chair. Bleeding. I can't see Kyle."

"How many other people?"

"Two. No, three."

"Okay, that's enough. We're calling for help."

As he was letting her down, he felt a pressure between his shoulder blades. "Don't move. Hands against the wall." Vanier froze, and Star lost her balance and fell. When he bent to help her, the gun pushed against his head.

"Don't move, I said. Joe, get the girl."

The shotgun stayed pressed between Vanier's shoulder blades, while another man came from behind Vanier carrying a pistol in one hand. He reached down to Star and grabbed the neck of her jacket with his free hand. When he pulled, Star rose into him and he grunted. His legs folded, and he collapsed, dropping the gun on the asphalt. Star grabbed the gun and ran in a crouch across the concrete, gun in one hand and the knife in another.

The guy holding the gun on Vanier said, "Shit."

Vanier felt the pressure in his back ease, as the man pulled back for a shot. He kicked back into where he thought the guy's knee would be and felt him buckle, the shotgun blasting into the sky as Star disappeared into the darkness. Then Vanier spun and grabbed for the gun, bringing his knee into the guy's stomach. Vanier connected, and the guy fell, grabbing Vanier and pulling him down with him.

Vanier rose up on his knees and head-butted the gunman in the face, and they both heard the crack of breaking bone. Vanier snatched the gun, but before he could get to his feet, they were both bathed in light as the back door opened. Vanier froze at the sound of a safety catch being released.

A man stood over them pointing a handgun. He said, "Drop the gun."

Vanier recognized the voice of Brasso. He did what he was told and stood up slowly.

Brasso said, "You move, you're dead."

He bent down and picked up the shotgun. Then he turned to the guy who was trying to stem the blood pouring from his nose. "Denis, stop fucking around and stand up."

Denis rolled over slowly and got to his feet. "Fucking bastard," he said, wheeling a vicious kick into Vanier's groin.

Vanier dropped, bent double, his forehead touching the floor.

"What's the matter with Joe?"

Denis walked over to the body. "Shit. He's bleeding bad. I think she stabbed him."

Vanier was still on his knees. Brasso said, "You. Get on your feet and put your hands on your head."

Vanier obeyed, and said, "Still playing soldiers?"

"Shut the fuck up and lean against the wall. Legs apart and hands up high."

Brasso pushed him against the wall, did a pat-down search, and took Vanier's gun.

"Oh, Christ, Paul." Denis was leaning over the body. "Joe's losing too much blood."

"Get him inside. Drag him if you have to." Then Brasso turned to Vanier. "Inside. No trouble. And keep your hands on your head."

Brasso stood behind Vanier while Denis pulled his buddy through the door. In the light of the doorway, it was clear that Joe was in bad shape. His shirt and pants were covered with blood, and he seemed barely conscious. It looked like the knife got him low in the belly and sliced. Vanier figured he wouldn't last long without help.

As soon as Joe's boots crossed the threshold, Vanier felt the pressure of the shotgun between his shoulder blades and followed them in.

Inside, Desportes was tied to the chair, bleeding heavily with his head drooping. His face looked like it had taken a pounding. Vanier could smell the stink of sweat and blood. Before he could see anything else, a bag was dropped over his head and someone plastic-cuffed his hands behind his back. When the cuffs were on, Vanier got a kick in the back of his knee, dropping him to the floor. Seconds later, he was hauled to his feet, and he heard another voice. Vanier was trying to keep track. Joe, injured. Denis who held the shotgun first. Paul Brasso who held the handgun on him. Now there was a fourth guy. The fourth guy said, "Put them both in the fridge. I need time to think."

Then Vanier was being pushed forward. He could only shuffle in the blackness beneath the hood with his hands cuffed.

"Stop."

He did. Then he heard a padlock being removed and the creaking of a door.

"Okay, move." Again the pressure of the shotgun between his shoulder blades.

Vanier shuffled forward, but his foot caught on a step, and he pitched forward, hitting the floor face first.

"Mind the step."

He felt a foot push at his shoes to move them out of the way, and the door closed behind him. He heard the padlock being slipped into place and pulled himself up onto his knees. Then he bent forward and shook off the hood. It didn't make a difference. It was pitch black inside the fridge, but at least he didn't hear a refrigerator motor running.

A few moments later, the door opened, and Brasso and Denis dragged Desportes into the fridge and dropped him on the floor.

Joe Lacroix was lying on a table bleeding out his life into a pile of red gauze and bandages, while Denis tried to stem the flow of blood and stomach juices. Knife wounds in the stomach are the worst. There are too many unprotected tubes behind the skin. The knife had entered cleanly – Denis found the tiny opening just below his rib cage – but Joe must've twisted on the way down, pulling his innards against the sharp blade.

Joe had stopped moaning once the morphine kicked in, but Denis had seen enough wounds to know that if they couldn't stop the bleeding, it was only a matter of time. In a hospital he might have a chance, hooked up to a never-ending supply of blood, while a surgeon opened him up and repaired the damage piece by piece. That wasn't going to happen on a dirty tabletop in an industrial park in Anjou.

Vanier's phone started to vibrate next to the gun they'd taken away from him. Brasso leaned over to look at the display. He said, "It's his partner, sir. Saint-Jacques."

"Don't answer," said a bald-headed giant in green fatigues, looking like he was dressed for war. He was standing next to Denis, watching him work.

He turned away from watching the work on Joe. "Paul, get Vanier back out here. I want to know how he found this place, and who he told. Right now."

Brasso moved to the fridge door and unlatched the padlock. Denis was winding a bandage around Joe. When he finished, he said, "What about the girl, sir?"

"She won't have gone far. If she came back, it was because of the dumb-fuck kid, her brother. She obviously doesn't have a phone, or she would have used it already, and we'd be finished. She's outside somewhere. Take the kid out and point a gun to his head. Tell her to get the fuck in here."

"But she has Joe's gun."

"So be careful. Stay close to the kid, and she won't shoot you. She won't take a chance of hitting him."

Brasso led Vanier out of the fridge and dropped him onto a chair. He had the hood on again. Denis went back into the fridge and returned with a blinking and shivering Kyle. He pulled out his gun and pushed Kyle out the door, shielding himself behind the skinny kid.

Vanier could hear the shuffling of people moving around, but he could see nothing under the hood.

The fourth voice, the one he couldn't identify, said, "Now, Mr. Vanier. Let's make this clear. You're a dead man. The only question is whether it's going to be easy or hard. And I can make it harder than you can imagine."

Vanier knew it wasn't the Colonel. Now he was wondering who was in charge. He said, "It's over. You're finished. Best you can do is …"

He was cut off with a punch to the side of his head that sent him to the floor.

"Like I said. You're dead, Mr. Vanier. Make it easy on yourself."

With the hood over his head, he couldn't anticipate the blows. He could only tense and wait. When the boot hit the soft skin of his side he had no defence, the air exploded from his lungs, and he felt the pain. He thought, maybe his kidney.

"Stand him up, Paul."

Brasso pulled Vanier to his feet. Vanier wondered where the next blow would hit. He didn't have long to wait. It was straight to his groin, and he dropped to the floor again. Then someone pulled the hood off and grabbed him by the hair, forcing him to look up. Vanier didn't recognize him.

"I'm Jan Prévost. And I'm in charge."

"Where's the Colonel?"

"Home in bed. If you've studied your history, Mr. Vanier, you

248

would know that every political movement needs a small group of dedicated people who'll do what's necessary to move things forward."

"The dirty work."

"Whatever is necessary. The Colonel is the acceptable public face of the movement. He's the leader. We just make sure that nothing stands in the way of progress. We're the hard men. And you're an obstacle that has to be removed. Now tell me, Mr. Vanier. How did you find the address?"

Vanier didn't see any point in lying. "GPS. The kid has a GPS on him."

The man looked over to Brasso. "I thought you'd searched them both."

"We did, sir. No GPS."

"Well do it again. And this time, find the fucking thing."

"Yes, sir."

Brasso opened the door and yelled at Denis to bring the kid back in.

Constable Richard Wallach reached into his pocket for his cell phone and checked the display. Then he held it to his ear. "Detective Sergeant Saint-Jacques. How are you?"

"I told you, call me Sylvie. I have a problem. I've had a couple of messages from DI Vanier, and I can't reach him."

"And how can I help?"

"I'm up in Tremblant. I took a few days off. If I was in town, I'd go looking for him. I was wondering – "

"If I would? Sure, but where do you think he is?"

"That's the thing. The last message said he had a lead and was going to look at a building on Rue de l'Innovation in Anjou. That was about an hour ago."

"I know the street. But why didn't you just call the local station and tell them he's gone missing? They could send a car to do a look around."

"Richard, we're in enough shit already. That's why I'm calling you. I don't need to make things worse. I just thought – "

"Got you. It's probably nothing, and you don't need to make a big story out of it. Why don't I drive by and check things out?"

"Would you?"

"Sure. It's not far. Give me half an hour, and I'll call you back."

"That would be great." She gave him Vanier's cell number in case he started answering his phone.

"Half an hour, forty-five minutes. I'll call you."

Star was sitting between two bushes, invisible in the shadows, watching the man holding Kyle by his collar and calling for her to come and help the kid. She still clutched the knife in her hand, but had dropped the gun on the ground beside her, after she realized that it wasn't like in the movies. She had tried aiming it at the man, holding it steady in two hands, but every time she squinted to shoot, she saw Kyle's blank face staring out into the night. She needed help.

When the man dragged Kyle back into the building, she stood up and ran to the back of the next building. Against the back wall, there were two steel containers on wheels, one overflowing with garbage, the other emblazoned with the recycling logo. Further along the wall were small piles of cut lengths of pipe. The recycling container was full of cardboard and paper, and she pulled a disposable lighter from her pocket. She hesitated before setting fire to the container. Instead, she pushed the garbage container a few feet along the wall until it was directly under a window, then she collected as much cardboard and paper as she could pile onto the garbage container. She grabbed a length of pipe, climbed onto the container, and used the pipe to smash out the window. Then she began lighting the folded boxes and paper. Each time she got a good flame going, she pushed the burning cardboard and paper through the window, letting it drop to the ground inside the building. The boxes and paper must have been falling on something flammable, because after a few minutes she saw more flames through the window than would have come from the boxes. The alarm went off.

She jumped down from the container, picked up the gun and the knife, and sprinted across the parking lot to where they were holding Kyle. She found two more containers at the back of that building.

Richard Wallach pulled into the parking lot next to the three trucks and killed the lights. He was wearing his usual off-duty outfit, leather jacket and jeans. He was careful about how he dressed. He walked to the door of the building and turned the handle. Everyone looked up as he walked in, including Vanier.

"About time you showed up," said Prévost, "Things are going pear-shaped in a hurry."

"Don't worry. Everything's under control."

He turned to Vanier, as if seeing him for the first time.

"Inspector. What a surprise. You really have fucked up this investigation, haven't you?"

"You've thrown your lot in with this scum? Didn't have what it takes to be a real cop?"

"A real cop? Like you? Don't make me laugh. I'm doing more for controlling crime than you've done in a lifetime. We're close to making Hochelaga a crime-free zone."

"You should know that the cavalry's on its way, and you're fucked big time."

"The cavalry? You mean Detective Sergeant Saint-Jacques?"

Vanier said nothing.

"Maybe the only friend you've got on the force. She got your

251

messages. And she's concerned about you. Not concerned enough to leave her little love nest in Tremblant, but, you know, concerned. She called to tell me. I offered to go look for you. I'll call her back in half an hour and tell her the place is quiet and you weren't around. You must have had the wrong address."

Prévost was pacing. "Wallach, we don't have time for this. We need to close this down right now. Get the other two out here. We're leaving."

"What about the girl? I thought she was here."

"She's still out there," said Denis. "I'm sure of it."

"We don't have time. We'll come back for her."

Wallach nodded in the direction of Lecroix. "What happened to him?"

"The bitch stabbed him and ran off," said Denis. He looked at Prévost again. "We need to get him to a hospital."

"I fucking know that, but it has to wait." Prévost was irritated. "We need to get rid of the baggage." He turned to Vanier. "You like flowers, Mr. Vanier?"

Vanier said nothing.

"Because that's where you're going. They're still fixing up the Alpine Gardens. Nice soft sand for a burial, and when they put the rocks in place, it will be a thousand years before they find you."

He turned to Denis and Brasso. "You two, get Joe into the truck, and come back for the others."

They lifted Joe off the table and struggled with him through the door. He was unconscious. Denis nodded to Brasso to look at his stomach. Joe's abdomen was swelling, a sure sign that the bleeding hadn't stopped, it just had nowhere to go. They put him in the back seat of the truck's cab and went back inside.

This time Brasso tried to intervene for Joe. "He's in the truck, sir. He's in bad shape. He's bleeding like crazy internally. Needs to get to the hospital."

"How many times do I have to say it? We get rid of these three first. Then you take him to the hospital."

He grabbed Vanier by the hair and pulled him out of the chair. "Brasso, you take the kid. I'll take this fucker. And you two – ," he pointed to Denis and Wallach – "get Desportes. Let's move it."

The procession shuffled out of the building towards the three trucks. Denis and Wallach were half-carrying, half-dragging Desportes across the lot. Brasso was frog-marching Kyle, and Prévost was bringing up the rear with Vanier.

Vanier smelled smoke and heard the sound of a fire engine, then two.

"Move it," yelled Prévost. Vanier watched them bundle Desportes and then Kyle into one of the trucks and slam the door. Prévost held a gun on him and gestured for him to climb up into the last truck. Vanier looked up. The bottom of the door was level with his waist.

"Can't be done like this," said Vanier, gesturing with the hand-cuffs behind his back.

The advance van from the fire station cruised past the driveway, its lights flashing.

"Get in the fucking truck before I kill you."

"Then take off the cuffs, I can't climb in with my hands tied behind my back."

A fire truck went noisily past the driveway, the noise from its air brakes indicating it was slowing down. The smell of smoke was everywhere, and Prévost reached into his pocket. He pulled out a knife and cut the plastic cuffs. "Get in the fucking car."

Vanier climbed up into the cab, and Prévost kept the gun trained on him as he walked around the front of the truck. Vanier heard the second fire engine pump its brakes and squeal to a stop. He looked out towards the street, and it was still clear. The fire must be in the next building.

Denis's truck was the first to start. Vanier watched as the reverse lights came on and the truck backed out to turn towards the street. Then it stopped. The driver's door opened, and Denis jumped down, turning to look at the tires. The truck was riding on the rims, and hanging shards of rubber showed where they had been slashed. He ran to Brasso's truck, and it was the same thing. Then he ran over to Prévost's truck, waving. Prévost lowered the window.

"Jan. She slashed the tires."

"Fuck," said Prévost. "Okay, everyone back inside."

Prévost turned to Vanier, "Any fucking problems, I'll kill you right here. And I'll kill you quietly."

Denis ran to Brasso's truck to tell him of the change of plan. Wallach was still sitting in the passenger's seat of Denis's truck, with Desportes and Lacroix bleeding in the back seat.

Brasso jumped down from his cab and was going around to the passenger side to remove Kyle. He heard a noise and looked back to see a flaming garbage container cruising towards him. He raised his gun and got off a shot just before being hit full-on by the steel container. Vanier saw Star move around the container, grab the gun that Brasso had dropped, and run off into the shadows. Prévost was walking around the front of his truck to pull Vanier from the passenger side. Prévost was distracted by the gunshot, the flaming garbage container, and the imminent threat of firemen appearing to douse it. He reached up and pulled the door open. Shouted, "Out, fucker. Now!"

Vanier swivelled in his seat as though he was going to jump down, then leaned back and brought his foot up powerfully under Prévost's jaw. He felt it connect with bone, but it didn't have much effect on Prévost, except to make him drop his gun. Prévost bent down to retrieve it, and Vanier launched himself out of the truck, stomping Prévost's head into the asphalt. They both reached for the gun, and Vanier was faster. He stood up with the gun aimed at Prévost. Then Prévost rolled and grabbed for Vanier's leg, pulling him off balance. The gun went off and half of Prévost's face exploded in a mist of blood.

Wallach and Denis were propping up Desportes, staring at Vanier. Vanier raised the gun and pointed it. Wallach took a step back and ran off into the darkness, leaving Denis bearing the load. Denis lowered Desportes to the floor and held his arms out, like he was waiting for crucifixion.

"Lie down. Hands in view, and don't move."

Denis obeyed the instructions.

Then Brasso appeared from behind one of the trucks. He was pushing Kyle in front of him, holding a sawed-off shotgun to his head.

"Vanier, I'm walking, or the kid's dead. Put your gun down."

Vanier saw movement behind Brasso. Star emerged from the shadows with a gun aimed at Brasso.

Vanier yelled, "Star. No!"

Brasso spun around with the shotgun, and Star froze. Vanier aimed and fired. The bullet hit Brasso between the shoulder blades, and he slumped to the ground.

Star rushed over, grabbed Kyle, and pulled him over to the grass at the edge of the parking lot.

Vanier heard a motor start, and saw Wallach accelerating towards him. He raised the gun again and aimed at the driver's seat. At the last moment, he spun out of the way and let the car speed by.

Star was back in the parking lot, helping Desportes to his feet and leading him over to where Kyle was sitting on the grass.

Seconds later, the lot was full of squad cars. A spotlight bathed the scene in light, and a speaker from one of the cars ordered, "Everyone. Put your weapons down and lie on the ground. Now! Everyone put your weapons down and lie on the ground."

255

Vanier was the only person standing. He made a show of holding his arms up and slowly getting down onto his knees and then lying flat out. He tossed the gun. Star watched from the grass, keeping her arm around Kyle.

The lot was still, except for the hum of engines from the squad cars and the boots of the officers approaching. Four of them walked cautiously up to Vanier. The lead officer dropped down on Vanier's back and started punching him in the head. Two others stared kicking him.

Vanier yelled, "I'm a police officer." It took a while before they got the message. "DI Vanier. I'm a police officer."

They cuffed him anyway.

Richard Wallach figured he had, at most, fifteen minutes to grab what he needed from his condo and clear out. He called Eddie Pickton on the way.

"Eddie, shit's happening. I need help."

"What kind of shit?"

"It's over, Eddie. The *Patriotes* are finished. Jan's dead, shot by a cop. Lacroix's dead. Brasso's dead. It's finished. I need to get away."

Wallach was doing his best to drive so as not to attract attention, but still gunning the accelerator when he could.

"I need a place to hide out for a couple of days. I need to arrange a new passport. Just a couple of days.

"Sounds like you're finished too, Richard."

Wallach sensed the hesitation. Why should Pickton help him if there was nothing in it for him?

"I'll pay, Eddie. I got cash in the condo. Eddie, come on. A favour. Remember, I'm the one helped you get where you were. Remember that."

Pickton remembered. And he knew what Wallach could do with that knowledge.

"OK, Richard. Meet me in half an hour. There's a parking lot behind the *Pain Doré* factory on Rouen Street. It's quiet. If I'm not there, wait for me."

"Sure, Eddie. I'll make it worth your while."

"Half an hour, Richard." Pickton pushed disconnect.

Wallach took ten minutes in his condo to dump cash and some clothes into a gym bag. His heart stopped beating wildly only when he was back in his car and turning out of the condo parking lot. He knew the bakery on Rouen Street and the lot behind it. It was only accessible by a laneway, bordered on two sides by old maples, and the fourth by the embankment for the train tracks. It was empty at night, and dark.

He pulled in and parked in a corner, almost invisible in the shadows. Ten minutes later, he saw headlights approaching up the alley and recognized Pickton's SUV as it turned into the lot. It cruised to a stop behind him, and Pickton got out. He gestured for Wallach to come.

Wallach grabbed the gym bag and walked towards him.

"Eddie," Wallach smiled, "I owe you big time for this." He reached out to shake Pickton's hand, and Pickton reached too. That's when Wallach noticed the gun.

"Ah, no, Eddie. Don't do this."

The screeching of a freight train slowly rounding a tight curve drowned out the noise of the shot. Pickton leaned down to pull the gym bag from Wallach's hand, placed the muzzle against Wallach's forehead and shot again. The body flinched slightly with the force of the bullet and lay still, blood pumping from the wound.

"The boy becomes the man, Richard."

Pickton opened the door to the SUV and threw the bag in. Then he climbed in after it and drove off.

Eighteen

Vanier sat alone in a dark corner of a semi-basement refuge for serious afternoon drinkers. He hadn't eaten all day and was rotating between beer and whiskey. The place smelled of years of spilled beer and damp carpeting, and there was a hush that had settled over the room like low cloud. Two television monitors were tuned to the evening news, one in English, the other French, and both were on mute. He didn't need sound to be able to follow the story.

The video they found at Prévost's place showed a convention of suppliers to Hochelaga's drug trade drawn together in a warehouse to celebrate their new business arrangement – where the hard men of the *Patriotes* would control the neighbourhood but permit business to continue under new rules. The deal was consummated by everyone participating in beating Émile Legault along the slow path to his death. It was meant to show they were all in it together. And the video was the *Patriotes*' insurance that people would respect the new rules. With the evidence of the video, the police had raided the homes and businesses of the leaders of the four crime factions that had joined the *Patriotes* in a show of solidarity. The television images switched back and forth from one group to another, handcuffed, sullen, and walking to cruisers and police vans. The Colonel wasn't among them. His face didn't appear on the video, and he claimed to know nothing about what Prévost and the others were doing. He said he had been betrayed.

Vanier didn't care about those who were arrested. Their places in the community, if they ever had to give them up, would quickly be filled by others, maybe even more brutal. He thought instead of the *Patriotes* and the work they had been doing. That side of the organization would collapse, and the whole edifice would crumble back to its nucleus of disaffected men with guns playing soldiers. The loss of the programs would create the same gaps that had allowed the movement to grow in the first place.

He knew that Hochelaga would go back to what it had been, decades before, an abandoned, dirt-poor neighbourhood that nobody cared about except for a few weeks leading up to elections, when promises flowed like honey.

The door opened, and Alex walked down two steps, scouted the gloom and walked over to Vanier.

"Hi, Dad."

"Hey. Want a beer?"

"No. Not today."

"How'd you find me?"

"You're pretty predictable."

Vanier smiled. It's good that someone knows you well enough to know where you go to get numb.

"How are you feeling, kid?"

"Okay. There's good days and bad days."

"And this is a good day?"

"It's not a bad day, Dad."

"Sometimes that's all you can hope for."

"I'm beginning to understand things. The moods, the flashbacks, the anxiety, the fear, even the good days. Talking to other guys is good. There's a group of guys that get together every week. That's good. Stress is bad. Alcohol's bad. The pills are bad. But just knowing that stuff, it's a start."

Vanier had done enough interviews to know when to talk and

when to shut up. He waited, letting the quiet settle.

"I've been thinking about good times. You know, unless you go looking for them in your memory, you don't remember. I mean, you remember shit day after day, even when it hurts to do it. But you have to make an effort to remember good stuff. Like fishing. Remember when we used to go fishing, Dad?"

Vanier looked up and smiled. He hadn't thought about fishing with Alex in years.

"Remember that spot in Vermont? The Missisquoi River, fishing off the rocks. We caught bass, but that was only part of it. I still remember how hot it was that day, and how cold the water was when you put your feet in, and the glint of the spinners in the water."

Vanier remembered the day, and wondered why he hadn't thought about it in years. He said, "Yeah. And there were about twenty cows downstream that had waded into the water up to their knees."

Alex smiled. "We should go fishing this summer, Dad."

It was as though a light went on in Vanier's head.

"Damn right, Alex. That's the best idea I've heard in months."

"And don't worry. I'm going to get a job, too."

"That can wait. Focus on getting better."

"It's part of getter better."

"Don't know where you're going to find a low-stress job, though."

"There must be some."

Vanier couldn't come up with one that easily. He looked up to catch the eye of the waiter.

"Wanna go home?" Alex asked.

Vanier thought for a moment. Said, "Sure. Maybe we can pick up some take-out. Indian?"

"Indian sounds great."

Vanier stood up, and they walked towards the door.

Nineteen

When spring finally takes hold of Montreal, it does it overnight, going from damp and grey to hot and sunny in a heartbeat, it's hardly a spring at all, more of day or two prelude to summer. The light pulls people out of the shadowy places, terraces sprout like flowers and fill with people, bikes are hauled out of storage, winter clothes disappear, and vast expanses of skin are exposed to soak up the warmth.

It took a week before Vanier was cleared to go back to work, and another to close the Legault file. Now, there was nothing unfinished and nothing of any significance to make him stick around. He had called Anjili and asked if she wanted to play hooky. Vanier had never been on a date to the Botanical Gardens, but, he thought, there's a first time for everything. She didn't take much convincing, but even though Barbeau's body had been removed, she made him promise to avoid the Alpine Gardens.

They followed paths that broke away from the asphalt pathways favoured by runners and stroller-pushing parents, and meandered through copses of thick woods that opened on wide vistas before arriving beside a pond where ducks were settling down to raise families.

The ground was mostly still dormant, but here and there flashes of colour from an advance guard of blossoms were breaking through. Anjili linked her arm through Vanier's, and they scanned as they walked, looking for evidence that the earth was waking up, for the patches of white, purple, red, and green rebelling against the dark browns of sleeping earth. Anjili pointed to a small cluster of blue flowers.

"Do you know what it is?

Vanier looked down, "All flowers are roses .... Except daisies. So those must be daisies."

She laughed and read the name stick beside the plant. "Woodland crocus."

"I was close," he said.

They sat on a bench next to the pond and watched the ducks. A few swallows were flying overhead, catching early insects.

"I love the smell," he said. "The dirt. It smells new."

"You know that it's microbes being released. That's what gives the musty smell."

"You're just being romantic."

"You're right. It's the smell of spring."

"And the noise?"

"No traffic."

"Yes. But if you listen, you can separate the different bird songs."

She listened. Above everything were the complaining noises of ducks and seagulls. But beneath them were at least three different bird songs vying for attention. It didn't take long for her to find the birds responsible for each call, and she pointed them out to Vanier. A brown bird flew down from a tree and bounced across the grass about six feet in front of them.

Segal asked, "What kind of bird?"

"All birds are robins ... Except owls," he said. "So that's a robin."

She turned to look at him, surprised. "Right."

He smiled.

A small green and yellow tractor pulled a trailer along the far side of the pond, too far away to hear the noise of the motor. It stopped near some large bushes, and they watched the driver get out and pull tools from the trailer. He went around the bushes, breaking out the winter debris, working methodically, leaning between the tall plants to pull dead vegetation out of the undergrowth. After fifteen minutes, he had a good-sized pile. He unhitched one wall of the trailer and began lifting the leaves and sticks into it.

"That guy looks just like … " She stopped herself, not wanting to break the mood.

"Alex?"

"Yes. Alex. Sorry."

"Don't be."

"He just moves like Alex."

"Let's carry on."

They got up from the bench and walked slowly around the pond. The worker saw them coming and stood looking at them, one hand on the upright rake. When they got close, he waved the greeting, and Anjili beamed a smile.

"Hi Alex," she yelled.

"Hey, Dr. Segal. Didn't know you came to the Gardens."

"Your father's idea. He has some great ones now and then. It's beautiful here."

"Yeah. I know." Alex was smiling, something Vanier couldn't see enough of.

Vanier looked around. "Lots of work to do here."

"It never stops, Dad. But it's great." Alex looked at his watch.

"I'm on break after I dump this stuff. Want to grab a coffee?"

"Sure. I'll give you a hand."

Vanier grabbed the rake and began raking the remainder of the pile together for Alex to load into the trailer. Then the three of them squeezed into the front seat of the John Deere, and Alex drove to the maintenance section. He let them off, pointing the way to the cafeteria.

"I'll see you there in ten minutes."

Vanier and Anjili linked arms and set off for the cafeteria in the Turkish Garden.

"Desportes?" she asked.

"He's the best employment agency in town. Alex likes it here. No stress, and he's outside all day. I think I'll talk to Mr. Desportes and see if they have a job for me in the Gardens."

"Why don't you do that?" she said, half wishing he would.